THE
TRUTH
IN
OUR LIES

OTHER TITLES BY ELIZA GRAHAM

THE
TRUTH
IN
OUR LIES

Eliza Graham

LAKE UNION
PUBLISHING

Text copyright © 2019 by Eliza Graham
All rights reserved.

Published by Lake Union Publishing, Seattle

www.apub.com

Amazon, the Amazon logo, and Lake Union Publishing are trademarks of Amazon.com, Inc., or its affiliates.

ISBN-13: 9781542044479
ISBN-10: 1542044472

Cover design by Debbie Clement

Cover photography by Richard Jenkins Photography

Printed in the United States of America

For Matthew

April 1943

We ran along the track into the shadow of the trees. Ahead of us another footpath cut in from the right, forming a crossing over which the boughs bent low. The crows cawed, their straggly black feathers flapping like mourning clothes. Some of the birds dropped to the ground, others landed in the lowest branches of the trees, showing no fear of us. Through my mind ran the word for a group of crows – *a murder*.

The gloom wrapped itself around us, the trees blocking the morning sun. Even the sheets of bluebells seemed oppressed, their vivid blue dulled to grey.

We turned down the track to the right. My legs pulled me onwards over the dead leaves, towards the pond. I knew what we would find there before we saw it.

1

December 1942

His hair was too oiled, his suit too sharp. I noted the man easing into the refreshment room at Liverpool Street Station as one to cold-shoulder. Too late. He was already coming over to stand on my left, proffering his cigarette case as I examined the dried-out scones on the counter. Without a word I turned to look at him, raising my veil so he had a clear view of the right side of my face too. He snapped the case shut and gave me a mouthful of Anglo-Saxon. As he walked out, the soles of his shoes beat out a brisk indignation at having been tricked by a female who'd seemed, from one side, worthy of his attentions.

'I've changed my mind about the scone.' I paid the cashier for the tea, the familiar mixture of malice and shame curdling inside me as I swayed my way through the crowd to a table with my tray. I was returning to my RAF station from leave over Christmas. It seemed half of London was on the move, too.

An attempt had been made to decorate the refreshment room for Christmas, but the paper chains were ungluing themselves in the soggy atmosphere. Several had already unravelled and dangled limply from pins stuck into the paintwork. A wag had pinned a small dried-out sausage underneath Father Christmas's nose in the poster on the wall. He looked like a bearded, jollier Hitler.

The middle-aged woman sharing my table peeped at my exposed right cheek when she thought I wasn't looking. The skin had lost some of its redness now and was stiffer than it had been in the weeks after the fire. If I touched the cheek, the scar tissue didn't feel like part of me but like something stuck on to my face. I stared into the cup of murky liquid.

'Anna Hall,' a deep male voice said. Alexander Beattie materialised like Mephistopheles out of the fug of cigarette smoke and steam from the café's tea urn. Except I'd always imagined Faust's demon as a finely drawn, nimble figure, whereas Beattie had heft – the station buffet seemed to shrink now he was standing in it. Not only did he look larger than most people here, his face lacked the winter-grey weariness most of us exhibited.

'Belated Merry Christmas. What are you up to these days?' His pupils dilated; he'd seen the scar on my face.

'WAAF.' I hated myself for sounding surly, but I didn't want him to ask me any questions about my face. I watched him for a further reaction but saw nothing in his smooth features.

'Bombers, I imagine, if you're heading to East Anglia?' he said in a low voice. He smiled at the middle-aged woman at my table and she beamed at him, drained her cup of tea, and stood up. Beattie sat down in the vacated chair. 'Last I heard, you were still sorting out the fighter boys at Bentley Priory, Anna. Filter Room, wasn't it? Where the sharper minds congregate? Good trigonometry skills and fast reactions and everyone keeping terribly calm under pressure. Why the move to the provinces?'

My job in the RAF's most important Fighter Filter Room had indeed been demanding, thrilling and terrifying.

'Circumstances changed.' I spoke the words shortly. I wasn't supposed to talk much about what I did in my WAAF roles, past or present. Beattie must know this.

'And your father and Grace?'

'Just my father now.' I could say it almost mechanically these days.

He raised an enquiring eyebrow.

'Grace died.' This made it all sound far too straightforward, but it would do for Beattie. He bowed his head briefly.

'I'm sorry. She was a wonderful girl.'

'I didn't know you'd met my sister?'

'You had a garden party, remember? The very last summer before the war.'

Beattie had been at my birthday party? I'd forgotten this. Too much champagne and a warm summer afternoon, everyone a bit raucous in the vicarage garden. Dad anxious about disapproving parishioners, probably wishing he'd insisted on limiting the drink to lemonade and tea. Grace wearing a tea dress in a soft rose poplin, the sunshine bringing a warm glow to her pale skin. She looked fresh and almost flirtatious as she chatted to my male friends. Mum was still alive, too, sitting in a bath chair under the old chestnut tree, smiling at everyone, too weak to eat much but enjoying the company.

'Oh yes,' I said confidently, picturing Beattie leaning up against the chestnut tree, cigarette in one hand, glass in the other, listening and nodding. 'Wasn't I lucky with the weather?'

He gave me a smile that put me in mind of a magician pulling off a sleight of hand. 'I wasn't there, Anna. You didn't actually invite me.'

I felt my one unburnt cheek turn pink.

'You lied. *I* lied. I was probably out of the country, visiting family.'

In Germany, he meant. But even if he'd been around, would I have invited him?

'I didn't mean to lie, I—'

'Oh, don't apologise for lying. You were convincing, Anna Hall. And that's good.'

'It is?'

'Certainly. For a second there you had me doubting my memory and believing I'd been at your party. Must be your well-lauded acting ability.'

'Those undergraduate plays, you mean?' I didn't want to take praise from Beattie. These days I found it hard to take it from anyone, even when, contradictorily, compliments were what I needed more than anything.

'My sources say you might have gone somewhere with your acting.' The woman behind the counter brought him over his cup of tea. She hadn't offered to do that for me. Beattie smiled a thanks at her.

'Squalid digs and a different provincial town every week?'

'You're probably right.' He looked me up and down. I pulled my veil over my face. 'Do you feel you're revenging yourself?'

'What?'

'Helping to send planes to Germany to drop explosives and incendiaries on their houses and burn them?' he asked, eyes wide and innocent. 'To pay them back for Grace?'

'What do you mean?'

'I'm guessing she was killed in an air raid, wasn't she?'

I gathered my things together. 'My train might actually leave on time.'

'Don't duck the question, Anna.'

'What business is it of yours, the way I feel about my work?' What he'd said stung because I couldn't completely deny the charge.

He put a hand on my arm, detaining me. 'You were a beautiful woman. Is that why you're burying yourself out there? The work's much quieter than it was at Bentley Priory, isn't it? So's the social life. I know the station you're based at. Nothing but fields of turnips for miles around this time of year.'

I hoped the look I gave him conveyed the disdain I felt. But he was only telling the truth.

'You should still be living on your wits. They're sharp, Anna – all you need. But your job is boring.'

'Boring?' If my commission came through, I might be working on codes and ciphers, which would be far more interesting. But I couldn't tell Beattie this.

'It's not nearly as challenging as the job you had at Fighter Command. And you can't really influence outcomes.' His grip still prevented me from moving. 'You can chart positions and of course that helps. But if a Messerschmitt has one of your bombers in its sights or flak catches one of your crews over Germany, what can you personally do in retaliation?'

My fingers tightened on my suitcase handle.

'What are you running away from?'

I looked at my half-empty teacup. For a second, I wanted to throw the liquid over his smooth face.

Beattie glanced sideways and lowered his voice. 'I might be able to offer you work where you can deal a more effective blow to the Germans.'

'What's your line?' I asked, knowing he wouldn't be able to tell me in a public refreshment room. He smiled at me.

'We'll be in touch.'

The station announcer called my train's platform number, saving me from the need to reply. 'I've got to go.'

I shook off his hand and fled for the platform, heart pumping. A bitter taste filled my mouth. I didn't think it was the aftertaste of whatever it was I'd just drunk. I crossed the concourse, dodging passengers laden with suitcases and pulling small children along with them. Normally enduring a wartime train journey would compound the low, exhausted mood that had afflicted me over the last eighteen months. Not today, though. Beattie had left me furious, but not tired.

Only when I'd pushed my way through the train to find a seat did I realise Beattie hadn't told me which train he himself was catching. In fact he hadn't really told me anything about himself at all. At university he'd always been like that: skirting questions, distracting you while extracting information.

Had he purposefully come to find me at Liverpool Street Station? How had he known when I was due back at work? When I'd told him about Grace's death he'd reacted as though it was news to him. But when he'd talked about me taking revenge for my sister through my work, it seemed, on reflection, like a provocation he'd thought up before we'd met.

My veil had ridden up. A Canadian officer in the seat opposite was staring at me. I tugged the veil down and opened my book, wanting to say something rude to him before he made one of the regular unsolicited responses to my appearance offered by complete strangers of both sexes.

I can tell you were a looker before . . . You should be grateful it wasn't worse . . . There are lots of disabled or disfigured men these days who wouldn't be too fussy.

'Everything all right, miss?' the Canadian asked. 'You cold?'

I must have been shaking. It wasn't because of the unheated carriage. Nor was it just because of my indignation. Perhaps I trembled because I felt change coming, an opportunity to take a more effective revenge, as Beattie put it. But I wasn't interested in Beattie or whatever job it was he claimed he could offer me, so why was I feeling rattled?

The Canadian passed me his greatcoat. I wore it as a blanket, smiling, in silent penance.

I heard nothing more from Beattie for a few weeks following the encounter at Liverpool Street. I concentrated on my work, spending any free time I had taking my landlady's dog for walks in a nearby forest. I received a letter telling me that my recommendation for officer training was finally going through to the next stage. It hadn't been possible to enter the WAAF directly as an officer when I'd first enlisted. Despite the events of less than two years ago, a small, ambitious part of me still wanted to rise above the rank of sergeant.

I'd made friends here at the RAF station in Suffolk. From the time I'd first turned up with my ruined face I'd enjoyed the kind, tacit support of other women and of the pilots themselves. Quite a few had lost friends to fire or seen the terrible facial disfigurements of survivors. Their response was to treat me with the usual banter and teasing. No concessions were made.

Beattie was right, though. Working out here wasn't as stimulating as my job with Fighters had been. No off-duty trips to West End nightclubs and theatres. Nightlife consisted of visits to the small local pub or an occasional cinema trip. All the same, I could see myself plodding on in the hope of my commission coming through.

Perhaps it was true that, as Beattie suggested, a tiny part of me rejoiced when our bomber crews returned from a successful raid on a German city and I knew I'd been a very small part of the team assisting them. I didn't let myself think about the consequences for the civilians on the ground. Sometimes an image of Patrick would flash through my mind and I'd touch wood. But Patrick was in Fighters, not Bombers. And he was no longer my responsibility.

The formal letter requesting me to attend an interview was sitting above the fireplace when I returned from a shift one evening. It was all very official, asking me to go to an office at the top of the BBC's Bush House premises in Aldwych in central London. I raised my eyebrows at the reference to my earlier 'meeting' with Mr Alexander Beattie. I wanted to pretend I hadn't received the letter but dared not. I decided to go and give lack-lustre answers to Beattie's questions. They'd have to let me stay here in Suffolk.

When I arrived at Bush House, I looked up at the Portland stone pillars above the entrance. The place looked commanding, purposeful.

Perhaps this job of Beattie's was worth taking seriously. To my surprise Beattie himself wasn't on the three-man panel, none of whom wore uniform. They introduced themselves and gave me the Official Secrets Act to sign, explaining briefly that they worked with Beattie on a political warfare project.

'Political warfare?' I asked. 'I thought he – Mr Beattie – was at the Ministry of Information?' He'd never actually told me this himself, but I thought it had been what mutual friends had mentioned him doing, ages ago.

'Mr Beattie is now employing his talents at what you might know as propaganda, sergeant,' the second man said.

'Those leaflets we drop over occupied Europe?' I'd heard about these drops, of course, as some of the RAF flights I'd worked on had sprinkled German cities with papers extolling the strengths of the Allies and detailing the weaknesses of the German forces.

They smiled at me. 'We've moved on a bit,' the first said. 'Though print still has its place. But what we're really talking about is communication over the wireless to occupied Europe.'

'Isn't that what the BBC does?'

The first man sighed. 'You seem to be asking us as many questions as we're asking you, Sergeant Hall.'

I started to apologise but the second man raised a hand, silencing me. 'The team we're recruiting for is – or will be – one part of an enterprise disseminating information to listeners in Europe.'

Radio broadcasts by an organisation that wasn't the BBC? I felt myself frown.

The third man spoke. 'You'd be based at a specialist unit outside London broadcasting to Germany and other parts of northern Europe. The work would be hush-hush.'

'Don't the Germans jam the radio frequencies?'

'We have ways of, erm, getting around that little issue,' the first man said. I remembered the pilots in Suffolk telling me how German radio stations in cities targeted by the RAF sometimes went off air in case the transmissions were helpful to bomber navigators. Perhaps these propaganda broadcasts of Beattie's took this opportunity to jump onto the German frequencies. The panel of men was looking at me.

'Why would you think I'd be good at this kind of thing?'

The second gave a brief smile. 'We've done a bit of research into you, Sergeant Hall. You took a modern languages degree and speak fluent German. You've acted. You worked as an advertising copy-writer before the war.'

Nobody had ever suggested that my acting or brief advertising experience was of any interest or use to the authorities. At least, I assumed these men were from the authorities.

The third man spoke again. 'We're looking for people who can convey messages naturally. Who understand the ways communications can be made credible.'

I looked at him. 'Credible?'

He shuffled in his chair. 'It wouldn't be exactly the kind of broadcasting the BBC does.'

'*Says* it does,' the first man said defensively. 'Everyone puts a gloss on things.'

'More than a gloss.' The second man sounded impatient. 'You'd be making things up sometimes, Sergeant Hall. And you'd work for what we call a research unit.'

Research unit? It sounded like a respectable academic outfit.

'That's a euphemism for a team based in the Home Counties but pretending to be a German station,' he said impatiently.

I felt like Alice falling down the rabbit hole.

'Would you be interested?' the first man asked. 'There's no compulsion, we're not Nazis. Your current job is obviously a worthwhile one. But Alexander Beattie thought you'd have a natural talent for this work.'

Beattie thought I'd be a natural at deception?

11

I left the interview telling them I'd think about the offer, taking deep breaths of what seemed like the clearer air of Aldwych.

~❊~

I was still uncertain I wanted to work with Beattie on this strange project of his when the second letter arrived with the offer of a job in a government information department. I smirked at the bland euphemism. Stroking the smooth black coat of my landlady's retriever by the fire that night, I bent my head down to him. 'Should I take the job, Pharaoh? Would you miss our walks in the forest?'

He let out a gentle sigh, seeming to acknowledge our parting. Accepting the offer could be a huge risk. I didn't know Beattie well; at university we'd been in different crowds. He'd been a year or two ahead of me, as well. At our last meeting he'd certainly rubbed me up the wrong way. But even so, there'd been something about him that day: an energy, a drive that quickened my spirits.

I'd miss the team here. But these days nothing was permanent; people moved around. Or suffered injury or death. If you stayed in one place too long, you could find yourself the only remnant of the original group.

The retriever rolled over for me to stroke him between his front legs. 'You don't care that I'm not pretty any more, Pharaoh,' I told him. 'Other males won't be as kind.'

I needed to rise to the challenge. I thought of my sister, born with, as my mother put it, a number of challenges, physical and intellectual. Despite always struggling with maths, Grace had mastered numbers and complex instructions by adapting recipes to what was available. She'd dug her wartime vegetable garden to strengthen her muscles, even though it must have been difficult – probably even painful – for her at first. My sister was an inspiration, but thinking about her was something I tried not to do too often.

The dog lifted his head and licked my scarred cheek. The nurses where I'd been treated would have been appalled, but I laughed. 'That's probably the most ardent male attention I can hope for, Pharaoh.'

Beattie also wrote a short letter to me, one paragraph in his spiky writing, telling me I'd be housed in a small but comfortable cottage in the same Bedfordshire village he operated from.

Plenty of walks over the Woburn Abbey estate grounds, among the wallabies and bison, Hall. I know you like that kind of wholesome activity. And the landlady of our HQ even has a dog she'll lend you. There's a pub, too, but you won't be allowed in there much or at all. London is an hour-ish on an indirect rail service, if you can justify the trip. All in all, not a glamorous place, but less turnip-ridden than your current location. And you won't be bored. And not being bored is the main thing, isn't it?

2

'We need more. More people, more material, more scripts.' Beattie rubbed his hands together. The two of us were alone in Mulberry House, his operations centre, as he termed it, but in reality a large red-brick Victorian villa on the south-western edge of the small village of Aspley Guise in Bedfordshire. 'There's a new and more powerful radio transmitter coming on board later this year. I won't bother your head with all the technical details.'

I stiffened. I probably knew more than he did about radio and perfectly understood the implications of a new medium-wave transmitter.

'Suffice it to say, we might have more airtime by autumn,' Beattie continued.

We had a new recording studio now, at Milton Bryan, a village just a few miles from here. I'd already been over a few times to admire the new broadcasting facilities. Working somewhere purpose-built and intact was a thrilling prospect. Three and a half years into the war most people had to put up with, at best, shabby and decrepit workplaces.

Beattie balanced his chair on its two back legs. I hoped they'd take his weight. 'We need more news, more material, more people to feed us information. Our audience is just lapping up what we transmit.'

Sometimes, looking out at the garden with its first crocuses and narcissi blooming, it seemed so incongruous that we were broadcasting to people in occupied Europe and Germany and sometimes below the sea in the North Atlantic. In fact, this apparently quiet corner of the country, fifty miles north of London, possessed excellent telephone connections with the capital. A large signals and ciphering centre a few miles away, at a place called Bletchley Park, seemed to employ a number of people. Though they kept the exact nature of their work to themselves, we received regular decrypts from them, delivered by courier. Beattie had selected this house as his research unit headquarters and personal residence, probably because it was large, well furnished and had covetable views of the woodland bordering this side of the village. I was getting used to Beattie, too: his sudden flashes of inspiration, his mood swings. I'd thought I'd miss using the mathematical part of my brain to position bomber squads, miss the way I'd fired calculations at the girls standing at the table in the Filter Room at Fighter Command. But I was becoming accustomed to this work and how it called on skills I hadn't known I'd possessed, not even when I was trying to write copy persuading people to buy a particular brand of custard powder.

He nodded at the door. I stood up and closed it. The only other person in the building was the housekeeper, but I was now used to the strict secrecy.

'We need more of everything, in fact.' Beattie all but licked his lips.

'We're going to interrogate another batch of POWs?' I asked. We'd already been down to the holding camps known as cages on several occasions to interview German and Italian prisoners. Some of them were prepared to provide information both military and domestic that we could use to add credibility to our broadcasts. We'd only just completed a round of interrogations. As far as I knew, nobody else of interest had arrived in the country since then.

He gave a dismissive wave. 'Better than that. They're sending me on a fishing expedition to scoop up German refugees who can help us.' His eyes shone in the same way I'd noticed when he got hold of a rare sirloin steak. 'And there's good news for you, too, Hall. You're coming with me to Lisbon. Today.'

I stared at him. This was the first I'd heard of a trip to Portugal. 'Me?'

'Don't sit there with your mouth open. There's someone out there who might be able to help us with material.'

Neutral Lisbon with its shops and restaurants. And Jewish and anti-Nazi refugees fleeing there from all over occupied Europe, looking over their shoulders in case the Gestapo or the Portuguese secret police were coming for them.

'I have a visa for you.' He tapped his chest pocket. 'Go and grab civilian clothes for a two-night stay.'

I was going to be liberated from my WAAF uniform?

'You'll need smartish frocks for daytime and night. Perhaps a pair of slacks for . . . more active pursuits, though the Portuguese are a bit old-fashioned about female immodesty.'

I knew better than to ask questions. Mentally I sifted through my wardrobe, selecting garments that still, more than three years into the war, looked smart. End of winter here, but already spring in Lisbon? Where exactly had I hung up my lighter-weight suits and spring dresses? Most importantly, did I have a hat and veil suitable for spring? For a few days I might be spared people gawping at my face. I could play the role of a normal woman.

The telephone rang. 'Answer that, will you?' Beattie said.

I listened to the caller and then placed my hand over the receiver. 'It's the BBC, you might want to—'

'Tell whoever it is I'm busy. They'll probably want something I don't want them to have.'

'It's the Director-General's office, they—'

'Definitely tell those blighters I'm busy.' His hand went up, forbidding further debate. I made excuses to the irate voice on the telephone. 'I'll expect you here again in half an hour,' he told me.

By now I was used to Beattie's impossible deadlines. Outside acute emergencies it was frowned upon to run in uniform. Even at a very brisk walk it would take me ten minutes to reach my own lodgings.

The landlady was far too astute to pass comment when I arrived red-faced, but I gave her a story about a trip to London, which made us both feel we'd observed the rules of discretion. She insisted on making me a cup of tea to gulp down while I packed a small suitcase. Thank God I'd handwashed underwear and stockings only the previous day and they were dry enough to pack.

Just nine minutes to make Beattie's deadline. I wouldn't have put it past him to drive off without me. As I rushed down the narrow pavement, suitcase in hand, satchel over my shoulder, I nodded at various villagers I'd come to recognise. They no longer stared at my face as much these days, but wearing my veil again felt good.

Beattie was waiting outside his front door. 'Good grief, Hall, you were quick. No need to kill yourself. The car is only just here.'

A large black Austin driven by a girl in Wren uniform pulled into the drive. 'Where are we flying from?' I asked.

'Whitchurch.'

I calculated that the aerodrome just south of Bristol was a drive of ninety-odd miles. These days it might take three hours, depending on roads. Then again, it might take a lot longer.

'Atkins, our driver here, is good at shortcuts,' Beattie told me.

As we headed west towards Buckingham my head was full of questions.

'You're wondering who we're going to see?' Beattie looked at me.

He wanted me to ask him, but I was still feeling peeved about the unnecessarily tight timing he'd imposed on me. He looked at me in a more pointed fashion.

'So, who are we going to see?'

'A wealthy Jewish industrialist from Hamburg who's been hanging around in Lisbon with his wife, waiting to fly to the United States.'

'If they're so wealthy, why are they still in Europe?'

'They holed up in Nice for a while, until the Germans arrived. They'd have moved on to Lisbon earlier to fly out, but the wife fell ill.'

'What industry was the husband in?' Technically I ought to drop the odd 'sir' into conversation, but Beattie didn't insist on it. Most of the time.

'Herr Silberman owned a large rubber-processing business specialising in seals used on German naval craft.'

We exchanged glances. I could already see the way we'd formulate the radio broadcast to the north Atlantic and Germany. *Officials refute rumours that seals on German vessels hundreds of miles offshore might be letting in water.* Of course, there were no rumours. Beattie and I would make them up.

Beattie read my mind. 'Of course, our slant would be that of good news: production errors on rubber-seal factory lines have *almost* been eliminated.'

Subtle and believable. German submariners beneath the surface of the freezing North Atlantic, wondering whether the seals on their vessels were part of the batch afflicted by production errors. Beattie's propaganda broadcasts in German, aimed at entertaining and informing listeners, often provided more truth than most Germans acquired from their own radio stations. Beattie and I researched the stories meticulously, checking all our facts, but included just the merest bending of the truth: usually a false piece of good news that wasn't really good news at all. Or a little nugget that introduced doubts. *Heartening reports from children's evacuation camps! Diphtheria rates have dropped to their lowest this year. Doctors are optimistic that mortality rates will sink to below a quarter of all infected children . . .* You were a German submariner whose house had been bombed, whose family had been evacuated. You heard that story over the airwaves and your attention was distracted away from British merchant shipping convoys towards the much-loved children you hadn't seen for months. Why the hell couldn't the authorities get a grip? Why was your family's life so unbearable? What exactly were you doing underneath the Atlantic when you should be protecting that wife, that infant son, that sweet daughter of yours?

I blinked, suppressing the thought of my father's face if he knew exactly what kind of work I was engaged in. 'Keep your tongue from evil and your lips from telling lies' – words from the Psalms I tried not to think about too often. When I'd worked on the defence of London from the Luftwaffe he'd been able to tell himself I was saving civilian lives. Helping British bombers drop explosives on German cities had been harder for him to comprehend. Deliberately deceiving people over the radio was something else.

'This kind of material also works on civilian broadcasts to the anxious mother or wife,' Beattie said. 'Makes her fear that her loved one will drown in a leaky submarine.'

Something else to worry about. Something else to make them doubt the value of the war they were fighting.

'Merchant shipping losses have never been higher,' Beattie said, sounding less bullish and – for him – worried. 'The pressure on British farms to produce food is more than farmers can bear. We need the convoys from the States.'

If we could persuade some of those submariners to waste time having their seals checked, more of the precious food cargoes might make it across the Atlantic. Last time I'd been in London I'd noticed how the walls were plastered with posters reminding people not to waste food, depicting stern-jawed merchant seamen facing waves the size of cathedrals or wolf-packs of German submarines to ram home the message.

I'd grown up assuming that food would always be available. My parents disapproved of gluttony and too much unnecessarily fancy food, but Grace and I had never gone hungry. Rationed food just about kept you going now, but wasn't abundant, unless you had a passion for parsnips and turnips. If rations were further cut, mothers would be sending hungry children to school. The Depression was a vivid memory for many people in industrial cities. Empty stomachs and lack of morale were bedfellows.

We passed Bicester and, after some twists and turns, what I thought was the town of Witney – the signposts had gone. Occasionally a shop front retained a place name, but otherwise it was almost impossible to know exactly where we were. I clenched my hands together, hating the feeling of disorientation.

'How are we doing, Atkins?' Beattie asked the driver.

'Making good time, sir.' She made a left turn at an unmarked cross-roads. On the front passenger seat a road atlas sat ready for her to refer to. Atkins hadn't even glanced at it.

'Broadcasting live from the new studio makes us sharper, more responsive.' Beattie was speaking to himself as much as me. 'No more transporting those damn records by Hillman Minx all over the place.' At the moment we pre-recorded our content onto discs and motored them to small radio stations set up in the neighbouring county of Buckinghamshire.

We made a sharp turn into a small lane somewhere north of Swindon. Or so I estimated. A late-winter mist swirling through the valleys made me feel even more disoriented. Beattie frowned. 'We seem to be heading north-east, Atkins?'

'Rumours of army convoys down here, sir.' She had an accent that suggested a smart school and a spell as a debutante. 'Bottlenecks on roads, they said.'

'Are you sure we won't end up in someone's farmyard? Or back in Bedfordshire?'

'I used to hunt around here, sir. Don't worry.'

The car overtook a slow-moving horse-drawn cart and turned left. Beattie nodded approval at the blond head under the peaked cap. He turned his attention to me.

'Submariners remain a key audience both for us and for our sister units. But Herr Silberman may also give us more material suitable for targeting civilians. Once you start talking to refugees it's amazing what pops up in conversation. I'm still hoping to persuade him to come to Britain instead of taking the Pan Am flying boat to New York,' Beattie went on. 'But his wife has family in Brooklyn.'

The mist lifted. We sat looking out at the Cotswold landscape, still washed in muted winter tones, but pleasing, I thought, with its pale gold stone walls and villages that seemed to have emerged from the earth.

'God, I hate the countryside,' Beattie said. 'At least we'll have a few days somewhere warmer and more interesting.'

Atkins slowed down to take a bend. As she accelerated out of it, the car's gearbox emitted a squeak. She tutted.

'Still giving you gyp?' Beattie asked.

'I'll have to look at it once I've dropped you off.'

She didn't always call him sir, I noticed.

I recognised what I thought must be the tower of Cirencester parish church. Dad had once had a friend who'd been vicar here and we'd visited as a family years ago. Atkins turned the car to the south. With her confident tone and whippet-slim figure she reminded me of some of the well-connected girls who'd joined the WAAF at the same time as me. Some of them had been posted to the large RAF station at Rudloe Manor in Wiltshire, less than thirty miles from here, to help with the defence of Bristol and South Wales. I wondered whether they were still there now that the Luftwaffe had eased its raids. Perhaps if I'd been posted to the south-west instead of Bentley Priory, I wouldn't have met Patrick. And wouldn't have been able to make a one-night visit to my family in south-west London in the spring of 1941. So many things would have been different.

The lack of signposts couldn't disguise the views and we were obviously now somewhere to the north-east of Bristol. The city had endured terrible air raids early in 1941. We skirted the centre, heading south-west, I estimated, through outlying villages and suburbs. Eventually we slowed and Atkins turned off the road towards a group of white buildings. This must be Whitchurch. The gearbox emitted another protest. My heart gave a thump.

'Been on a plane before, Hall?' Beattie asked. He probably knew I hadn't.

'No.' I hoped the single word didn't convey the mixture of emotions churning inside me. How many aircraft had I helped position in my previous job? How many crews had I protected with my rapid, accurate calculations, my use of trigonometry? And yet I had never myself set foot in a plane. Would anyone be watching over us as we headed across the Bay of Biscay? I reminded myself that the pilot would have radio contact. The flight would be listed. But radar wouldn't extend into the Bay of Biscay. There'd be no early warning of the enemy's approach. And the Luftwaffe was highly active down there.

'Passenger flights these days aren't as comfortable as the films would have you believe,' Beattie went on, sounding less smug than I might have expected. 'But it's reasonably rare for difficulties to be experienced.'

Atkins drove towards the white buildings. 'The terminal's here.' She got out to open the boot for our suitcases.

'No time to hang around,' Beattie said, examining his watch. I murmured a thanks to Atkins and followed Beattie inside, where we joined a short queue of people waiting to board the Lisbon flight.

Our tickets and passports checked, I walked up the steps into the Dakota behind Beattie, feeling nothing like a movie star, hoping the funk didn't show on my face.

As we seated ourselves, Beattie patted his slightly bulging jacket pocket. 'A quick nip of brandy before take-off eases things, Hall. There's a blackout on the windows so you won't see anything, anyway.'

He could be kind, when it suited him. On several occasions he'd helped refugees working for us who needed papers or assistance with locating other family members who'd fled Europe. He'd presented me with exotic objects such as oranges or tins of shortbread, but liked to keep me off balance, surprising me with sudden changes to routine, this trip to Lisbon being an extreme example. Perhaps his true kindness had been giving me this job, though. Even if I'd never admit this to him.

Only eighteen passengers on the flight. The rest of the cabin was piled with bags of what looked like mail. A co-pilot gave brief, clipped instructions. Beattie passed his flask to me. I took a small sip, feeling the warm liquid hit my stomach. As the Dakota accelerated up the runway, I clutched the edge of my seat, but felt the nip of brandy taking away the edge of my nervousness.

'Fatalism,' Beattie told me, voice carrying above the Dakota's engines. 'If we run into a patrol, you and I can't do anything about it so we might just as well relax.'

I gave a grim internal smile, imagining how this philosophy would have gone down in the Filter Room at Bentley Priory.

He settled into his seat, tugging the belt over his solid middle and letting out a deep breath. 'I'm a bit funny about water,' he said. 'Don't like the thought of having nothing between me and the Atlantic.'

It was an unusually frank admission. 'Can you swim?' I asked. Not that it would make much difference if we were shot down.

'They tried teaching me when I was a child, but when I was about four I had a bad experience, lost my footing in a lake and my head went under. I prefer to keep away from situations where being in water is required.'

'You chose a good landlocked place to work, then,' I said. 'Apart from the pond in the woods there's not too much water near Mulberry House.'

I understood about phobias. My fear of fire had lessened only slightly as months and years passed. I tried not to think of my previous work, of the last radio exchanges I'd heard with pilots screaming as flames engulfed their cockpits. I could see this Dakota dropping to the bottom of the Atlantic, the passengers sitting in their seats as the cold water rose above our faces. I could feel my lungs filling with salty water and not experience the terror that afflicted me when I considered death by fire. My scar seemed to burn more painfully. I closed my eyes and made myself think about Lisbon. Would there be blossom on the city's trees? What might there be to eat? Could I buy presents for my father and my landlady?

Beattie and I didn't say a word during the six-hour flight apart from when we thanked the steward for the mugs of coffee and sandwiches. The latter looked like the usual curly-edged offerings but were actually filled with ham that didn't have the texture of carpet lining.

As the plane descended to Lisbon, some of my stomach churning returned, but when the Dakota came to a stop and we were allowed to lift the blackout, I blinked. It was night but I saw lights. Brightness everywhere. Lisbon called itself the City of Lights, just as Paris did. First time I'd seen an illuminated metropolis in over three years.

Beattie seemed to guess what I was thinking. 'Shame it's slightly foggy, but it's always cheering to see peacetime civilian life, isn't it?'

Of course he'd been over here 'harvesting', as he put it, several times in the early years of the war, during the first refugee rush from Europe.

'Tonight you can just relax, Hall,' he said as a taxi drove us from the airport. 'Nothing on the cards until we meet Herr Silberman at a café for a mid-morning coffee tomorrow at the seaside.' I looked at him. 'Not my choice of venue, but they were adamant it had to be out there.'

It almost sounded like a peacetime jaunt. I sat, still blinking in the taxi. The brightness: street lamps, light shining from apartments and houses, the multi-coloured glare from neon advertising on the top of buildings, all blazing out, unafraid. On a hilltop I saw a floodlit castle. 'What's that?' I asked.

'The Castle of São Jorge – St George to you.'

'It's so . . .' Words failed me.

'Blatant?' he suggested. 'You're feeling the liberation of getting off a small island, Anna. Heady, isn't it?'

Darkness and a sense of geographic confinement had become natural.

'Lisbon has seven hills, like Rome, so there are some good views.'

I watched the brightly lit trams whistle and rattle next to us, some of them curving off the road we were on to shoot up- or downhill like fairground rides. We turned onto a wide avenue, fronted by lit-up hotels and restaurants. The taxi slowed. I clung to the edge of the seat, feeling exposed, half-wanting to glance skywards to check nothing was going to attack me from above.

'Here we are,' Beattie said. 'Not the Aziz or the Tivoli, I'm afraid – bit over budget for us. But this establishment is only mildly infested with the enemy.'

I stopped, half in and half out of the taxi. 'Germans are staying here?'

'Everyone's cheek by jowl in Lisbon. Don't let it worry you, Hall.'

I walked into the lobby feeling like an antelope approaching a pride of lions.

3

Inside the hotel smartly dressed people crowded the reception desk. The staff appeared almost overwhelmed. 'The embassy recommended this place, but they warned that standards mightn't be as they were before the war,' Beattie told me. 'Hotel rooms are scarce in the city now.' He lowered his voice. 'Half of Europe's Jews who are still free and have any money left are here in Lisbon, trying to get out by ship or aeroplane. Half of Germany's here spying on them.' He ran a finger over the reception desk and nodded approvingly. I was looking at an obviously German party at the far end of the lobby, two of the men in uniform. 'Don't scowl at people, Hall, even enemies. I booked rooms next to one another on a floor that's tacitly for Allies only. One does hear stories about our Teutonic friends.'

My skin prickled. Tonight there'd be reassurance in knowing he would sleep in the neighbouring room. I was still blinking at the lights and the chatter of people coming and going, the sounds of motor engines on the avenue outside. 'It's a bit livelier than Aspley Guise, isn't it?' Beattie said.

Once inside my room, I didn't turn the light on – wartime habits being hard to break – and walked to the windows. I stared at the street lights, fascinated by the neon advertising strips for watches, cameras and cars. I craned my neck but couldn't make out the fort on the hillside to the south-east. If things had been different, if I'd been here with

Patrick, we might have planned sight-seeing and some shopping. The only demand placed on us would have been choosing a restaurant. I told myself not to be so foolish but couldn't stop my imaginings. Would we order nightcaps from room service: a couple of brandies? Perhaps I'd run myself a bath and he'd sit on the edge, chatting to me. Or sit in the tub with me . . .

Or perhaps we'd just stand at this window, arms round one another, looking at the lights.

Damn him. Damn Patrick for still being so much in my mind, after all this time. I'd purposefully not read any of the RAF death notices in the newspapers. I prayed he was alive, but I didn't want to know anything about him. And I didn't need him in my head, especially not now, in this new city. Let him be happily entangled with another woman, safe from danger. But let him perhaps think of me sometimes? No, I didn't deserve that. Let him have forgotten me completely.

I turned away from the view to unpack the few clothes in my suitcase. One of the Czech refugees I'd worked with in Bedfordshire had swapped a pot of cleansing lotion for a pair of my warm lisle stockings. The lotion was supposed to be good for damaged skin, but the pot was almost empty. Was there anything in Portugal that might be good for my face? They said olive oil was soothing. Did the Portuguese produce olive oil? Or would almond oil work better? I was desperate to strengthen the small muscles on the right side of my face, and massaging it might help. When I looked at my reflection, my attempts at smiling still looked lopsided. Often the damaged skin woke me up at night, seeming to recall the fire in its cells, the pain cranking up my mind, filling it with fears.

∼❧∽

I woke to hear car horns on the street outside instead of the muted late-winter birdsong of Lily Cottage's garden. Checking my watch I saw it was quarter to eight. No mention of breakfast had been made. Beattie wasn't one for early morning meetings. I washed and dressed quickly and headed out of the lobby onto the street, relieved not to see any Germans hanging around, nodding at the concierge. The tree-lined avenue on which the hotel sat stretched left and right. I read the name on a signpost: Avenida da Liberdade. Liberty Avenue. It seemed an appropriately positive name.

A motorist hooted at me as I crossed the road without looking. So many cars. So many people driving around on non-essential business: shopping, visiting friends, going to non-war-related jobs.

Businessmen headed by foot for work. Some of them stepped into cafés where they were obviously in the habit of buying the tiny cups of what looked like very strong coffee. Small boys buffed their shoes as they drank. All around the bustle of a peacetime city made my eyes widen. No barrage balloons. No signs directing pedestrians to air-raid shelters. No sandbags, boarded-up windows or shattered glass.

A side street leading uphill promised a good view. I followed an elderly woman carrying a wicker basket, admiring her stamina as she briskly tackled the walk up the cobbled pavement. The street opened up into a small square, where more men sat at tables, plates of pastries in front of them. My stomach gurgled. I wished I had the nerve and the Portuguese to order coffee and pastries for myself, but there were few other women sitting outside at the tables and I was wary of drawing attention. I checked my watch again and decided to head back down to the Avenida and our hotel for breakfast. As I turned towards the street leading steeply downhill, I saw a single woman sitting at a café table, probably a refugee, perhaps Jewish, from France or Belgium. Something about her clothes, the navy slacks and the silk blouse, worn half tucked in, half out, caught my eye. A long string of pearls was wound twice round her neck. Two curves of vermillion marked out her lips, through which she drew on a cigarette. In front of her was one of the small coffee cups. Our eyes met. She gave me a half-smile and raised the cup. I nodded at her.

Perhaps she was a German spy. There was something in that salute that made me think not. She'd been proud, yet wary, perhaps on the defensive. That lipstick was her shield against the world. The slacks were an act of defiance. Did she feel she needed to assert herself in Lisbon, where so many of her enemies walked around?

I'd dressed in a light wool-blend frock, cut on the bias, falling just below my knees, with a veiled hat trimmed in the same navy. Grace had made the dress for me in the spring of 1940, using the last of a precious piece of fabric and a pre-war paper pattern. She'd been a promising seamstress and had briefly taken tailoring classes before Mum had become terminally ill. I'd frequently been asked where my dress had come from. It had been the last thing she'd sewn for me.

Patrick had never seen me in this day dress because our courtship had played out either at night, or on days out when we'd gone for walks to country inns. I'd started to borrow his knitwear for these excursions. *I love to see you bundled up in my old jumpers, darling. So wholesome and yet so alluring . . .*

It struck me that dressed in civilian clothes rather than uniform I was technically a kind of spy.

As I approached the Avenida a solidly built young soldier in German uniform came towards me. My muscles stiffened. An enemy, right in front of me. Half of me still expected him to stand to one side and let me pass, as most men would. This one smirked and continued to walk directly at me. I jumped aside, missing his grey-uniformed shoulder by an inch. A tram bell rang out in warning. My nerves jangled. 'Lovely manners,' I called after him in my best High German accent. His shoulders stiffened and he turned around to glare at me. I wanted to ask him if his mother had brought him up to be so discourteous, wanted to scream at him that his people had taken my sister's life – had murdered a good, kind person. I reminded myself that we were supposed to be keeping a low profile. I looked away and walked on.

There was no sign of Beattie in the hotel reception. I'd have to eat my breakfast alone.

It was served in the smaller dining room of the hotel, a tiled room full of morning light. Fresh bread rolls with real butter, pastries, coffee, a small plate of fruit. To my left a couple sat talking quietly to one another in French. In the corner a single man read a *Frankfurter Allgemeine*. From time to time he lowered the paper and studied the other guests in the breakfast room. When our eyes met, he bowed his head, eyebrows raised. At least this one was pretending to be civil. I found this more unsettling than the uncouthness of the soldier earlier on. I gave a curt nod and returned to my pastry, which was worthy of attention, being one of the most delicious things I'd eaten in over a year.

When I'd finished I walked past a middle-aged couple coming into the room, he in uniform, she in a severely cut suit. They looked me up and down. I felt an urge to ask them who the hell they thought they were.

The woman eyed me with distaste and muttered something about the veil being a good idea for one such as me. A childish part of me wanted to tell her that if I had a piggy face like hers I'd be wearing a bag over my head. The thought made me smile. I was glad to see her eyes narrow with irritation. Then I felt a pang of embarrassment at my schoolgirl response.

I returned to my room to clean my teeth and waited for Beattie in the lobby, mercifully less crowded now. He appeared in a lightweight suit and greeted me with a grunt. Still too early for him to want much conversation. At a nod from Beattie, the doorman found us a cab, which drove us through a large square with a statue in the middle, tiled in an unusual wavy pattern. 'Rossio Square,' Beattie said. 'The railway station here is where most of the refugees arrive in the city. We'll come back later.'

The taxi turned off into a quieter street, heading south-west, I estimated. We passed shops selling leather goods, embroidered linens and books. 'There may be time for some quick shopping tomorrow,' Beattie said, 'but probably not from that establishment.' He pointed to a corner. '*Alemanha*', the sign said. Germany. A propaganda office with window displays. I glimpsed photographs of uniformed men and posters of saluting youths.

'We might examine the displays in detail another time,' Beattie said.

'How can the Portuguese bear having the Germans here?'

Beattie shrugged. 'They probably feel the same way about us. We're supposed to be their old allies, but keeping us happy while preventing the Germans and their Spanish friends from invading Portugal is a tricky business.'

The Germans wanted Portuguese wolfram, I remembered, a metal used in munitions manufacturing.

'We've got a propaganda centre in the city, too,' Beattie told me. I wondered what our shop displayed: pictures of the King and Queen? The Trooping of the Colour? Henley Regatta? Was our version more or less acceptable to the Portuguese?

The Tagus was in front of us. My heart lit up at the sight of the river, glittering in the spring sunshine. We turned into a modern-looking road. 'Newly built and makes it much quicker to get to the coast,' Beattie said.

'Where exactly are we going?' I asked.

'A resort called Estoril,' Beattie told me. 'It also boasts a rather interesting fortress, but the main draw now is the casino.'

'People still go to casinos?' The world was in turmoil, but people still bet on black or red?

'Don't be such a vicar's daughter. Even in the trenches men place bets. And you yourself must have played rummy or whist off-duty or down in an air-raid shelter.'

'Not as glamorous.'

'The more prosperous refugees catch the sun, while the Gestapo watch them. Cat and mouse. For a period in 1940 the refugees included our very own Duke and Duchess of Windsor, until they were sent to the Bahamas.'

The Duke, our king until his abdication, had long been rumoured to have friends on the German side.

'Herr and Frau Silberman have a favourite café on the front – not my favourite rendezvous with all that damn water around, but whatever makes them happy.'

The city started to fall away, replaced by suburbs. It was market day in one of the squares; stalls were set out with cabbages, cauliflowers, beetroots and fish in a variety of shapes and sizes. Oranges, too. My mouth watered as I recalled the taste. 'Stop gawping, Hall,' Beattie said. 'You're like a child outside Hamley's toyshop at Christmas.'

When we arrived at our destination in Estoril, the middle-aged couple were already sitting under a sun umbrella on a hotel terrace. I noted a smartly dressed young man and woman on a table nearby. Tanned. Blue-eyed. Athletic. German. Beattie didn't seem to notice them. Again I felt uncertain how to respond. Enemies, close enough to touch, and we had to eat and drink as though this were normal? My eyes were blinking in the bright seaside light. Thank goodness I'd thought to pack a pair of dark glasses in my satchel.

Frau Silberman was thin; pale, despite the sunshine, eyes flickering from one spot to another. Her husband appeared more relaxed, but I noticed how he clutched a small leather case on his lap, probably containing their visas and money. Good, he had his back to the Germans. Good, also, that I could sit with my right side in the shade. I'd have to pull up the veil to talk to the Silbermans but wouldn't feel as exposed.

Beattie seated himself so he was facing the young German couple. He removed a small potted plant from the table, placing it on the wall beside us.

'Probably bugged,' he mouthed at me. He ordered coffees and pastries for the four of us in what sounded like rough but effective Portuguese. Frau Silberman looked at my face and then away to the beach.

It was a peacetime scene. A vendor wheeled an ice-cream cart down to the sand, where a young female gymnast performed perfect cartwheels and somersaults in the air, ending each set with a graceful handstand.

'I have our Pan Am tickets,' Herr Silberman said. 'We fly to America tomorrow.'

'We can't persuade you to stay here longer and help us?' Beattie spoke in a low, gentle voice.

The waiter appeared with a laden tray. '*Pasteis de nata*,' he said, smiling at me. I hoped my greed hadn't been too obvious.

'We have to get out.' Frau Silberman spoke under her breath as the waiter left, eyes on the German couple. 'I don't feel safe here. People are watching us. At night I hear footsteps outside our hotel door.'

'Anything you can tell us today will help our efforts.' Beattie sounded soothing. The young German couple continued to stare at the four of us. Even if we were out of earshot, it might be conceivable that either or both of the pair could lip-read.

Beattie's hand swept a linen napkin off the table. 'So clumsy. Excuse me.' He bent down. 'Who were your biggest clients?' he asked the man quietly while he was out of sight of the German couple. 'What were the names of ships or submarines that used your rubber seals? What kind of manufacturing error would cause a fault in the processed rubber?' He sat up again.

Herr Silberman stiffened. 'When I was still running the factory our quality was first rate. We never let our seals leave the plant unless they were perfect.' Beattie took out a cigarette case and offered him a cigarette. Herr Silberman took one and muttered names and details.

I took notes, writing pad out of sight on my lap, careful to use a form of shorthand. The industrialist's wife never ceased her restless eye sweeps. 'Why exactly do you want this information?' she asked, covering her face with her hand as she spoke.

'I can't tell you,' Beattie said. 'Rest assured that anything you give us is gold dust.'

But Frau Silberman was distracted. 'That girl on the beach is attracting the wrong kind of attention,' she whispered. 'She's Jewish. I've seen her before, here and in the city.'

The girl's tangle of thick reddish-brown hair certainly made her stand out.

'Sometimes people shout after her, saying she's stolen their money. Is she mad to be so obvious?'

Her husband pressed her right hand. I noticed an indentation on Frau Silberman's ring finger. Had a valuable ring been sold or handed over to a border guard in return for turning a blind eye?

Beattie glanced at the gymnast. 'Probably the kid's best chance of earning enough to buy a ticket to Palestine on some old steamer without a proper visa.'

Herr Silberman resumed his descriptions of the naval chiefs and junior ministers he had dealt with, those he had taken to lunch, to dinner, to the opera. 'They didn't boot me out of my own company immediately,' he said. 'Until 1938 I carried on almost as usual. Then they stole everything from me but kept me working as an adviser in one of my own factories, on a pittance until we made a run for it.'

'Nobody knows more about the industry than you, Frank,' his wife said, suddenly sitting straighter and setting her chin. Beattie motioned with his hand that she should keep her voice down. The sea breeze was blowing my hat brim up and down, exposing more of my scarred skin.

Herr Silberman squeezed his wife's hand. 'I spent years perfecting our rubber seal. I designed it to save lives. I know this sounds strange, but part of me still wants my products to keep German seamen safe.'

'For God's sake, remember your brother and that camp,' Frau Silberman said. 'He was sent there before the war. When they let him go, he'd lost two front teeth and one of his kidneys no longer worked,' she told us.

'Where's your brother now?' Beattie asked.

'We last saw him in Hamburg. He was supposed to be heading to Switzerland – there's a priest, a naturalised German who helps Jews. But my brother doesn't reply to letters any more.'

The young German couple put coins on the table and got up, seemingly losing interest in our group. A tabby cat slunk onto the terrace and curled up on the tiles in the sun. The industrialist's wife looked at it. There was something in her eyes I understood.

'Can you give me the priest's name?' Beattie asked in a voice so quiet Herr Silberman had to lean forward to catch it. He nodded at me to pass over my writing pad and wrote 'Fr Paul Becker'.

'He's a good man. I don't want him compromised,' Herr Silberman told Beattie, handing me back the writing pad.

'We'll be discreet,' Beattie said. 'We want the war to end, the killing to stop, the gangsters in charge put on trial. We want sailors and submariners to surrender to us because it's hopeless.'

A young man entered the terrace and sat down in a wicker chair close by, seemingly absorbed in a book.

'We want German servicemen and civilians to have doubts about the system and what's going on at home.'

I was actually working on a radio play with that very goal in mind. I'd brought my notes so I could fill in any quiet time with writing a few more scenes.

Men in what must have been Portuguese police uniforms were moving the gymnast off the beach. She wasn't taking it well. I could almost see the sparks flying off her. She'd be a good character in a play. Fully conveying the force of rage emitting from the girl would be challenging, though.

Herr Silberman stood up, briefly eyeing the young man in the wicker chair. 'They're everywhere, listening in. If they think I'm helping the British they'll take it out on my brother.'

Beattie had told me about assassinations and kidnappings in Lisbon – Gestapo agents seizing people from the streets. The Portuguese secret police raiding hostels and taking refugees off to internment camps. And as for what might happen to the brother if he was still in Germany, well, Herr Silberman's fears were understandable.

'When exactly do you fly?' Beattie asked, although he'd have known the flight time.

'We can't see you again, Mr Beattie, we have packing to do.' Frau Silberman picked up the handbag – an expensive pre-war Parisian-looking model. The edging was peeling off the soft tan leather straps, which were starting to fray. Frau Silberman had probably sat in train carriages at border crossings, her fingers worrying away at those straps. 'Thank you for the coffee and good luck with your endeavours.' Her eyes met mine. 'I wish we were braver people. We were once, before I first became ill in France. Before we had to cross the Pyrenees by night.' She shuddered.

I held Frau Silberman's gaze. 'I hope the future brings you peace of mind after everything you've suffered.' I pictured the couple in an American diner, admiring the architecture of Manhattan, feeling lost and free all at the same time.

Herr Silberman stopped. He turned around to me. I noticed just how stooped his shoulders were. '*Fräulein*, do you think you can begin to understand what we've been through?'

I met his weary gaze. 'I've never experienced what you have,' I said. 'But I can try to imagine.' An ironic smile covered his face. I half-closed my eyes. 'Going out to buy provisions and feeling nervous because there's a new face on the street or someone in a shop queue who shows an interest in you. Flinching every time you see anyone in uniform.

Packing up – again – and abandoning more of your possessions.' I looked at Frau Silberman. 'Even your cat. Saying goodbye to people, not knowing whether you will ever see them again. Telling one another it will all be fine, even when you can hear police cars rumbling over cobblestones towards you.'

He frowned. I'd gone too far, presumed too much, but what the hell, I went on. 'Some mornings when you wake up, the sun's out and you forget. And then you remember again.' My voice shook. I'd put too much of myself into the last sentence. I woke up happy most mornings now, but moments later memories ambushed me. The other words I wanted to say dried up inside me.

Frau Silberman touched my right cheek. I froze. Nobody apart from a doctor or nurse touched my skin like that. '*Liebling*, you have lost someone, haven't you?'

A girl lying crumpled beside a burning velvet curtain.

Nobody said anything for a moment.

'Give me that.' Herr Silberman sat down and put out a hand for my pad.

He turned his back on the wicker lounger and scribbled down words. 'Technical details,' he murmured. 'Names of the wives of some of the people in the ministry and navy I used to sell to. The months of their birthdays.' He gave a brief smile at my surprise. 'Well-judged presents kept us safe for a while. A senior submariner had an elderly Pomeranian he adored. I gave him a leather collar for the dog. He wasn't such a bad man.'

'We did have an old cat,' his wife said, addressing me. 'We brought him with us from Germany. Jews were barred from owning animals.' Her voice grew harder. 'Did you know that our pets were confiscated and destroyed? Even young and healthy ones, just to punish us?'

I noted it mentally for weaving into a future broadcast. Sometimes the truth threw us more useful lines than the lies we created.

'We kept Noodle indoors. Our servants in Germany were loyal. But then we had to leave him in France.' She put a hand to her throat. 'We should have taken him to the vet to . . .'

'He'll be well looked after,' her husband told Frau Silberman.

She frowned at me. 'How did you know?'

I nodded at the tabby asleep in the sun. 'The way you looked at him.'

'You're sharp, young lady.'

With a nod to us, Herr Silberman led his wife away.

The gymnast had shaken off the detaining arms of the police and slunk away between the parasols on the beach, not unlike a cat herself. I watched her run up the steps to the hotel terrace in a few easy bounds. Her auburn mop of hair was cut with a fringe falling just above her eyes, which gave her an intense, questioning look. She wore a shabby lower garment that looked like a divided skirt, presumably to preserve her modesty when she was upside down, and a faded blue shirt. An old jacket was tied round her waist. The girl met my gaze boldly as she dodged between the tables, evading the waiter who moved towards her.

Beattie blinked, checked one pocket, then another, looked under the table. 'Damn, my wallet.' He frowned in the direction of the street. 'That little devil must have taken it as she brushed past.'

I undid my handbag and drew out my purse, which contained the *escudo* Beattie had handed to me on the plane.

Beattie looked at his watch. 'On to our lunch now, I think. Let's get away from the damn sea.'

My heart lifted at the thought of even more unrationed food.

'I booked a place near the city centre. They say the fish is good. Afterwards there are some cafés in Rossio Square where we might find other persons of interest. Though the Silbermans alone have made the trip worthwhile, especially with their mention of a tasty Swiss cheese.' He rubbed his hands and gave me a searching look. It was either the case that he was pleased with my performance with the Silbermans or felt that I had over-exceeded my brief. He would find a way of making his pleasure or otherwise known to me over the next day or so.

We had lunch in a restaurant round the corner from the German propaganda centre. I ate fish fresher than anything I'd seen for over two years and relished the scent of the lemon wedge I squeezed over it. Beattie regarded me over the wine carafe with benevolence. 'You did well, Anna, getting them to open up.'

I blushed, annoyed with myself for being so pleased.

'It feels so strange,' I said. 'Being in such proximity to people we've been fighting for years now.'

'Use it as research,' he said. 'Some of these people are your audience.'

'I suppose so.'

'But . . . ?'

'When I think of our listeners I have to like them. Or at least empathise with them.'

Beattie nodded. 'You need to get under their skin. And they need to get under yours.'

We finished our wine in silence. Beattie threw down his napkin. 'No need to hang around wasting time. Shift yourself, Hall.'

He summoned the waiter, giving him the name of someone official sounding who would settle the bill. We walked up into what Beattie told me was one of the older parts of the city, the Bairro Alto. To the left the soaring walls and arches of a ruined church caught my eye, making me stop to stare up at them. 'A Carmelite church hit by the earthquake in the eighteenth century,' Beattie told me. Our expedition involved multiple sets of steps. Beattie took them in his stride, though I noticed he insisted on pausing a couple of times to admire the view, taking in ragged breaths of oxygen. Again I admired the São Jorge fortress on the opposite hillside and a huge monastery adjacent to it.

'No time for tourism.' Beattie led me on, turning off one of the stone stairways into a narrow side street, hardly more than an alleyway.

'Finckler is a dress designer,' Beattie told me, pressing the bell. 'He owned a studio in Paris but used to live in Berlin.'

Like Beattie himself.

'He does all kinds of things now while he waits for a visa.' We knocked on the black door. Footsteps pattered down. Finckler was small, neatly dressed even though his suit fabric had faded. Beattie introduced me and Finckler showed us upstairs. Rolls of fabric were laid out on long tables for pinning and cutting. Draped over mannequin dolls were dresses and jackets, their folds falling into elegant lines. I hadn't seen so much silk and linen for years and felt an urge to bury my face in the new garments and breathe them in.

'We can still find quality fabrics here.' Finckler was watching me. 'Cottons, linens, wools. And refugees lug bales of silk across Europe and sell them here. I can offer those with money clothes as good as they ever had in Berlin and Paris.'

I wanted to run my hands over a roll of soft ivory linen but wouldn't risk marking the fabric.

'You're right to admire that, Miss Hall,' he said. 'I thought a dress with a pleated skirt, with a few rows of this above the hem?' He pointed at a reel of narrow midnight-blue satin ribbon.

'How long would the skirt be?'

He looked at my dress. 'Just to where your hem is. If we were in Paris I'd say above the knee, more modern. Young women with legs like yours should show them off.' He said this dispassionately so I didn't mind the comment. Finckler shrugged. 'But here? Portugal is a con-servative place.'

'And what are you making with this?' Beattie asked, his attention apparently on a folded piece of satin. I knew he'd been taking in the discussion of my legs.

'An evening gown for the German mistress of a senior diplomat at their embassy.' Finckler gave a deep laugh. 'Ironic, no? She's actually married to one of the diplomat's juniors.'

'The German mistress comes up here?' I felt myself stiffen. How could Finckler bear to measure her, pin the satin round her?

He nodded. 'Bizarre, isn't it? And she doesn't mind climbing up all the steps to this studio. She pays good money so I'll ensure her new gown has the diplomat panting.'

I stared at a little cardboard box full of what looked like small, round bullets. Lead weights for dress hems. 'It's breezy down by the seafront,' I said.

'Could lead to all kinds of exposure,' Beattie added.

But I was thinking of something else. Lead bullets. Shortages. Malfunctioning bullets. Could we claim slave labourers in munitions factories had tampered with them? A story formed in my mind. I pulled out my notebook again and scribbled a few ideas for a quick radio news item. *The authorities have pounced on a group of slave labourers in a munitions factory wilfully sabotaging ammunition to endanger our soldiers.* Any troops picking up the broadcast might waste an hour or so inspecting their bullets. At best, whole cartons might be recalled. 'Sometimes you'll be the fisher and sometimes you'll be the spinner of tales,' Beattie had told me when I'd started this work. 'Your listeners may be military or civilians, but the objective is the same: to make them act in Allied, not German, interests.'

Finckler turned to Beattie. 'The fancy woman is my main news. There's always a chance she's been planted to keep an eye on me, but I don't think so.' I couldn't help looking out of the window to see whether anyone was hovering on the street. He went to one of the mannequins and slit open the long hem of the skirt it wore with his scissors, removing a piece of paper. 'It's all in here.'

'Thank you.' Beattie took the paper.

Finckler looked again at the roll of ivory linen I was still admiring. 'Years ago I made a dress from a very similar linen for your mother, Alexander.' I blinked at the old man's use of Beattie's first name. 'Uta's dress was longer, of course, as was the fashion then, and the waistline was lower. But the skirt had a navy trim, too.'

'Mama always loved her clothes. I remember her dressing up to go out with my father.'

'You must miss her.'

'Yes.'

I'd never heard Beattie talk about his mother before, hadn't known she'd been called Uta. I moved towards the folded satin to avoid intruding on the more personal conversation. The afternoon light falling through the window brought out the fabric's pearlescent shimmer.

'That peach would be a good shade for you, wouldn't it, Miss Hall?' Finckler said.

I smiled. 'My sister used to say I was hopelessly weak when it came to beautiful clothes.'

'What's wrong with that?' he asked. 'Beauty has its place in the world.'

'You're both coming over terribly philosophical,' Beattie complained. 'Where's that writing pad of yours, Hall?'

I handed it to him. He flicked through the pages and gave it to Finckler. 'Have you heard of this man of the cloth in Zurich?'

Finckler took out a pair of reading glasses and peered at the words. 'I have. They say he's helped people.'

Beattie took the pad back and gave it to me without further comment.

⁓❦⁓

'He liked you,' he said, when we were out on the street again.

'Will Finckler stay here much longer?'

Beattie didn't answer for a moment. 'Finckler needs to get on a boat. He's made too many clothes for dangerous people, knows too many secrets.'

'Is he still saving for a passage?'

'For his niece in Germany.' Beattie looked over his shoulder. 'She's in hiding. He needs to bribe people. He knows it's probably too late, though.'

At least we could help him by paying for his intelligence. 'And it's from your time in Berlin that you know him?'

He said nothing.

I was about to apologise for asking when he spoke. 'He was a friend of my mother's. When I found out he was here it seemed like Providence. Run a tape measure round someone, wrap fabrics round them, and you find out all kinds of things.'

Beattie made an impatient tutting noise as though he was wasting his own time. 'Let's get down these diabolical steps and go to Rossio Square for a coffee.'

My nerves were jingling. I certainly didn't need any more caffeine, a substance I'd only been drinking in small quantities at home. But I knew better than to demur.

The café he chose on Rossio Square was large, probably packed at night and still busy enough now. I ordered a cup of tea. Beattie looked on as I added milk. 'For God's sake, Hall, you might as well be in Cheltenham.'

I added a sugar lump to spite him.

I spotted a slight figure moving over the wavy-patterned tiles and tensed. 'It's her – the girl who took your wallet.' I was out of my chair, slinging my satchel over my chest, moving through the café door, not even waiting for Beattie's reply. I had the advantage of surprise and my shoes were rubber soled, almost silent on the square's tiles as I ran after her. The pleats in my dress made it good for running in, something Grace probably hadn't thought of when she'd made it. The girl turned, heading back towards the Bairro Alto and I followed her, the breeze shifting my veil as I sped up. An elderly woman stared at my suddenly exposed right cheek and hissed a word like '*bruxa-anjo*'. I didn't know much Portuguese but could guess it wasn't a compliment.

The girl must have heard the old woman's exclamation and guessed that someone might be coming after her. She accelerated into a sprint towards another set of stone steps. Two workmen carrying planks into a run-down shop blocked her path. Without breaking her pace the girl sprang neatly around them. I was fit but this sprint was turning into a steeplechase. My heart pounded as we continued uphill. To the left and right, lines hung with washing over the alleyways and lanes. Paint was scuffed off walls. The smell of the drains made my nostrils twitch.

I'd left my map on the café table. As my lungs protested I tried to memorise slogans painted on the walls. The pair of red children's trousers hanging from a line. The bush flowering carmine behind a crumbling wall. We reached the top of the steps. The girl shot right, along a road curving round the hillside.

Brakes squealed. A man on a bicycle nearly toppled over. Again the girl sprung nimbly around, but it cost her a second. I caught up with her and grabbed the frayed sleeve of her jacket. 'Wallet – now,' I gasped before I doubled-over, lungs empty.

The girl blinked beneath her thick auburn fringe, perhaps in surprise at the use of German.

'The wallet.' I said it loudly.

She put a hand into her jacket pocket. I caught the glint of metal before she pulled the knife out.

4

My right knee caught the girl's wrist. She gave a gasp of surprise and the knife fell to the ground. The man on the bicycle muttered an oath and cycled away.

'The wallet. Now,' I said, stooping for the knife, but still holding on to her sleeve. 'Before I start shouting for the police and complaining that an illegal alien has turned a knife on me.'

At the mention of the police the girl's eyes widened. She pulled Beattie's wallet out from an inside pocket and handed it over, her face blank. Perhaps she was bracing herself for the arrival of the feared Portuguese secret police. I placed the wallet and knife in my satchel. The girl eyed the street; she would dash away any second.

'Jewish?' I asked, in a low voice.

A slight nod of the head.

'The police will lock you up or worse if you steal from tourists.'

'You're not a tourist,' the girl said. 'Nobody's here for a holiday at this time of year. Everyone wants to go somewhere else.'

'I'm a law-abiding visitor. With a visa.'

The girl looked amused.

'Whereabouts in Germany are you from?' I asked.

She said nothing.

'That's a northern German accent.'

'Berlin originally,' she muttered. 'I moved around.'

'I expect you did.' I tightened my hold on her. 'How did you get here?'

'Enough of your questions.' She tilted her chin upwards. 'What happened to your face?'

'Incendiary.' I could almost recite the word now without feeling the emotion that went with it.

The expression in the girl's face was unreadable. 'Where?'

'London. In the Blitz.'

'Does it still hurt?'

I was surprised that the question didn't bother me particularly. 'Sometimes, yes.'

The girl nodded. 'That woman called you *bruxa-anjo*, didn't she? Know what that means?'

'Something-angel?'

'Witch-angel. Was she right?'

'I'm certainly no witch,' I said. 'I mean you no harm. We're on the same side.'

The chin jutted up again at that.

'I saw your acrobatic show on the beach. You're very good.'

'I was a circus performer at the beginning of the war,' the girl said. 'The family who owned the circus managed to keep me on for a few years. When they were forced to sack me I went from port to port as a dancer and performer. Not doing . . . that . . .' she added, flushing. 'You know, going with men.' I was leading her downhill now, her sleeve still in my hand.

'So you performed splits and cartwheels for naval types. Sailors, submariners?' I could see the grimy bars, smell the smoke and spilled beer, hear the raucous shouts and whistles. And in the midst a small, supple figure contorting herself into all kinds of shapes, then whipping round a glass for them to fill with coins, ducking male hands as they groped at her body, or tolerating them if she had to.

'Seamen are generous tippers,' the girl said, appearing to relax a degree. 'Even here. You can let go of me now. I won't run away.'

I dropped her arm. My skin was pricking as scenes played in my imagination. I could almost overhear snatches of the seamen's gossip, the juicy bits they couldn't resist letting out, even while they kept an eye open for the informer who might betray a joker or rumour-monger. This was what it felt like when things came together – ideas, people, histories, messages; when the magic began to work. I watched her closely as we descended the steps in case she made a dash for one of the side streets, but she walked just in front of me, keeping a steady pace. I wasn't entirely sure I knew where I was going.

'Calçada do Carmo,' she said, pointing at a steep zigzagging cobbled street below us. 'It takes us to Rossio Square.' A flash of amusement passed over her face. 'In case you're lost?'

'Tell me the names of ports you worked in,' I said, to stop her from enjoying herself too much.

'Kiel. Bremen. Hamburg. Saint-Nazaire in France, too, for a bit, when I managed to leave Germany.' The girl was talking quickly now, seeming almost relieved to tell her story. 'Some sailors are more . . . open. They're at sea, they visit foreign ports, hear people talk in a way they don't at home. Some of the poison misses them.'

I motioned her across the road.

'Where are you taking me?'

'To meet my colleague. He's in a café in the square.' Her body tensed, but I tugged gently at her arm and we crossed over.

Beattie was still sitting at the table where I'd left him. I felt a sense of pride that he'd trusted me to catch her alone. Or perhaps it was simply that he'd decided to let me do the sprinting. Around him waiters wiped down tables, darting curious looks at us. I had the distinct impression they recognised our new friend. 'Three coffees,' he told them. 'And a plate of pastries with the custard in them.' He got up and pulled out a chair for the girl. 'You look hungry,' he said in German.

'I've been starving since we left France,' she said, appearing younger and less feral.

I handed Beattie his wallet, knowing he had noted the 'we' she'd used, too.

'What's your name?' he asked the girl.

'They call me Micki.'

'You steal because you're hungry, Micki?'

Micki started to say something but stopped, looking down at her shoes: dancer's pumps with rubber soles. A silver sports car I recognised as a German BMW Roadster slowed as it passed us. A man with short fair hair leered at us before accelerating off.

Beattie turned his head to watch it drive away.

'I hate them,' Micki said.

'You're stealing for someone?' he said softly, looking back at her. 'Who is it, Micki? A man?' He shook his head. 'No. Someone more vulnerable.' He put a hand on the girl's chin and tilted her head, looking into her brown eyes. 'Your baby?'

She tried to look away, but Beattie wouldn't let her. 'My little brother,' she said at last. 'He's sick. We can't get a visa for him the ordinary way. I thought a bribe might help.'

Probably not. Visa numbers were limited, strictly controlled. 'You might be better off spending your money on a doctor for him,' I said. 'Was he with you when you worked in the bars of Bremen, Kiel and all the other places?'

I said the names of the ports quietly but deliberately for Beattie and felt a buzz of interest from him even though his expression remained neutral.

Micki nodded. 'Maxi wasn't too sick at first. I had money and there was still a doctor who'd see him.'

'How long ago did you leave Germany?' Beattie asked.

'Nine months ago. Feels like much longer.'

'You've done well to survive so long.'

'It's been hard,' she said shortly.

The pastries arrived. 'Eat up,' Beattie told her. 'Then take us to your brother.'

She stuffed two of the pastries into her mouth, and placed the remaining one in a pocket.

A taxi took us to a tenement in a south-east quarter of Lisbon called, Beattie told me, the Alfama. The driver let us out before we reached the front door as the house was positioned up yet another set of steps. We ascended, Beattie managing to keep up with us. Micki pointed at a faded and chipped sign on the door advertising a *pension*. 'Maxi and I have a room to ourselves. And use of a basin on the same floor. Most of the refugees have been shoved into tourist centres on the coast, but we're in the centre of town.' She made it sound as though this hovel were the Tivoli hotel.

I felt a pang for the girl. Despite her tough appearance, she put me in mind of Grace. It was something about the expression her dark eyes took on when they didn't blaze with defiance: humorous, self-mocking.

I resisted the urge to place a handkerchief to my nose as we climbed the stairs. The girl took a key from her pocket and unlocked a door to a windowless room that was probably really a cupboard. There were two beds, or, more accurately, a mattress and a small pallet on the floor. On the ceiling above the mattress someone had screwed in a series of hooks to attach a curtain for privacy. A small, thin boy lay on the pallet, covered in a faded quilt, eyes closed, his skin the colour of paper, his lips slightly parted.

'What's the illness?' I asked.

'Tuberculosis.'

Beattie and I exchanged glances. Short of sending Maxi to a sanatorium in the Swiss Alps, little could probably be done for him now. Even at home people who looked as far gone with the disease seldom survived.

Beattie took bank notes from his wallet and placed them on the bed. 'Buy Maxi the best food you can find.' He turned away from the boy and lowered his voice. 'Your little brother can't travel overseas. We'll pay for him to be transferred to a hospital.' His words became softer. 'He'll be well cared for. We'll find a room for you close by.'

Over Micki's face emotions flickered one after the other: disbelief, grief, resignation and then burning curiosity.

'You want to know why I'm offering this to an impoverished refugee – a pickpocket I've never met before?'

She nodded.

'Here's the answer. When your brother no longer needs you, you'll have a visa to fly to Bristol in England. You'll work for us.'

'Who are you?'

He put a finger on his lips. 'This work will, however, commence while you're still here in Lisbon.'

'I never said I'd work for you.' She gave him a sideways look.

He ignored her. 'Actually, you'll start this afternoon, while we wait for your brother to wake up. Sergeant Hall will take notes.'

'Sergeant Hall?' She rolled her eyes. 'Is that what he calls you?' she asked me.

'My name is Anna,' I told her, ignoring Beattie's frown.

'What is this work, Anna?'

Beattie coughed. 'German sailors and submariners.' He pointed to the single chair by the bed. 'Sit down, Micki, and start recollecting.'

'What do you want to know about the sailors?'

He smiled at her. 'Everything. Beer or schnapps? Their children's nicknames, whether they tell rude jokes about important men and their whores.'

She scowled at him. 'Are you some kind of pervert? What do you want to know that stuff for?'

Beattie and I looked at one another. We couldn't tell her who we worked for, what we did. But there had to be some way of reassuring her that it mattered. That we could use the names to make our broadcasts more personal. If we knew which men served on which crews we could ask Ciphers to keep an ear open for information about promotions. Congratulations could be sent across the airwaves, further reassuring submariners that we were an official source. Sometimes birthday wishes went down well, too.

Beattie leant forward. 'We want to trip them up,' he said.

'Who's *them*?'

'German combatants. And civilians. We want to make them believe things that aren't true.'

'Germans have been doing that for years.'

He laughed. 'But our lies will help us beat them.'

Some of the tension went from her shoulders.

'So we need all the gossip you picked up as you juggled, cartwheeled and sat on their laps.'

⁂

Beattie and I ate dinner that night in a restaurant that almost made me want to weep with its perfect white tablecloths, its aromas of cooking meat and fish, and replete menu cards. 'We've earned a slap-up meal.' Beattie filled my wine glass. 'You'll like this; it's a red we rarely see in Britain, even in peacetime. This trip has been all I hoped for. And more.' He sounded warm. When he'd taken an appreciative sip of his wine he nodded at me. 'You did well catching the girl.'

'Micki.'

He gave me an amused glance. Of course he remembered Micki's name. The waiter came over to light the candles on our table. As his lighter flicked in front of me I tried not to flinch. Beattie looked at me. He must have noticed my phobia before, every time he lit up in front of me. These days I didn't smoke as much as I had done and when I flicked my own lighter, I held the flame as far away from me as possible.

'That little brother of hers looks so ill.' I swallowed.

'I wouldn't give poor old Maxi more than a few days. No reason for her to hang on here after that.' Beattie helped himself to another piece of bread from the silver basket. 'I'll push things along so we have Micki on British soil within a few weeks.'

Micki spoke barely any English and would be mourning her brother as she arrived in a strange country at the end of winter. My concern must have shown.

Beattie sniffed. 'Don't worry about that one. She's a spitting little alley cat.' He blinked at my face. 'I'll find an expat to give her English lessons while she's still in Lisbon,' he said. 'She looks like a survivor. She'll pick the language up fast.'

'She'll have to.' The broadcasts we produced went out in German, of course, and the teams working on them were all either native German speakers or fluent, as I was. But when it came to ordering couriers or cars to take scripts or personnel to the studio or interrogation centres, English was essential. Apart from anything else, we were forbidden to speak German in the village itself. Too alarming for the locals, who might think we were all a bunch of spies.

A waiter ushered in a musician carrying a guitar like no other I had seen before – one with a very round body and more strings than usual.

'Keep your attention on the mission, Anna,' Beattie said. 'The bigger picture. We can't afford sentimentality about Micki and her brother. She's a tool we can use. What do you think would become of her if she stayed here? I doubt she'd have a hope of getting on a ship.'

As though in mockery of Micki's hopes the guitarist in the corner started to play. He plucked at the strings with his thumb and index fingernail, singing one of those mournful Portuguese pieces I couldn't understand, but which made me think of love, loss and betrayal. Beattie had promised us a celebration dinner, but melancholy swept over me.

'It's called *fado*, this music,' Beattie said, taking another sip of his wine. 'Gets to you, doesn't it?'

I nodded.

Sentiments like those evoked by the music were what we played on, too. We touched people's emotions: those whom we persuaded to work with us and those we targeted. Often these emotions were unpleasant ones because they were the most powerful, Beattie said. We made people feel afraid or contemptuous or triumphant at believing they'd found out something the authorities didn't wish them to know.

We ate the remainder of our meal in silence. I tried to remind myself to savour each bite – I wouldn't be dining like this in England in the foreseeable future – but I longed for the solitude of my hotel room.

As we walked through the hotel reception the concierge called out to me, '*Senhorita*, something has arrived here for you.' He handed over a flat parcel.

'Give that to me, Hall,' Beattie said quietly. 'Carefully. I'll open it on the balcony of my room.' I was about to question him when I caught a glimpse of the concern on his face. 'We'll take the stairs, not the lift.'

But when he stood on his balcony and examined the handwriting on the address more closely, his face relaxed. 'It's from Finckler.' He handed it back to me.

'You thought it might be a bomb? From the Germans?'

'Stranger things have been known, though I admit it's the wrong shape.'

I undid the string and unwrapped the parcel on Beattie's bed. It opened to reveal white tissue paper, which I unfolded. A nightdress, little more than a slip, what Hollywood stars called a negligée, in the peach satin I'd admired in Finckler's studio. I stared at it.

'I told you he liked you.'

There was a sheet of thin writing paper in the parcel.

I wish I had more of this satin to make you an evening dress. F.

'I should write and thank him, but . . .'

'You can't.'

Best not to draw any more lines between us and Finckler, I supposed.

'What are you thinking?' Beattie asked.

'I was wondering why he liked me.'

He looked at me curiously. 'That's probably the only completely truthful answer you've ever given me, Hall. You like to keep your thoughts and feelings to yourself, don't you?'

'It's how we're encouraged to be, isn't it? Stiff upper lip, mustn't complain, keep your chin up . . .'

Beattie laid a hand on the gown and ran his fingers over it.

'But you'd never want to unburden yourself to me, would you, Anna?'

I decided to be truthful again. 'No.'

My negligée was still spread out over Beattie's bed. I folded it.

'I'll find a way of getting word to him that his present went down well,' Beattie said. 'The talent of the man – to run something like that up so quickly.'

I picked up the gown and the wrappings. 'I suppose I should turn in now.' I might have been fifteen again, aware of my developing body, of the eyes of the boys I passed on the street to and from school, longing to run home and hide in my bedroom.

'I can see why Finckler does well here,' Beattie said. 'The Portuguese do good embroidery, but their nightgowns tend to be like something your grandmother would wear, neck to toe.'

As I said goodnight, I almost wished Finckler's present had been a modest Portuguese garment. All the same, when I unwrapped it again, I had to try it on. It fell over my body like a second skin – simple, with small, capped sleeves, without lace or anything other than the glimmering soft satin, covering my legs to mid-thigh. In the mirror I saw how the peach cast a gentle glow over my skin. Even the burnt side of my face looked softer.

No wonder Finckler was so in demand, even among his mortal enemies.

I brushed my teeth and cleaned my skin with the precious last drop of lotion. I would wear the nightgown tonight. Hard to imagine how it would be received by the landlady at Lily Cottage on my return. I smiled, almost hearing concerned comments that I might find the house too draughty for such nightwear. This was a negligée for a starlet to wear lounging on a chaise longue, cocktail in hand. Almost against my will, I saw myself wearing it for Patrick, seeing his eyes light up, his hands reach for me. But what was the point of indulging these thoughts? The garment couldn't hide my ruined face.

Tomorrow morning, if there was time, I would ask Beattie for an hour off to shop for more practical clothes. My landlady would appreciate a present, and any foodstuffs I could pack into my small suitcase would be welcomed for padding out the rations.

Someone knocked on my door. I hesitated, stories about the Gestapo or Portuguese secret police dragging people from their hotel rooms filling my mind.

'It's only me,' Beattie called.

I opened the door on the chain. 'What is it?'

From the corridor came the sound of voices approaching from the lift. German voices, male, a group of four or five. Instinctively I undid the chain, opened the door and beckoned Beattie into my room. I closed the door and heard their footsteps pass.

'Trying to put the wind up us by coming to this floor,' Beattie said. 'I'll have a word with reception.'

'Somewhat unnerving,' I said, aware that I was wearing nothing more than the negligée. I cast my eyes around the room, looking for my dressing gown.

His eyes were on me. My skin prickled where his gaze fell. 'My God, Hall,' he said. 'I just came to ask if you had some spare paper. I need to make notes. You . . .' He sounded choked.

Before I could blink, his arms were round my waist. My brain was whirring, trying to process what was happening and whether it was what I wanted. Had I ever regarded Beattie in a romantic – an erotic – light before? My mouth felt dry. The wine at dinner wasn't the cause.

'You look as though you belong in Hollywood or Cap Ferrat before the war.' He released me and looked around my room.

I reached for the towel I'd left on the bed and wrapped it round my shoulders. The very act of covering up made it obvious how exposed I actually was.

'This is a strange set-up for us both,' he said.

I laughed, feeling tense rather than finding it funny.

'Don't laugh at me.'

I looked at him. He was completely serious.

'Oh, ignore me, Anna. I'm in a strange old mood.'

I didn't like to say I'd noticed.

'I thought we were celebrating.' I was trying to skirt over the awkwardness because it was our last night in the neutral city. I wasn't certain what I felt about Lisbon now, though. For all its lights and shops there was a sense of danger here I hadn't felt since the Blitz.

'We are. But don't you find that the moment of triumph is very fleeting? The best bit is when you're hunting – when the person, the story, the slant is just within your grasp.'

'And then it's on to the next target, trying to recapture the same moment again?' I knew what he meant. At times when he opened up about work like this a connection formed between us.

He nodded. 'Never feeling satisfied for long. Perhaps that comes from when humans were hunter-gatherers, always on the move, always searching.' He studied me. 'You're another restless soul, aren't you, Anna?'

'Am I?' I had always prided myself on sticking to tasks, whether they were pursuing academic challenges or work targets.

'Even if the fire hadn't happened you'd have been getting restless in that RAF job of yours.'

'They said I was good at what I did.'

'*Calm and accurate under pressure* was how they phrased it in your reference. I can just see you at a table pushing around those bits and pieces that look as though they belong in a board game.'

He knew that my job in the Filter Room hadn't been like this. He was trying to bait me. The connection between us had faded away again.

'Approved for officer training, too, so you must have been promising. But there's more to you than that, Hall.'

'Is there?'

'The kind of talent you'll only uncover in a job that turns you inside out to reveal what's hidden there.'

'Like this one?'

'Yes. And believe me, it's only just warming up. War's good for people like us.' He was leaning towards me. 'Our more unusual attributes are what's needed. You and I may find peacetime harder.'

Peacetime. Street lights in London. Whipped cream on strawberries. Moonlight that didn't feel treacherous for what it might draw from German skies. Beattie moved closer.

I could tell him I was tired. He'd return to his room. I knew him well enough to doubt he'd push me into doing something I didn't want to do. But if I turned him down would he hold a grudge against me? Was it worth risking an atmosphere for the next month or so? Hopefully he had something in one of his pockets that would make the encounter safe. Years now since I'd slept with Patrick. Beattie looked at me, asking a silent question.

I removed the towel from my shoulders. Clad only in the negligée I lay back on the bedspread, which was made of thick white quilted cotton. Through the fine satin of the negligée I could feel its little ridges under my buttocks and shoulders. Beattie let out a sigh. 'I've put you in a terrible position, haven't I, Anna? Sleep with the boss or risk offending him. But you won't offend me if you say no.' He sounded suddenly young, more vulnerable. I told myself not to be taken in but still lay there on the bedspread.

'I'm saying yes.' *Why?* I didn't have feelings for Beattie. But wasn't there just a tiny bit of curiosity about him, which the wine and brandy had freed me to explore? Or was I reassuring myself that a man might still find me attractive?

He moved quickly and smoothly, surprising me for a man of his size, taking me in his arms again. 'I could breathe you in all night.'

His breath was warm on me. I felt myself let go, inhaling and exhaling in time with him. Perhaps we could just stay like this without the need to do anything more. Being with him wasn't as dizzying and magical as it had been with Patrick, but it wasn't unpleasant; relaxing, really, almost companionable. Beattie moved his fingers under the negligée to my breasts. I felt like I had on the diving board in school swimming lessons: just close your eyes and do it.

I pushed him away gently and pulled the negligée over my head. Sometimes words complicated things. I reached out for his tie and undid it, letting its silk length slide down my naked body to the carpet.

His sigh was almost a gasp.

Beattie and I sat side by side in our seats in the Dakota. The hum of the engines made me drowsy; sleep had come late to me after Beattie had left my room in the early hours. I'd tossed in my bed, the negligée I'd replaced twisting its way round my thighs like a silken serpent. I'd woken just in time for breakfast and rushed out to do some shopping, feeling distracted and bleary-eyed.

Beattie was absorbed in reading a *Times* from the previous day that had come over on the outbound flight, yawning occasionally, his eyes pouched and shadowed. Perhaps he hadn't slept well, either. I had no work that I could safely take out of my satchel here where curious eyes might glimpse it. The French novel I'd brought with me to Lisbon was still in my satchel, barely opened during this trip. I appeared to have fallen into a French novel myself, I noted, sleeping with a man I wasn't even in love with just because . . . ? Because I was spoilt goods: a woman with a disfigurement, a female most men felt sorry for. Sometimes I felt their eyes on my back as I walked ahead of them in the street in my uniform. When they passed me or if I happened to turn around, the pupils of their eyes would constrict. *Nothing of sexual interest here.*

I was shallow to worry about my lost looks when innocent people raced to the very edge of Europe in an attempt to avoid imprisonment and death. I felt weariness at the immensity of what we were fighting. Or perhaps it was a reaction to Lisbon itself, to its dappled fatefulness and light. The plane lurched as it hit a pocket of turbulence. My left shoulder and leg fell against Beattie's. His newspaper trembled, but he didn't look away from the print.

As my eyes grew heavy and my head began to nod towards my shoulder it seemed that the propellers and engines were throbbing to the rhythm of my own thoughts. *What have I done? What have I done? What have I done?*

5

Micki put the battered duffle bag on her bed. 'All my worldly goods are in there,' she said. 'Beattie gave me some money before you left Lisbon so I could buy clothes. I only had what I was wearing when I met you for the first time.'

'"Met" sounds very polite,' I said. As though we'd been introduced at a party instead of first encountering her when she stole Beattie's wallet and pulled a knife on me.

She grinned. 'I was polite after the first time.'

'You were.' I touched her arm. 'It's good that you're here. Sorry the room's so small.' I grimaced as soon as I said the words; she'd been in far smaller and less wholesome accommodation in the last few years. That hovel in Lisbon she and Maxi had shared had probably not been the worst of it.

'I like this room very much. I can see the trees in the garden.' She said the words in a halting English, clearly making a big effort. Something in her accent puzzled me for a moment.

'Of course, an Irish crew on that boat you came over on.'

She grinned again. 'They told me they'd give me a brogue to confuse the English.'

'I'm impressed. And it could be a useful disguise around here.'

She sat on the bed, looking smaller and younger. 'I'm going to have to pretend I'm not from Germany, aren't I?'

I sat next to her. 'Probably best not to draw attention to the fact.'

'The villagers wouldn't like knowing there are Germans among them.' She nodded. 'I don't like having the bastards around, either.'

I didn't know what to say to that. 'Tell me about the voyage,' I asked in German.

'The ship was really just a "coaster" boat. That worried me when we were so far off land, in open seas. It carried wheat and sugar from Lisbon to Dublin. The crew were kind to me. I slept in a cubicle the size of this bed, but it was pretty clean. We had fresh fruit from Lisbon. So I ate oranges and tried to improve my English when the crew had time.'

She was putting a good spin on it. The Irish boat would have been at risk from the U-boats and Luftwaffe, who had sunk a number of neutral vessels. The crew would have felt on edge. If the sea had been rough, the coaster would have tossed on the waves. No Dakota to Whitchurch for Micki – I'd had the devil's job finding this passage for her. In the end, I'd gone to London to see an Irish friend of Beattie's, taking with me a bottle of brandy and a box of cigars to secure the ticket.

'Then the ferry across the Irish Sea.' She grimaced. 'That was worse – everyone was seasick apart from me. A woman met me in Liverpool and took me to some kind of camp. Questions, questions, questions for days and days.'

I could well imagine. A stateless girl of German origin, albeit Jewish? I'd heard Beattie on the telephone shouting at someone, telling them that a much-needed resource was being held up. Finally he'd stomped up to Liverpool on the train himself.

'When Beattie appeared I could have hugged him,' she said quietly.

'He can be kind,' I said.

She turned to me. 'But not to you?' There was a questioning expression in her eyes.

I stood up. 'I'll let you settle in. Lunch will be downstairs shortly and then we'll walk to Mulberry House, ten minutes away. It's Beattie's lodgings and our workplace.'

'We work in a house? I thought there would be an office.'

'It's a bit unusual. But we try to keep a low profile in the village.'

Micki sniffed. She had perhaps been thinking her new life in Britain would involve living and working somewhere more metropolitan.

She was pulling her possessions out of her duffle bag when I left her. A few shirts, the skirt that looked like a games skirt she'd worn in Lisbon, underwear, a single jumper. A toothbrush and hairbrush. An unframed photograph, which she placed on her bedside table. 'I have a ration book now,' she said, looking at the small pile on her bed. 'Perhaps I can buy some new clothes in due course.'

'I have lots of clothes I don't wear,' I said. 'They're at my father's house in London but I'll ask if—'

'I don't want charity.'

The uninjured part of my face felt hot. 'I'm sorry. I didn't mean to offend you.'

'Ignore me, Anna.' She fingered the edge of the quilt. 'Your clothes are always lovely. I'm just not used to, well, people being kind to me.'

'I can understand that.'

She frowned, obviously doubting this. And she was right. What would I know about being Jewish, hiding in my own country, then fleeing with a small and sick brother? I'd grown up as a comfortably off middle-class girl, never moneyed but never lacking shelter and love.

'I remember what you were wearing in Lisbon,' she said. 'The beautiful dress and hat.'

'I've always had a bit of a weakness for clothes. Not that I get much chance to wear them during working hours.' I looked down at the hated WAAF skirt and made a face.

'You could make anything look good,' she said, 'with your figure. Don't mind me being snappy,' she added quietly. 'I owe it to you, Anna, that I'm here.'

'Enlightened self-interest,' I said breezily. 'We need you, Micki.' Her knowledge of those bars in German naval ports, the things the seamen talked about, the slang they used, the jokes they told, they would add veracity to our broadcasts.

'You can rely on me,' she said as I left the room.

6

A lunatic asylum.

Mrs Haddon, the housekeeper of Mulberry House, frequently told us that this is what the redbrick villa had become. She'd worked for the family who'd lived here previously. They'd been the type to sip Darjeeling under the cedar tree or hit croquet balls through hoops. Her grin gave her away, though. She liked us, even though she frequently added that most people would have us all locked up and that was no word of a lie.

This afternoon, looking around what Beattie called his operations room – formerly the drawing room – I saw Mrs Haddon's point. Micki was standing on her hands on the edge of her desk. Luckily she was wearing a pair of slacks.

She was observed by our most recent recruit, Father Becker, the Roman Catholic priest persuaded by British intelligence to leave Zurich to work for us in England. He had Swiss citizenship, through his father, so it had been easier to obtain papers for him, although the priest hadn't been terribly keen on coming to England at first, Beattie told me. Fortunately he'd changed his mind. '*Fräulein*, your hip is too far back,' he said.

'Do you know much about gymnastics, father?' I asked, in German.

'Not personally, Sergeant Hall.'

'Just call me Anna,' I told him, as I'd done several times before. As usual he looked embarrassed at the very suggestion, perhaps because he was a cleric, unused to being on first-name terms with a non-related woman. Or perhaps just because he was German, and so very formal.

'Certainly true that you can't see a hole without falling into it, father,' Micki said, still upside down, her hair – now worn in a single plait – dangling down like a reddish-brown rope. She seemed completely at ease being inverted.

He shook his head. 'God didn't grant me the gift of physical grace.'

'You have other talents. An ability to communicate with the almighty.' Micki lowered herself to the floor slowly and with complete control.

He nodded.

'I can see the attraction,' Micki said. 'Even though you know it's all complete lies.'

'Micki . . .' I needed to assert authority before a theological argument began. I'd refereed and broken up several since Micki and Father Becker had started working together. Micki would of course be doctrinally and philosophically outgunned by Father Becker, but she wouldn't concede defeat.

'If I killed you I'd put a stake through your heart to be sure you wouldn't jump up again,' Beattie had told her soon after she'd joined us. Micki had beamed.

Now that the first week of her new job had passed, she reminded me of a tiger cub: simultaneously cautious and bold. Shopping in Bedford on a rare Saturday morning away from the village I'd found a second-hand silver frame that looked as though it might fit the photograph she'd brought with her, and left it on the end of her bed. She'd never mentioned the frame, but when I came in from a Sunday afternoon walk, I'd found my work shoes polished to a gleam they hadn't enjoyed since my WAAF days.

Tyres scrunched on the gravel outside. For a moment the three of us froze. Beattie didn't mind shenanigans, as he termed them, didn't actually give a damn about anything that more conventional employers might have frowned on: drinking, swearing, women wearing trousers, mucking around in work hours. As long as the intelligence was pulled out of those we interviewed or interrogated and twisted into material for our nightly broadcasts. But Beattie's moods could change by the second, if he felt a task had been less than perfectly carried out.

It would be all right today, I told myself. Father Becker had produced yet another excellent religious broadcast script for the fictional radio priest character of Father Josef, as performed by Gerhard Meiner, a refugee actor from Bremen.

I'd sat up straight when I read the script. As usual the sermon lulled listeners into thinking it was just another state-sanctioned religious broadcast, albeit more reflective than most of them. But a few minutes in came a brief mention of the rigorous investigation of immoral behaviour on the part of some men training young German children at various holiday camps.

The script ended with a direct quotation from scripture: 'He that shall scandalise one of these little ones that believe in me, it were better for him that a millstone should be hanged about his neck, and that he should be drowned in the depth of the sea.'

'I have stretched the truth in my script,' Father Becker said, rubbing the side of his head.

'That's exactly what you're supposed to do,' I told him.

'You haven't exaggerated at all,' Micki said. 'There really are perverts in those camps. My non-Jewish school friends went off to them each summer. They told me about youth leaders coming into tents at night. Or supervising shower sessions, hard-ons visible through the *Lederhosen*. One of the few times in my beloved homeland I was grateful for being Jewish.'

An expression of distaste covered the priest's face.

'You may look as though you've found a weevil in your bread, father, but you know I'm right.' She glowered at him.

'I think perhaps we are overdoing it,' Becker said, studiously keeping his eyes on mine.

'We need to plant a seed of doubt,' I said. 'To germinate in listeners' minds.'

'But to speak of such wickedness, is that not too much?' he said.

'We just want them to think that little Joachim might have a bad *Erkältung* and should stay at home for the camp fortnight,' Micki said. 'If enough of the fools do that, the Party will have a problem on its hands.'

'I do not think you understand the audience—'

'Oh, I understand them perfectly.' She scowled at Father Becker. 'And I can tell you that their husbands and sons aren't prudish when they're drunk in a bar groping prostitutes.'

'It's a question of whether a parent can trust an organisation that lets these unsavoury things go on.' The voice, deep and melodic, spoke like us in German, from the door. Beattie. He'd let himself in silently. As always when I saw him again after an absence of whatever length, and to my irritation, I felt my blood pulsing round my veins. How long had he been standing there?

'*How reassuring that the Party has not let these accusations run on for any longer than was necessary for a thorough investigation*, perhaps?' Nice. Suggest that originally the Party hadn't shown any interest at all in sorting this out, had hoped it would all go away until angry parents insisted on something happening and a scandal was brewing.

'You've had the script checked?' Beattie asked me. We had to have all our material signed off by Beattie's own boss, Sefton Delmer, before broadcast. Only Beattie was authorised to make or approve amendments after this stage.

I opened my mouth, but he raised a hand to stop me. 'Of course you have, Hall.' Yet again he was reminding me that he was my boss.

Since Lisbon it had been like this: he'd assert his authority, then chide me for not showing initiative, for not getting on with things. He'd praise me for the way I'd got Micki working so quickly for us: not just sharing her own information about German and French naval ports and the people who frequented them, but going on to interview other German refugees herself, laughing and weeping with them, reminiscing, picking their brains. Moments later he'd tick me off when the motorcycle courier I'd organised to pick up a script arrived three minutes late because she'd had to stop to mend a puncture. Sometimes I wondered whether I'd imagined that night when he'd stroked my skin and told me he wanted to breathe me in. And then we'd brush past one another in the narrow hallway and I'd feel a frisson between us.

'And you've ordered the courier to take the script to Gerhard Meiner?'

'Of course.'

'Cancel it.' He looked at me. I knew not to show surprise or annoyance.

'Why?' Micki asked.

'Gerhard Meiner will no longer play Father Josef,' Beattie said. 'He has pulmonary trouble, finds it hard not to cough on air.'

'I could perhaps assist.' Father Becker made the suggestion with a shrug indicating he knew the offer would be turned down.

'I'm sure your sermons were masterpieces, father,' Beattie said. 'But you preached from the pulpit, not over the airwaves. We need a professional actor. Someone who sounds like more of a priest on air than you do.'

Father Becker stiffened. 'But I—'

'You're a real priest, yes. You just don't sound as much like one as Gerhard Meiner did.'

What was true often sounded less truthful than what was a lie. At least, that was the way it went in Beattie's fiefdom.

'That is troubling,' Father Becker said. He frowned.

Micki sniffed. 'Gerhard Meiner is a terrible lecher. He sounds like a kindly old uncle but he has his hands down your knickers before you can say *"Ave Maria"*.' She'd spent some time with Meiner, I recalled, working with him and Beattie on a possible play about German submariners.

'Then I am relieved I cannot stand in for him.' Father Becker smiled, but I noticed a little twitch around his right eye.

I squinted at Beattie. 'Can't we patch Meiner up for this evening?' We had so little time to sort out a replacement. Mentally I scanned the Germans and Austrians in the village, trying to recall the sound of their voices, whether they could pick up a part speedily. But they were journalists, editors and writers, not actors I could imagine in this role.

'We couldn't stop him medicating himself,' Beattie said primly.

Micki snorted. 'You mean he's overdone the dope.'

I glanced at the clock. Six hours before the evening broadcast. It would only irritate Beattie to point this out. We'd have to use some pre-recorded dance music to fill in the gap left by cutting the religious slot. Or there might be a spare Gerhard Meiner broadcast recorded onto a wax disc we could use. We'd produced additional recordings for emergencies, but we'd already used up two of them to cover previous pulmonary incidents.

'I have a replacement.' Beattie gave a modest little smile.

I sat up straight.

'He's too young to act the same Father Josef role, so we'll need a new character, but that's to our advantage. Poor Father Josef went too far and needed helpful correction.' He nodded at Father Becker. 'Add something at the beginning of your script about state and religion working together, blah blah blah.'

Father Becker started writing notes on his pad, his eyes sharp as he concentrated. Not for the first time I remarked on his adaptability. Plucked from his life as a priest in Switzerland, transferred to this strange little team, two members of which were women and very unlike the devout female believers he'd previously known. Until 1942, when

69

he'd moved to Switzerland, Father Becker had worked in a parish in Cologne. It was this pastoral role as much as his help with refugees that had made Beattie so keen to bring him over here.

'Our new radio priest – shall we call him Father Friedrich? – will be played by this recruit to our cause.' He looked at me. 'Don't glower like that, sergeant. No time for me to get you involved. The housemaster only found Meiner paralytic on his bedroom floor this morning.'

The German refugees and former prisoners of war working for us were housed in private accommodation in the village. We called the people who kept an eye on them housemasters or mistresses because their role was to allow their charges enough freedom to do their best work, but not enable them to get up to anything that might have the locals muttering about spies. The system was not unlike that of an enlightened boarding school.

'When I realised Gerhard Meiner was out of the game, I immediately telephoned my contact at the cage,' Beattie went on.

The cages were centres run by the Prisoner of War Interrogation Section, or PWIS, though PISS was Beattie's preferred acronym. PWIS detained the more *interesting* German prisoners. There were several cages within easy driving distance of the village, but when Beattie used the definite article he was only ever referring to the Kensington cage in the prosperous London borough. It housed SS and Gestapo prisoners, along with some particularly vicious Wehrmacht regulars. He'd worked hard, easing his way inside the fiercely guarded holding centre with hard-won paper sign-offs, supplemented with some of the bottles of whisky kept in his office. 'There's nobody in the cage suitable for broadcasting,' he said. 'Though PISS did tell me something else interesting, more of which in a moment. Then I remembered William Nathanson.'

'William Nathanson?'

'British subject, served in the RAF until he was injured, but born and schooled in Prague for the first nine years of his life, speaking both

German and English. A bilingual upbringing not unlike my own or that of our esteemed chief.'

Beattie was referring to Sefton Delmer, born to an Australian father and German mother, growing up, like Beattie, in Berlin.

'Nathanson could do a radio padre who sounds educated but can talk in punchy sentences, without—'

'Ridiculously long sentences that make you wait five minutes for the verb,' Micki finished for him.

'Theological, but of the people,' Father Becker said.

'Good way of putting it, father.' I was trying to cheer him up after the earlier rejection.

'When you've finished.' Beattie was staring coldly at me.

I stared back at him, staying just on the right side of insubordination.

'Can this William Nathanson act, though?' Micki asked.

Good question, I thought.

'Yes, he's had some stage experience and did a bit of radio before he joined up. He was the navigator in a Halifax. Survived a crash landing but can't fly any more.' Beattie turned his gaze to my desk. I didn't like to keep all my papers tucked away in a drawer out of sight. That was the way ideas, cross-references and interesting connections slipped from your mind. Unless you were Beattie, of course. The man's mind was an enormous portmanteau internally and ruthlessly organised by sorcery.

'May I brief Lieutenant Nathanson before this evening's broadcast?'

'I need him this afternoon.' Beattie looked at his watch. 'For the other business in Kensington I mentioned.'

He was taking this newcomer with him to the cage. Not me.

'What's that face for, Hall?' We'd switched to English.

'Nothing, sir.' He'd know by my use of the address that I was stewing over something, as he put it. 'Is the lieutenant going to be working with us here as well as doing the radio part?'

'That's what I was planning. He's talented.'

He rearranged the papers on top of my desk, lining them up on the blotter, setting the fountain pen parallel with the top edge. 'Those places . . . A lot of the men who operate the Kensington cage are . . . Not the finest of English manhood. It'll be hard enough getting Nathanson in, but a woman would be out of the question.' Micki was watching us, forehead puckered, trying hard to keep up with the conversation.

'They think I'd faint? Need smelling salts?'

He scowled. 'I nearly passed out myself last time I was there. I interviewed some poor sod who hadn't been given access to a lavatory for forty-eight hours while he was made to stand.'

Bad smells. Bruised and bloodied men. Fear. Anger. Too much for a woman. I'd shown Beattie what I could accomplish when we'd been in Lisbon, but now he was pushing me back into my basket. My right cheek seemed to throb as it did at times of emotion, something to do with damaged nerves, the doctor had told me. I prayed the throbbing wasn't visible.

'Can I at least come in the car with you to Kensington?' I switched into German. 'Sir? I can brief Lieutenant Nathanson while we drive.'

'What about Father Becker's script?'

'It's nearly ready,' I said.

Father Becker gave a gasp.

'There's time for you to finish it before we go,' I said. He moved to the desk on which his German language typewriter sat. 'The lieutenant can read it as we drive. If he has any questions I'll be there to answer them.'

I felt a need to protect my position. Beattie frequently praised me for my editorial work. But in the early hours of the morning, when red ants seemed to run across my scarred face and I couldn't sleep, I worried that he'd discover an appalling error in something I'd written and send me back to East Anglia.

I wanted to see Beattie with William outside the office, assess this newcomer's relationship with him, note any potential threat to my position.

Beattie was still rearranging my desk. I wished he'd stop. He might like papers neatly piled one on top of the other, but I preferred my own system. 'Can't I come with you? Sir?'

'Oh, all right.' Sometimes Beattie would suddenly accede to a request for something stretching the bounds of what was allowed. Then he'd follow by refusing something silly: his signature on a pencil order or a few hours off to visit the dentist. 'You can always go for a walk in Kensington Gardens.'

I was about to say something in riposte but stopped myself. If Beattie's interview went on for hours I could find a bench and work. It was a fine spring day, a good time to sit in a park. Outside the window the budding boughs of a chestnut tree were rocking in a gentle breeze.

Thinking of captive men who'd done awful things having the details beaten out of them didn't match the atmosphere engendered by the garden. Or match the framed embroidered biblical quotation hanging on the wall above my desk: 'There is deceit in the hearts of those who plot evil, but joy for those who promote peace.' The words were so inappropriate for a room full of people like us that Beattie had laughed when he'd first seen the embroidery and insisted on it remaining.

Beattie was fiddling with the pencils on my desk. Despite his bravado, he hated the Kensington cage. He preferred to use what was given to him freely, often willingly, from men who'd had enough of the war or Hitler. Beattie was devious – a liar, some might say – venal, over-ambitious. But I knew violence wasn't his bag. Brain power and a kind of electrical energy got him what he wanted. And obsession with detail. On the occasions I'd accompanied him to the studio I marvelled as he double-checked everything, from the electrical plugs and the microphones to the broadcasters' warm-ups. I'd seen him eyeing the sound-proofing tiles, pulling a chair from under a desk so he could stand on it and rub a finger round the tile edges to make sure they were adhering to the wall properly. He'd check the locks on the studio doors – on both sides. The studio technicians would give him detailed daily reports on their equipment inspections. He'd talk to the guards outside and to the girls who operated the switchboard just inside the front door.

Beattie did all this with a seeming lack of tension, cigar lit, hands in trouser pockets, but he and every one of the staff at the studio knew a mistake could ruin everything. A second's delay in starting a broadcast could alert listeners to something not being quite right. A background sound might give away the fact that the people on air were sitting in a studio in Bedfordshire, not Germany. Or a problem with the telephone lines connecting us to the transmitters might mean our so carefully composed and delivered words went nowhere.

Live broadcasts gave us the opportunity to jump on news stories as they emerged. And they spared us the rigmarole of prerecording onto records. But if a slip was made while you were on air, there was no way of correcting it. Getting our hour-and-a-half programme safely broadcast every night except Saturday, when the slot was given over completely to a live concert band, was our responsibility. 'If we fuck it up, it's the end of our unit,' Beattie regularly warned us.

'Before I go, tell me how the circus piece's going?' he asked Micki.

'Nearly finished.' She'd done so well at interviewing and suggesting stories that he'd asked her to write up her own idea about German circuses successfully replacing the dwarfs who had formerly entertained crowds. She read what she'd written. '"It's been decided that it is more humane to remove such sadly deficient specimens and offer them a kinder alternative to working for the rest of their lives."' Micki paused. 'I don't know whether I should replace "It's been decided" with "The authorities have decided"?'

Usually we were at pains to keep our language as simple as possible – not always the case with German state radio broadcasts. Active case, not passive. Snappy. Easy on the ears.

'I like the distancing effect,' Beattie told Micki. 'Those monsters washing their hands of their crimes, shilly-shallying, as we say in English. Read the rest of it.'

Listeners would know that the euthanasia programme for the handicapped had supposedly been suppressed following public protest, but would suspect it was continuing in secret. Micki's story cheerfully stated that orphans from Hamburg were being assessed in juggling and comedic skills. *Good news for circus lovers: the smaller children are just as funny as the dwarfs!* And as child talent was not hard to find, the supply would not dry up. Micki had left the listener to infer why this was.

Beattie nodded at the last point as she read it. 'It'll remind listeners of how many mothers died in last week's bombing raids,' he said.

'Won't it make German civilians loathe us even more?' I asked.

'They'll hate the RAF,' he said. 'But they'll hate their own authorities even more for letting the bombers through and not encouraging evacuations.'

I looked again at the embroidered biblical words on the wall. Grace had sewed similar quotations for Christmas bazaars, so neat in her stitching, so good at choosing colours.

'Five minutes,' Beattie said, leaving the room.

Micki wrote on the margins of her script. She stopped, resting a hand on her chin, a rare, faraway expression on her face. Perhaps the mention of small children had made her think of Maxi. She still hadn't spoken much about him. I didn't like to pry. 'Your work is excellent,' I said. 'I can't believe how quickly you've picked it up.' She wrote fluently and with precision. And she was obviously very intelligent.

Father Becker's fingers tapped away. From time to time the typewriter emitted a dull metallic jarring as the keys tangled themselves up. Since his arrival, priest and typewriter had been fighting a daily battle of good and evil, as Beattie termed it. And that wasn't the only battle fought. Father Becker regularly misplaced his ID papers, his glasses, his scarf. Sometimes I marvelled that he'd been able to organise himself sufficiently to follow the travel itinerary from Switzerland to Bedfordshire put together for him by Intelligence. It was a miracle he hadn't ended up in Berlin or Moscow.

He released the lever and carefully pulled out the typed sheets and carbon copies with the air of someone detonating an explosive. He handed me one of the copies. In his typewriter the carbons always seemed to slip out of place and were usually smudged.

'Here you are, sergeant,' he said, proudly handing me a copy.

I just hoped this new team member of Beattie's would be able to do justice to the script.

7

In the car, driven once again by Atkins, Beattie told me that the prisoner he was going to see was a lieutenant captured in North Africa and shipped here from a Middle-Eastern POW camp. He'd been accused of involvement in the execution of British prisoners near Dunkirk in 1940. Beattie folded his arms, indicating that he wouldn't tell me more.

I read through Father Becker's script. Of course I wasn't a native speaker. At a push I could pass for a German who'd lived in southern Africa or South America since early childhood. But a sharp ear would pick out a stressed consonant or drawn-out vowel that wasn't quite right. No broadcasting in German for me. I'd been disappointed when Beattie first explained this to me, but as the weeks passed, the work I did writing and editing scripts and interviewing prisoners had consumed me. My mind felt stretched and challenged. 'Intelligence,' Beattie told me when I first started working for him. 'In the usual sense of the word. This war will ultimately be won by what's between people's ears.'

Sometimes I suspected it would be won by the side who could tell the best lies. And that was where I came in with Father Becker's script: making sure the lie had been inserted seamlessly, which it usually was – for a religious man he wasn't a bad liar. My work was often more anodyne than lying: inserting a fact that might seem like a lie but wasn't. Sometimes I wondered whether the line between truth and lie was blurring itself in my mind. If I could almost convince myself that these stories I inserted or twisted were true, what else might I have convinced myself of? Hadn't I told myself that I'd been kind to Patrick when I'd written him that last letter?

A tall, upright figure in RAF uniform stood on the roadside at the village's edge. My heart wanted to jump out of my chest at the sight of him. William Nathanson, I reminded myself. Not the other tall RAF pilot I'd been thinking of. I hoped Beattie hadn't heard me gasp at the sight of this man.

The car halted. Atkins opened the door for Nathanson. He sat beside me, sandwiching me between the two men. 'Just as well transport gave me the larger car,' Beattie grumbled. It was on the tip of my tongue to point out that they always seemed to give him this Austin Twelve.

The blue uniform suited Lieutenant Nathanson – almost an exact match for his eye colour. His hair was a chestnut brown. Before the RAF had got hold of him a lock of it had probably fallen over his forehead. He adjusted his tall body stiffly, perhaps still suffering pain from his crash landing. Atkins cast her eyes over him before she closed the door. Most women would have done just the same.

He appeared surprised to see me with Beattie but greeted me politely, convincingly masking anything he might feel about my face. Nathanson was an actor, after all. Though perhaps he simply couldn't see much of the scarred side, positioned as he was to the left of me, his long legs neatly arranged so they didn't invade my space.

'Just in case you're wondering, Sergeant Hall's not actually my secretary,' Beattie said. 'Don't ask her to make the tea – she produces a kind of insipid puddle. God knows how we'll marry her off when this is all over.'

I decided to ignore Beattie. 'Sorry to drop this on you.' I passed the script to Lieutenant Nathanson. 'But it's for your first broadcast tonight. Time is tight, so you might like to have a quick look now.'

'Ah.' He sat straighter in the car seat, flicking through the pages, eyes scanning the text. 'It's always helpful to get scripts in advance.'

'I gather you've done this kind of work before, lieutenant?'

He glanced at the driver. Beattie gave a reassuring nod. 'Not black broadcasting,' Nathanson said. 'But the . . . ordinary kind, yes.'

Black was what we called our broadcast mixtures of lies and truth; black not only because of what we said but because we pretended to be something we weren't: a German radio station. Grey was propaganda, mostly truthful but unattributable material. White was the BBC and, according to them, attributable and truthful. 'At least we in Black are honest liars,' Beattie said sometimes.

'Call him William, Hall,' Beattie said. 'You know me, never stand on formality.'

'I'm Anna,' I told William, who blinked as though my uniform made me in some way unfeminine and undeserving of my name. Or perhaps he'd just noticed my scarred face.

'Before the war I did a bit of stage work,' William said after a moment. 'A few performances in repertory in provincial towns and cities.'

'Hall is a thespian, too,' Beattie said. 'Or was. Before she moved to a job in advertising.'

'Advertising?' he said. 'Sounds very glamorous, very Manhattan.'

'I was only a copy-writer. No dry martinis at six.'

'Look at us all now,' Beattie said. 'A team of misfits, liars and geniuses.' William Nathanson didn't look as if he belonged in the first two classifications. He probably played cricket in the summer. But perhaps he'd come to England too late to master the game? No, not that late: his English was uninflected – you had to live in a country from a young age for that to be the case. He was reading Father Becker's script, a slight frown on his brow. From time to time he reached a hand to his lower spine, rubbing it as he concentrated.

He finished scanning the script and turned to the first page again, moving his lips as he read. He stopped when he saw me looking at him, but it was me who blushed.

He grinned. 'It helps to speak the words to myself.'

'The script may change before this evening,' I warned. 'If new intelligence comes up, we have to tweak.'

'The motorcycles bring us information at all times,' Beattie said. 'I hear their tyres on the gravel and the couriers in their black boots trip-trapping up to the front door and my heart misses a beat.'

In the front of the car Atkins coughed.

'A bit like being on the stage,' William said. 'If a director gets it into his head to make changes an hour before curtains up.'

For a second I was nineteen again, on a stage in an Oxford college garden, praying I'd remember the latest amendments to a script made by the enthusiastic third-year student director.

'Nearly at our destination.' Beattie's voice had grown grim. Or it might have just been the view of the western end of Bayswater Road out of the car window, the stuccoed houses opposite Hyde Park looking tired and shabby.

'Sorry you can't come in, sergeant. But you may find the air outside fresher in more than one way.'

'I'll manicure my nails.' I blushed at Beattie's furious glance. 'Sorry, sir. I'll get on with the play.'

The car turned right into Kensington Palace Gardens: Crown property, exclusive, with the palace itself sitting on the south-eastern side. Before the war some of Queen Victoria's children and grandchildren had lived in the palace. It had been bombed, I remembered. If the royals were still in residence, could they have any idea who their neighbours here were?

We stopped at the sentry point set into a barbed-wire fence enclosing three of the houses. Surely this couldn't be the cage? Remove the fence and it looked like somewhere you'd go to visit an ambassador and worry about a speck of dirt on your white kid gloves.

'Looks too gracious to be involved in anything dirty,' William said.

Like its neighbours, the house was huge and white-stuccoed, with the air of something imported from a more exotic landscape, yet possessing a very English kind of respectability, in keeping with the plane-tree-lined road and Victorian lanterns. Even with the overgrown garden and barbed wire, it was hard to imagine anything more violent than a disputed lawn tennis point occurring here.

The sentry examined Beattie's papers and nodded at William and me to hand over ours. 'The young lady's not going in.' It was spoken as a statement. I bit my lip. 'She'll wait in the car with my driver.' We drove in, halting in front of the door, and the men got out.

'I'll stretch my legs,' I told Atkins.

'Don't go too far.' She'd driven Beattie long enough to know that the job of chauffeuring him was subject to sudden changes of plan. Beattie might burst out of the door within twenty minutes and announce we were driving to Bermondsey to talk to a refugee from Poland. But Beattie knew we had to have both William and the script at Milton Bryan in time for the evening broadcast.

The sentry eyed me suspiciously as he let me out. 'I won't be long,' I told him.

He nodded, eyes screwed into a scowl before widening as they spotted the scar tissue on my cheek. For men like him I fell into that strange category of being neither a male nor a female with a normal face. For William Nathanson I seemed to inhabit the category of human being. It was too soon to be certain, but so far I approved of him.

I walked down the avenue. Its pavements needed sweeping, but blackbirds sang in bushes; there was little sound of traffic and probably hadn't been even before the war. A pair of schoolgirls strolled past me in the opposite direction – some London schools had returned to the city since the air raids had eased. I caught the scent of warm leather satchels, dusty, rubbery classrooms and a snatch of conversation – *beastly* Mrs James and a grim arithmetic test. For a minute or so life felt ordinary, in a way it hadn't for years.

I reached the palace railings and peered through. Guns and sand-banks filled the gardens. How naive I'd been to imagine peacetime lingered here.

Eyes, green, glaring, met mine from behind a tree. A fox. I'd heard they were colonising London, living on bombsites, relishing the rats that had also moved in. This was a big fellow, probably a dog fox. He smouldered at me. I couldn't move my eyes from his. I was on his territory. His upper lip stiffened into a growl before he slipped between two bushes and disappeared.

I clung to the railings, feeling dazed. Ridiculous. I'd survived a fire and yet a small wild animal had shaken me. Vermin in Kensington Palace Gardens. I smiled – an anecdote to relate later. Something more useful too, perhaps? I let go of the railings and took my writing pad from my satchel, mind whirring. I rested the pad against the trunk of a plane tree and scribbled a note to myself.

German cities were experiencing an increase in animal invasions – not just foxes, but perhaps wolves? *Good news: authorities have succeeded in reducing the numbers of invading wolves in whatever-the-city by almost a quarter this week. New ways of dealing with the problem continue to be researched.* Or would rats be less newsworthy but more worrisome to a German housewife? I replaced the pad in the satchel and retraced my steps to the fenced-off mansions. The sentry scowled at me again. 'Papers?'

I handed them over.

'These don't give you access to this centre if you're not accompanied by someone with clearance.'

'I'm one of Mr Beattie's team.'

'Where does it say that?' He made a play of squinting at my papers.

'You know I'm with him.'

'Do I?'

'You saw me with him in the car just half an hour ago.'

The guard stared at the scars on my face again without even trying to hide his smirk. If only I could wear civilian clothes and my veil, keep my face hidden. Damn Beattie for not getting me properly transferred over to a civilian role when he took me on. It suited him for me to be uniformed. Perhaps it gave the unit a note of respectability.

'Dear me, someone's had a bit of a burn,' he said. My hands curled up into fists.

Atkins was still leaning against the car, smoking and watching us. She walked over slowly towards us.

'Everything all right?' She raised a well-shaped eyebrow at the sentry. 'Mr Beattie will be expecting Sergeant Hall to be waiting in the car.'

He grunted and opened the gate for me. I muttered a 'thanks' to her as we returned to the Austin. She shrugged it off. 'The man's an idiot.'

I took a breath, annoyed and shaken by my reaction to the guard. I needed to pull myself together. Millions facing death all around the world and Anna Hall was still over-sensitive about her face?

I sat back in the car and took out my writing pad, as much to calm myself down as for work purposes. 'I saw a big dog fox,' I told Atkins. 'Bold as brass, just standing there.'

In the rear-view mirror, Atkins' eyes widened. 'I've heard they're moving into cities.'

I returned to my notes. This was a quiet workplace, away from Father Becker's unrhythmic typing and Micki's commentary on the landlady's West Highland terrier chasing squirrels in the garden. Atkins took knitting needles and wool out of the glove compartment. 'Shouldn't do this in uniform,' she told me, 'but I'm desperate to finish.'

'A jumper?' I asked.

'For my old dog. It may be spring, but Millie feels the chill, so I unpicked this old cashmere cardigan to make something for her.' Her eyes, a child's light-blue, met mine.

I slipped into the world of my play, feeling better. Atkins had given me an idea. She wasn't unlike the subject of my radio play, Clara.

Clara lived with her elderly father in a castle in an unspecified part of central Europe in an unspecified historical period. Her brother was absent fighting an unnamed, remorseless enemy on the country's borders. Her fiancé was a prisoner of war, threatened with death. Clara herself had once been a gifted archer and rider, but now took care of the castle and its inhabitants. Not a day passed without her carrying out some act of sacrifice. Her dresses had been turned into children's outfits. Her bedclothes had been given to the homeless. Clara used her bow and arrow to shoot rabbits and deer, which she cooked for the poor and for the wounded soldiers who needed feeding up for their return to the front.

Clara could have been a sanctimonious pain in the arse, as Beattie put it, but for the fact that she possessed a sense of the ridiculous, sparingly, but, we hoped, sharply displayed in each episode. Clara noted that the donation of her last pair of rubber boots to a soldier with small feet hindered her work in the variously muddy or snowy vegetable patch. How was she supposed to provide potatoes and turnips for those in her care? Donating the family's thickest furs to combatants meant that she and her father needed to burn more precious wood to keep themselves alive in the winter.

'Never too heavy, never too obvious,' Beattie would tell me. 'Just enough parallels with everyday German life to raise questions.' I was growing to like Clara, even hoping that she and her father would survive, that the enemy would not reach the castle and that her absent menfolk would return safely. I'd suggested making Clara into a more brazen rebel against the tyrannical king, but Beattie thought that might be laying it on a bit thick. Perhaps William would have a view.

My fountain pen was running out of ink. I searched the satchel for a pencil and caught sight of my fingernails. My hands with their long fingers were still in reasonable condition. I usually managed to find hand cream but missed seeing varnish on my nails. Nazi women were supposed to forswear make-up, but photos of officials with beautiful actresses on their arms showed that their men still savoured red lips and sultry eyes. If Clara brought down a deer with her bow and arrows and they had venison for dinner, might she apply cosmetics to complement her gown? A woman's face was hers to do with as she wished, Clara would explain to a prim servant who expressed disapproval of her poppy-red lips. I glanced at Atkins' blond head, bent over her knitting. Clara might knit her wolfhound a jumper out of fine cashmere for the hell of it, too.

I scribbled notes for the next episode, five days away. It wouldn't take me long to write the script and then it would be translated by the German team.

Something was happening outside – the heavy front door to the mansion opened. Beattie himself was coming out of the house now. William followed, looking pale. I could see the outlines of uniformed men behind them.

I stuffed my writing pad and pencil into the satchel and opened the car door. Atkins muttered a warning to me. 'It's fine,' I told her.

I may not have been inside this cage but I'd frequently been with prisoners of war in interview rooms, confronting the anger, despair or faint hope. This prisoner coming out smelled raw, but not desperate. His eyes burned in a face still displaying a tan acquired in the desert. He met my gaze. I was the one who looked away first. The prisoner examined me as though he were the interrogator, taking in the ruined section of my face without obvious shock but with keen appraisal. This man was just like the fox I'd seen at the park railings. As he came closer I saw he was young, probably the same age as William. His vulpine expression was probably the result of exhaustion and scanty rations. Fed and in clean clothes he might look as I'd imagined Clara's brother in my radio play.

'You remember the deal?' Beattie said in German, turning back to him.

The prisoner shrugged.

'I didn't hear your answer.'

'Yes,' he muttered.

The sergeant guarding him gave him a nudge with his rifle. A truck was coming through the gates behind me. Beattie must have ordered it. The prisoner got into the back and the truck drove off.

'An intense but interesting session,' Beattie said as he joined me. 'The interrogators here think he's telling the truth when he says he had nothing to do with the shooting of the prisoners.' He settled into his seat. 'But while they were interrogating him he let slip something about his family. They run a hotel on Lake Constance, quite a pretty spot, apparently, popular with Party officials.'

I'd never visited Lake Constance, the large stretch of water at the bottom-left side of Germany, very close to Switzerland, but I'd heard about its balmy climate and scenery.

'Quite a few people of interest still come and stay at the family hotel,' William said, seating himself beside me.

SS. Senior Nazis. Off duty, relaxed, enjoying the mild climate and views, drunken and indiscreet, perhaps. I felt the skin on the back of my neck prickle. Beattie looked at me and grinned. 'You're salivating, too, aren't you, Anna?'

The use of my Christian name indicated I was in favour again. Beattie always liked me most when I was showing what he called my under-surface, the part of me that liked to exploit and spin, the part that hadn't lived up to my vicarage childhood. I felt the same connection with Beattie we'd shared in my hotel room in Lisbon.

'Where are they taking the prisoner now?'

'They wanted to ship him to Canada with the others, but I persuaded them to send him to an Italian POW camp not far from us. He's quite a fellow. Told me I could hang him for all he cared if I let him have a shower first.'

'How does he know who's staying at the hotel if he's been away in the army for years?' I asked.

'The pay book shows he's had several leaves at home,' Beattie said. 'And his sister writes to him using a family code.'

I knew the kind of thing – references to pets and uncles and aunts. 'Can we verify his information?'

'We have a contact, a mushroom seller, would you believe,' Beattie said. 'He's just across the water in Switzerland but crosses over regularly. He can tell us if the information Schulte passes on sounds reasonable.'

Who ordered what at the bar, or from room service? Favourite champagne. Cream cake preferences. Already my mind was racing ahead, composing snippets about high-ranking Nazis tucking into pastries, town dignitaries showing off local wines and fish freshly caught in the lake, while most Germans found their rations shrinking by the month. Women – who exactly popped up to the bedrooms with these men after dinner when their wives didn't attend the conferences?

Beattie nodded at me, reading my mind. 'We'll milk him.' He took out a linen handkerchief and held it to his face momentarily. 'That place,' he said.

'But interviewing him in a POW camp?' With other prisoners curious about what was going on, even if they were Italian, not German?

'I'm arranging for him to get some farm work so we can talk to him by himself.'

'He's an officer.' Officers weren't obliged to carry out labour.

'If he volunteers, he can work. And he will because he'll be bored out of his mind alone with the Eyeties.'

Keep an intelligent man digging up root vegetables or spreading muck in near solitary conditions and he'd be glad to have someone to talk to. 'He'll have to work somewhere where there are other prisoners,' William said. 'So the military police can watch him.'

'Isn't there a farm not too far from us where the son was taken prisoner in France and then the father died?' Beattie tapped his fingers on his attaché case, waiting for me to pull the name out of my memory.

'Waites Farm,' I said. 'They were talking about it in the—'

'Blue Anchor,' Beattie finished, smirking at my expression. 'I know you sneaked off there with Micki, Hall, disobeying my orders.'

He could only know this because he'd been in the pub himself on that same occasion two nights ago. He let me stew for a few minutes. 'Now, how's our priestly broadcast shaping up, Nathanson?'

William took the script out of the leather folio case he carried and set himself to studying it.

'You need to sound like that kindly priest who muttered Latin over your dying mother and made you feel better.' Beattie paused. 'When you meet our real-life Father Becker he'll provide the role model. Avuncular, speaking more in sorrow than in anger. Keep that tone up until the end when you drop the little bombshell, or should we say, millstone, about the nonces in youth camps feeling up the children. Then sound like the righteous and angry voice of God. But don't overdo it.'

William swallowed.

'You'll get used to it.' Beattie folded his arms. 'Hall did, and she came from a vicarage.' He smiled to himself.

I scowled at him. Was the dig at my background meant to remind me of that night in Lisbon? He glanced at me again and for a moment I thought I saw something more serious in his eyes.

As we left London behind, I became aware of William watching me. This time he was sitting to my right. Was he fascinated, as some people were, by the rippled skin on my cheek?

I busied myself with my pencil and writing pad.

8

William shifted in the rear of the Austin as we drove to the studio that evening, checking yet again that the script was safe in his folio case. He really hadn't had much time to read it. We slowed at the gatehouse. Atkins wound down the window and we showed our papers. I felt the familiar rush of pride as the guards waved us through and we pulled up outside the main door. The building consisted of a central three-storey, tower-like brick structure, stepping down on each side to a two- and then one-storey level. The plain lines and metal-framed windows were modern and quietly confident in appearance, a contrast to ostentatious Nazi architecture. Even the guards' Alsatian dogs appeared calm, if alert.

I'd probably never be able to tell anyone about this studio and what I did here, but I could still revel in its existence and the fact that people from all over Europe worked together in it. I drew in a breath as we entered. The studio still held on to its new-building smell, too: clean metal, linoleum and fresh wood – an increasingly rare and morale-boosting feature.

Beattie, as usual, spent some minutes talking to the girls on the switchboard situated just inside the entrance. Sometimes he brought them bars of chocolate. Most of them were former General Post Office telephonists or had worked for Thomas Cook. Dealing with travellers whose *wagons-lit* tickets had been wrongly allocated was good preparation for handling furious air marshals ringing up to complain about coverage of air raids on German cities. More importantly these women had experience in switchboard technology and telephony and understood how the complicated wires and connectors to the transmitter masts worked.

I took William through to the studio, on the way pointing out the rooms housing the files and research, which all kinds of people came to read, and the soundproofing tiles. 'Nobody could get through the guard post, but even if they did, they wouldn't hear a word of what we broadcast here.'

'A secret world.' He shook his head. 'What an achievement.'

'It is. And the public will never really know what went on in here.' For that matter, I didn't know half of what went on at the studio.

'Excuse me.' A uniformed girl dashed past us, sheets of paper clutched to her chest, on her way to hand the latest intelligence to someone or other. Everyone had signed the Official Secrets Act and it had been made clear that the consequences for blabbing would be unpleasant, possibly even deadly. I still found it hard to believe that British authorities might shoot a kid of nineteen or twenty. We weren't as bad as the Nazis, were we?

The studio housed a scrambled telephone line, linking us to someone anonymous but high up in the RAF who'd pass on details of bombing raids in Germany for Beattie to insert into the evening news broadcasts. Names of streets badly hit, names of residents – taken from telephone directories – we could provide all the details before the official German radio stations could. Sometimes we'd add a little comment about the Luftwaffe facing penalties for its failure to shoot down British planes.

I showed William the shower block and lavatories and studios. 'We often use live bands or classical ensembles – the Germans do love their music. Our musicians are some of the best you'll hear. We captured a whole touring orchestra in North Africa and persuaded them to play for us.'

William laughed. 'I'm picturing double basses and saxophones being solemnly taken into captivity and interrogated.'

'Stranger things have happened here.' I looked over my shoulder, aware as always that I needed to keep my voice down. 'We've also got an American swing band when we want something jazzier. That kind of music's been in short supply in Germany. It seems to be going down well.' The aim was to make the programmes coming out of Milton Bryan irresistible.

'Doesn't swing music give the game away that we're not broadcasting from Germany?'

'We tone it down so it's a little more . . . Chemnitz than Chicago. The bandleader doesn't approve but it's a fine balance.'

We passed Sefton Delmer's office. 'That's the big boss's room,' I said, in the same lower voice. 'Our Mulberry House research unit will move over to an office here eventually. Much more convenient.'

'But no more throwing the ball for the terrier in the garden?' The distraction therapy seemed to be working on William. He'd met the dog and the rest of the team very briefly in Mulberry House before coming over here.

'We'll need a studio mascot,' I said. Again I lowered my voice. 'I was thinking of a German-speaking parrot. A good mimic of someone like Himmler. Imagine the havoc we could cause on air.'

He laughed again.

I took him into the studio we used each evening for our hour-and-a-half schedule and showed him how to adjust the microphone height.

'Good quality equipment,' he said, looking closely at it.

'Nothing but the best. It's so much better broadcasting live than using all those records. I was always bracing myself for the needle to get stuck in a groove and play the same words over and over again, though the technicians know their stuff and would have jumped in.'

'You can't always rely on the equipment. Sometimes it comes down to humans doing their bit.' He ran his fingers over the edge of the desk, looking pale.

'Would you like a few minutes to rehearse?' I asked him.

'Please.' He gave me that boyish grin. 'I don't know why I feel so self-conscious suddenly. It'll be fine once the light comes on.' He nodded at the bulb that would switch to red minutes before the broadcast and then to green as we went on air. 'This isn't like the stage, is it?'

There was nobody to feed off. 'The announcer's a steady hand and we'll be just there in the cubicle.' I pointed at the small glass-windowed control room, where I'd sit with Beattie. 'I know you'll do a grand job.'

'That means a lot, thank you.' He massaged his temple. I noticed his hands trembling.

'It'll be over before you know it.'

William took his notepad out and wrote something. 'It helps,' he said, 'to have it all in writing. Then I can't get mu—' He rolled his eyes. 'Don't listen to me. I'm not a flapper, honestly.'

I left him to rehearse and went to talk to the studio technicians. Everything was well prepared, as always. The weather had been checked: no storms expected that might affect the performance of the transmitter or masts. I found Beattie in another of the studios, eating what smelled like a freshly baked meat pie.

'Sorry, Hall, I grabbed the last one from the canteen hut.' He looked down at the plate. 'Actually I think I might have had the last two. They might be able to find you a biscuit?'

I hadn't eaten since lunch and my stomach suddenly remembered this. Micki would have asked the landlady to save a portion of the rabbit stew she'd cooked for us, but I wouldn't get that until much later. Hopefully the canteen might have something left.

'Lieutenant Nathanson's nervous,' I said, 'but seems well prepared.'

'Good.' Beattie nodded at me to sit down with him. 'I know Nathanson.' He pushed the plate away. 'You've made a bit of an impression on him. Not just because of your famed intellect, either.'

I tried to give him a hard stare.

'What with Father Becker making eyes at you as well, it could get complicated in the front room.'

'Father Becker?' I heard the incredulity in my voice. 'He's dedicated to a life of chastity.'

'Perhaps he wants to take this opportunity to let rip a little. Bedfordshire has that effect on some people. It's the breezy air and all those pine trees. Ask that lot up at Woburn Abbey.'

'Don't be ridiculous.'

'Because priests can't have normal masculine responses to attractive women? Or because you've got it into your head that you're now irredeemably flawed?' He said the words gently but I felt them like a slap.

I looked at my watch. 'Much as I value your analysis of my situation, there's no time for this now. Sir,' I added, hoping he couldn't hear anything in my voice that might suggest what he'd said had shaken me.

'Pity,' he said. 'I may not have time to help you again.' As I stood up, he put a hand on my arm. 'Anna,' he said. 'You've done a good job taking him under your wing.'

I looked at him.

'I mean it.'

Five minutes to go. I left Beattie with his empty plate and returned to the studio. An engineer was examining the microphone, glancing at the control room where his colleague would be checking amplifiers and circuits. Watching this calm, methodical routine always reassured me. I knew the exchange with Beattie was part of a process of antagonism that Beattie himself sometimes needed to go through when he was under pressure. First night with a new radio character. And a new actor. We were all on edge. William still looked pale. I poured him a glass of water.

'Thanks.' He took what might have been an aspirin from a pill box and swallowed it with a sip of water. 'I feel better now it's nearly time.' He glanced at the clock.

'Waiting around's the worst bit. But you've prepared very thoroughly for this.' I couldn't do much to help him from within the glass box, but I hoped my presence would be reassuring. The announcer, a German from Saxony, came inside and introduced himself to William. 'Break a leg,' I said.

I moved into the control room, Beattie coming to join me. We put on our headphones, waiting for a radio station in Hamburg to go off air, at which point we'd jump onto its frequency, seamlessly assuming its identity. Eventually, Beattie said, when we were using the new transmitter, we'd have our own frequency, and there wouldn't be this moment of heart-racing as we took over from Hamburg.

The announcer would commence with the news. Then the audience would be expecting to hear the broadcast – sermon, you could call it – by the kindly, ageing German priest Father Josef as performed by Gerhard Meiner. Meiner had probably now been transferred to a discreet clinic for the addicted. He might reappear in Aspley Guise again at some point.

As always, I pictured our listeners. A middle-aged couple, perhaps. He too old to fight but drafted into some civil defence job. Sometimes he came home too late to listen to us. His wife always tuned in, though. She'd be knitting something warm for their son on the Eastern Front. There was a daughter, too. She was younger, doing her homework, half an ear on the wireless, having attended a League of German Maidens session earlier in the evening. Perhaps she'd find the religious broadcast a bit staid, preferring the upbeat music, an antidote to the stodgy old League meeting. Or she might enjoy my Clara play. I felt a connection with this imagined family, almost an affection for them. I spent so much time trying to enter their heads.

Just before William started, the announcer would briefly explain why a new priest was taking over the slot, using Beattie's words about correction and gratitude. I looked at William in his blue uniform – surely Beattie could find some way of letting him wear civilian clothes, so much more suitable for broadcasting? William rubbed his back in slow circles. The legacy of the crash landing?

As the last minute trickled away William seemed to change in front of me. His pallor left him, his posture became more upright. Yet simultaneously his face almost lost its smoothness, turning into something more wrinkled and lined.

Seconds to go. William straightened the script in front of him and adjusted the microphone again. Three seconds. Two. One. The announcer pressed the button illuminating the green light on the control position beside us. The engineer pushed a key to switch off the green light and replace it with the red one. We were live.

'*Guten Abend*,' the announcer said. I felt the usual relief that the jump onto the frequency had worked. He read the news. We still obtained quite a bit of it from an official German teleprinter accidentally left behind in the London embassy at the start of hostilities. 'The audience actually gets more truth from us than they do from their own broadcasters,' Beattie liked to tell us. 'When we're not lying to them, that is.' We'd added to this evening's news with our own intelligence: accurate, but not necessarily what the German authorities wanted the public to know. Accounts of bomb damage provided by RAF reconnaissance and verified on the ground by people who supplied information to British intelligence, specific as to street names and numbers. Commendations for members of the armed forces. A little piece about a Berlin film studio Beattie was particularly pleased with. We'd probably informed the actors, director and producer that they'd be filming a new production of a Grimm's fairy tale before the propaganda minister Goebbels himself had had time to tell them. I hoped this infuriated him.

I pictured the announcer's voice turning into electrical impulses as it passed through the microphone, running through amplifiers in the control room, along telephone lines to the transmitters and from there pulsing above English fields and then the sea, eventually to be picked up in Germany. We couldn't easily fight the Germans on their own soil. Even the arrival of the Americans into the war hadn't seemed to bring an invasion of Occupied Europe much closer. Until it happened we had bombers. And we had the war of minds, a part of which was fought here.

The announcer introduced the religious programme, explaining what had happened to Father Josef, using Beattie's suggestions. Being sent to a camp would do Father Josef good, he explained, making the ordeal sound like a kindly if robust educational experience, until he added that Father Josef had requested listeners' prayers for a quick recovery from a bout of dysentery.

And then he introduced the new Father Friedrich, who would provide the radio flock with fresh spiritual nourishment. With a final nod to the newcomer, he sat back. William was on.

What came from his mouth, from his whole body, astonished me. I had known some good student actors, one or two who'd gone on to act professionally. I'd seen Laurence Olivier onstage several times. I'd expected William to be satisfactory.

He wasn't satisfactory. It wasn't a good acting performance. It didn't seem to be a performance at all. William *was* Father Friedrich. I couldn't even see his blue RAF uniform any longer. I was seeing a shabby German priest in his late thirties who was pleading – subtly, carefully, but intensely – for his radio listeners to think about what was going on in their country.

A bead of perspiration fell down William's neck. He twisted a hand to wipe it away. I held my breath. He paused, coughed. Good. Father Friedrich wasn't a professional broadcaster, coached to perfection; he was a cleric.

William followed Father Becker's script exactly, without a mistake but with an occasional slight hesitation to make him utterly believable. It was one of Becker's best creations. Not for the first time I wondered at how our somewhat bumbling team member could produce such well-tailored pieces.

William blessed the audience in Latin. *In nomine Patris, et Filii, et Spiritus Sancti*, he concluded. The announcer introduced the swing band. When the switch to the music studio had been made and the technician gave us the thumbs-up, Beattie let out a sigh. 'Told you the lad would be good.'

'More than good,' I said.

'I know how to choose people.' Beattie took out a cigar and scowled at me as though implying I was the exception to the rule.

'I'll go and get him something to eat and drink.' William had been too nervous to eat beforehand.

The meat pies had not been replenished but the canteen hut gave me a plate of sandwiches and a mug of coffee for him. I returned to find William in the corridor outside the studio. 'You were wonderful.'

'Thank you.' He looked triumphant but as though every particle of energy had been pumped out of him.

I held out the sandwiches. 'Let's get you some fresh air and refuel you.'

'You make me sound like a plane,' he said.

Another man might have made a joke about me changing his oil or checking his plugs, but not William. He seemed relaxed with women, holding doors open for the uniformed girls and secretaries rushing past, seeming to note, like any man would, the pretty, shapely ones, but not leering at them.

There were a couple of folding seats we sometimes took out of the studio to sit on if the guards were amenable. While we were outside the sealed studio we couldn't talk about what had been broadcast; it was strictly forbidden, and if another team of broadcasters appeared we were not supposed to talk to them at all.

'Do you miss flying?' I asked.

He thought about it for a moment. 'I miss the crew. Crews. I was on several.'

'Switching over must have been hard.'

He nodded. 'I started to feel like a bit of a Jonah, to be honest. I was the only one of my first crew who survived. Then, when they switched me to the second Halifax, we lost two men. By the time I moved to the third crew to replace the navigator they'd lost, everyone must have seen me as an albatross.'

'That's tough.' I remembered how superstitious flying crews were. Everything had to be done the same way, each time. Same lucky charms and mascots. Same meal. Same drink. Same jokes. Survivors could be irrationally blamed for all kinds of ill luck.

'The last crew were a good bunch.'

'You must miss them.'

'Sometimes, yes.' William gazed up to the sky, where the Milky Way blazed. 'Even in London you can see all these stars some nights,' he said. 'I don't remember it being like this before 1939. Some religions believe that people become stars when they die, don't they?'

'"When like stars his children crowned, all in white shall wait around,"' I quoted.

'"Once in Royal David's City", my favourite carol,' William replied.

I stared heaven-wards. Was Grace a star now? My mother? Such a childish fancy, but appealing.

'Who did you lose, Anna?' William looked at me. 'It's the question we're not supposed to ask, isn't it?'

'My sister. She died when . . . After an incendiary hit us.'

'I'm sorry,' he said.

'And someone else. He didn't die, but I . . . couldn't face him.' I twisted my mouth. 'Literally.'

'Do you miss him?' His eyes were full of concern.

My sigh was a little puff of mist in the cool air. 'Sometimes.'

He stared down into the contents of his mug. His hand shook. Some of the tea splashed onto the grass. Noticing my eyes on him he appeared to flip out of whatever was troubling him. 'Those sandwiches were good. Do you remember coming in after a performance and suddenly feeling ravenous? I used to raid the larder at my landlady's.' He spoke jovially but beads of perspiration had formed on his brow again. He shook slightly. Post-performance release, I remembered, could make you feel shaky with relief. Or was it his back? He rocked forward slightly, clasping it with one hand. That malicious companion, pain, always lying in wait. I hadn't thrown it off completely myself.

I smelled Beattie's cigar before I saw him. 'Nothing more we need to do here tonight. Let's get home, kids.' The black car was pulling up in front of the studio. I took a last look at the Milky Way streaming across the night sky.

Atkins got out to open the doors. She really didn't need to. 'Good for me to jump in and out of the car, sergeant,' she said, reading my mind. 'Need to keep fit.'

'Atkins is missing her riding,' Beattie told us.

'When I'm on motorbikes it's almost as good,' she said. 'Perhaps I'll get some time at home soon. We've got lots of American officers in the house. Bit of a change for my folks, but they'll survive.'

Atkins said it drolly, but I thought we'd all fallen into a fast-flowing river. When we surfaced again we'd find ourselves washed up in places we didn't recognise.

9

'Let me come with you to Waites Farm,' Micki said. I was packing up my satchel with notepad and pen. The nib on the latter had started to scratch. I took a spare pencil as insurance.

'Not this time.' A fortnight had passed since William had joined us and Schulte had been transferred to the farm. William and I had prepared our interrogation approach just as we might have rehearsed scenes from a play. We would extemporise according to the answers we pulled out of Schulte.

The corner of Micki's mouth twitched. I'd come to recognise this as a sign of deep displeasure. Her initial quietness had definitely faded. It was a relief to hear her sing to herself or chatter to the terrier in her rapidly improving English. But as her confidence grew, so did her boldness.

'I could ask that Nazi the questions that would really show him up for what he is.' She folded her arms.

'I know.' William was already standing outside, waiting for the car. Father Becker was smoking in the garden. I could speak freely. 'But it's not your project. You're not authorised. Sometimes we have to keep our work in separate boxes. Even among ourselves.'

'You don't trust me.'

'I do.' I put down my satchel. 'In due course Beattie may have you working on projects that I'm not authorised to know about, things you can't mention to me. He may even lend you out to research units I've – he's – never even met.'

Her eyes widened. 'I might not always work with Beattie?'

'Quite possibly. We aren't supposed to ask questions about the other units, though.'

'This place.' She shook her head.

I touched her arm. 'It seems mad, I know. Like Alice falling down the rabbit hole – you know that story?'

'Of course.' She flashed a look at me. 'I did actually grow up in a house with books, you know.'

'I'm sorry, I didn't mean—'

This time it was she who touched my arm. 'Forgive me, I'm over-sensitive. It's still so strange, all this . . . what we do. I do not always know how to behave. Part of me still thinks I need to defend myself, take what I can from other people to survive.' She looked down. 'I am trying not to be like this.'

'You're doing well. It's a big change coming from Lisbon to here.' I looked at her, trying to establish whether I could say what I wanted to. I took the plunge. 'And Maxi, you must miss him.'

She swallowed. 'At first I didn't. It's so different here. But now, I think of him, Anna. At night, in bed.'

'That's always the worst time,' I said softly.

Micki looked up. 'Beattie said you had a sister.' I hadn't mentioned Grace to her before. I'd told William about my sister, so why not Micki?

'Did she . . . ?'

'She died in the Blitz, yes. In one of the last raids.'

'Same time your face was burned?'

I nodded.

She spread out her fingers on her desk and looked down at them. 'I keep wondering whether I could have done more for him. If he'd got better food when he first fell ill, perhaps he might have put up more of a fight.'

'I blame myself for my sister's death, too. She wasn't strong. She was born with some handicaps.'

She looked startled. 'Surely not, Anna – it was a bomb, it was the Nazis—'

I could have told her, but there wasn't time, not when the car was already crunching up the drive. 'Oh I blame them, too. Part of the reason I came here was to get my own back.'

'Me too.' She gave me a conspiratorial smile.

Car doors were opening outside. I picked up my satchel. 'Do me a favour and read through my Clara episode? I'm not sure I've got the locals quite right. William and Father Becker don't quite understand what I'm trying to do with the female characters.'

'Comment on your play?' She sounded startled. 'Me?'

'It's not restricted, so anyone in the unit can read it and I think you'd have very useful comments.'

'Really?'

'Pencil any observations in the margin.'

Beattie came in. 'Haven't you gone yet, Hall?' He looked at Micki. 'You're coming with me, get your jacket. Some German sailors have washed up in the local cage. I want you to talk to them.'

'I'll look at the script later,' she told me, looking excited. 'If you don't mind, Anna?'

⁂

Schulte, the German prisoner, didn't look as much like a fox this morning as he sat in the farmhouse kitchen. Spring had given way to winter again. It had rained – the drops turning to sleet – since dawn. Through the window I could see the mud-strewn tractor. The two Italian prisoners prodded at the engine, their expressions bleak, perhaps wondering if they'd ever again enjoy the sunshine of their homeland.

Fresh air and better rations had filled out some of the sharpness in Schulte's face. His boots were muddy. Sewn to his uniform were strips of coloured fabric identifying him as a prisoner in case he tried to escape. I could see by the way he glanced down at them that the strips and dirty footwear weren't to his taste. Let him feel uncomfortable, on edge.

The Waites's daughter, Mary, who looked about seventeen, wanted to set up a trestle table and some hay bales in the barn for our interview of the prisoner, but Mrs Waites had intervened, quietly clearing the kitchen table, placing a log in the stove. Mrs Waites was a well-preserved woman in her forties and would have been pretty if she hadn't lost her son to a prisoner-of-war camp in Germany and her husband to a heart attack.

'Thank you, both of you,' William said. 'Please stay out of earshot until I come and tell you you may return.'

'See if Giovanni and Carlo have got the tractor going yet, Mary,' her mother told her.

Schulte turned his head at the mention of the tractor.

William gave the girl the apologetic smile I'd already noted. Her frown softened as she left with her mother.

It hadn't taken long for me to see why Beattie had wanted William to work for the research unit. William's emollient skill and ability to read people meant he could do far more than act out the part of a radio padre. It had only been a few weeks, but it felt as though he'd always sat in the front room of Mulberry House with Micki, Father Becker and me. Only last week that bashful smile had worked its charm on the stationery officer when we'd run out of envelopes and were informed that no more could be obtained for two weeks. William had strolled over to the cottage housing the supplies office and returned an hour later carrying half a dozen envelopes and knowing more of the private history of the stationery office clerk than I had gleaned in months.

He closed the stripped oak door behind the two women and sat down beside me, facing the prisoner.

I slung my satchel over the back of my chair. Light from the kitchen window streamed in, casting the men's shadows against the wall to my side. Only a wooden kitchen table, its surface worn smooth by decades of use, stood between them. The young men's silhouettes were almost identical: both formerly enemy combatants, both tall and athletic, still in uniform, though Beattie had agreed that William should wear civilian clothing and was negotiating with the RAF on this concession. He still hadn't made a similar move on my behalf.

A cat stretched out in front of the stove. The animal ought to be removed. Yet I had a hunch that carrying out the interview in this warm but homely room might work in our favour. Let the prisoner think that this session would be gentler than the interrogation in the cage. Let him relax.

'You're being well treated by the family?' I asked, in German. 'And by the Italian prisoners?'

He nodded.

'Please give me spoken answers.'

'Yes, they treat me well.'

'Dull work, though, pulling up turnips? Mucking out the pigs?'

'Better than being indoors.'

'You prefer the outdoor life?' We could use the threat of keeping him indoors at the camp, if necessary.

He eyed me curiously, still seeming puzzled that I was running the interview, but nodded.

'Your parents didn't need you to work inside the hotel?' I continued.

'No. I mowed the grass and fixed the mower.'

'Anything else?'

'We had boats, too,' he said grudgingly. 'For the guests. I varnished them and serviced the motor boat when I was home from university.'

'What did you study?'

'Engineering, but only for a year.'

'How much contact did you have with the guests?'

He shrugged. 'Not much.' Something in his tone made it sound as though he hadn't minded this.

'You didn't serve them food and drink?'

He straightened his back. 'I wasn't a waiter.'

'A family hotel? And you the only son? You must have played quite an important role.' I tried a more flattering tack.

'Sometimes I took guests' wives out on the lake if they didn't want to row themselves.'

I raised my eyebrows encouragingly.

'And if they wanted to sail, I took them out in our dinghy.'

Something pulsed through my nervous system.

'Who exactly did you take out in the boat?'

His expression took on the vulpine quality I remembered from Kensington. 'Whoever asked me.'

'Including?'

'Guests from all walks of life.'

'Even once the war started?'

'As time went on we lost some of the regulars,' he admitted. 'We'd always been noted for our food and our location. And we were famous for our red shutters.' A faraway look passed over his eyes.

I noted these points.

'I'd imagine it was more important political types who came?' Fewer pleasure trips for everyone else in wartime.

He nodded.

'Answer me properly. You know the deal we made with you. You can go back to the cage for more questions about exactly where you were at the time of Dunkirk if you prefer.'

He glowered at me. 'I had nothing to do with the shooting of those British prisoners, I—'

'Who were the guests?' I asked.

'Some fairly senior SS men,' he muttered. 'And their womenfolk.' He listed them. William took notes.

'What did they talk about?'

He gave us snippets of gossip that could have come from anywhere, most of which we'd already heard. And a joke about Hitler visiting an asylum and complaining that one man didn't salute him. 'I'm the nurse,' the answer came. 'Not one of the lunatics here.'

William put the lid on his fountain pen. 'I've heard that one before.' We liked jokes, fresh jokes, pulled from the factories and bars and made – unwisely – on public transport. Often we broadcast them before they'd gone beyond the confines of the neighbourhoods where they'd started. Spreading an obscene or unflattering quip about some Nazi bigwig gave Beattie particular pleasure. He'd add a little twist about people being arrested for passing on the joke. Without any evidence that this had happened.

Schulte crossed his arms.

I forced myself to breathe slowly, picking up the scent of prisoner: wet wool, leather and sweat. Not unpleasant, not quite. He'd obviously been availing himself of the shower block at the POW camp.

'None of this in the cage.' I gestured at the cat by the stove.

'I'm telling you what I know, sergeant.' A note of mockery as he used my rank.

'You've had days to rake your memory. When you get letters from home your family use a kind of code to pass on more interesting information, don't they?'

He looked at me silently.

'So, tell me, Lieutenant Schulte, why are you giving me this shit?'

He blinked at the language. Good. 'The man who came to Kensington to see me . . .' He looked down at his hands.

'What about him?'

'He seemed to understand what it was like in the hotel, how we had to go through the pretences.' Schulte seemed to relax as he talked about Beattie. 'It was as though he were a sorcerer,' he murmured, almost to himself.

Ah, so he was pining for Beattie. Wouldn't be the first time. Beattie had a way of making himself feel like the solution to people's problems. He would actually be the cause of very many problems if Schulte didn't talk. I closed my eyes, trying to draw on the internal energy needed to float into someone else's world, inhabit their hopes and fears. I was as good as Beattie. No, I was better. I was a woman, and a scarred one at that, more reliant on imagination and empathy than power.

I hadn't ever been to Lake Constance in the far south of Germany, but I could picture hotels like the one the prisoner had grown up in: locals working in the kitchen and garden and as chambermaids, the owner-managers who knew the best local butchers and bakers, who'd once welcomed returning guests year after year. Now they were hosting a different kind of clientele. Some of the staff would love the proximity to the powerful. Others would despise the bragging, the vulgarity.

'Some of the middle-aged female guests, the wives, are lonely,' I said slowly. 'They see their husbands flirting with the pretty young things brought in each night to wait on them and entertain them. You went home a few times on leave, lieutenant, didn't you?'

He nodded.

'The last time being June last year. And some of the wives of important men asked you to take them sailing out on the lake. You're a nice-looking young man.' He folded his arms, but I watched his face carefully as I went on. 'A good listener. I imagine you've always got on well with your sister.' I looked closely at him. Schulte's face softened almost imperceptibly. 'She confides in you, doesn't she? So do the wives. They tell you their worries about their husbands. The conversation with the chief that went the wrong way. The threatened posting to the east. And about the heavy drinking, and the pills so many of these senior men take.'

William shifted his position on the kitchen chair.

Schulte tilted his head, eyes on the table, his body very still. I continued. 'And here's this handsome young man on leave, handling the boat so neatly, nodding so sympathetically.'

A log inside the stove fell. Schulte jumped.

'How did you know all that?' His face hardened; he reminded me once again of the fox.

Some of it was inference based on a close reading of Beattie's notes. And the rest was that growing ability to pick up on the emotions playing out behind someone's expression. The loss of my looks had caused me to pay more attention to other people than I had as a self-absorbed young woman who never, frankly, needed to make much of an effort to draw people to me. 'People are always interested in you, Anna,' Grace had told me once. Perhaps if my face hadn't been so disfigured I'd never have had the patience to enter someone else's head. Or the inclination.

'You were this handsome boy who wasn't judgemental about the drugs and alcohol,' I went on.

William glanced at me, eyes narrowed. I'd overstressed the point, scared Schulte off continuing. We waited.

Schulte let out a breath. 'Actually, there was this woman, a Frau Lauder.' He shook his head. 'But it's frivolous, it can't be—'

'We'll be the judge of that.'

He paused, looking down at the fingers he was steepling on the table. 'She said something about drugs given to senior officers in the army and Luftwaffe, to keep them awake at night. And another kind given to make them sleep off duty. Frau Lauder joked that there must be whole factories producing uppers and downers for the same people.'

'And?' William's voice had an edge to it. 'What else did she say when she was mocking these drug users?'

Schulte looked around as though worried we'd be overheard. 'We were out in the middle of the lake, nobody could hear us. She said some of the pills her husband had been given by their doctor had made him . . . unable to . . .' He shuffled in the chair.

'Have intercourse with her,' I said. A more Anglo-Saxon expression had come to mind, one which Beattie would undoubtedly have used, but I'd censored myself, perhaps because of William's presence.

Schulte looked down at his hands.

Nice. Not a new story, but close to the bone. Our colleagues broadcasting to German troops might be interested . . . *Doctors have found a way of counteracting a side-effect of the medication prescribed for those brave men needing to keep themselves on full alert . . . German fighting men will no longer be distressed by lack of amorous ability . . .* It would work for civilians, too. The wives sitting at home might prick up their ears, but it would have to be discreetly phrased for our audience.

The leaflets people might also like the story for some of the more pornographic printed material the RAF sometimes dispersed above German troops. Their artists could produce some interesting illustrations.

The prisoner's face was set, probably worried he'd said too much.

'Tell me what's on your mind.' I dropped my voice, trying to make it sound sympathetic.

'My sister . . .' He shrugged. 'She's seventeen.'

'Quite a bit younger than you,' I said. 'You must be worried about the groups of drunken men milling around in the bar when there are receptions and parties.' Through my mind flashed an image of Micki at the same age, ducking lecherous drunks in bars. I looked him directly in the eye. 'Surely your parents must want to rid themselves of these unseemly guests?'

'On that last leave of mine, we thought of claiming manpower shortages, closing the hotel. But the local Party wouldn't let that happen. They'd insist on bringing in their own staff to serve in the restaurant and bar.' He pursed his lips. 'And that would be worse.'

'You're wondering how they're managing now?' William said, his voice soft. 'Worrying that you can't do anything to help?'

'Yes.' Schulte's face had lost some of its stoniness.

'You can help Grete,' I said, folding my papers, sounding as casual as I could.

'What do you mean?' Schulte asked.

'We might be able to put in a word for your family when the war ends.'

Schulte's eyes widened. He tapped his fingers on the table. William and I let the silence sit there. Perhaps Schulte thought the war's end was so distant that he couldn't even imagine it. To be honest, I couldn't myself. Beattie said he'd put money on an Allied invasion of Europe taking place next year, but who knew how long it might take to reach Berlin.

'There were many conversations like the one I had with Frau Lauder,' he said slowly.

'But?' William asked.

'Suppose what I tell you is linked to my family, *Fräulein?*' He swallowed, looking younger and less certain of himself.

'Sergeant,' I corrected him as I stood up. 'We make no promises, Lieutenant Schulte, but this must be better than the cage.'

'If I thought I was endangering my parents and sister I would have to go back to the cage.' He spoke calmly.

I looked at William. 'Would you take the lieutenant out? Mrs and Miss Waites can come in now. Mrs Waites will be wanting to cook the lunch.'

William went into the yard, returning with Mary. Schulte walked off towards the barn.

Mary had recently completed school, I recalled from our notes on the family.

'Is Lieutenant Schulte pulling his weight?' I asked her.

'He's very fit. Quite practical. Hasn't worked with farm animals like the Italians have, but learns quickly.' Mary was trying hard not to look at the right side of my face. She was probably feeling the mixture of pity and relief some attractive women felt when a competitor was out of the ring.

'He's not like the Italians,' she said. 'They're cheerful. They don't feel like enemies, really. This Nazi should be doing something harder.'

'He's a regular army officer, not obliged to work at all.'

She made a scoffing noise. I stared at her. 'Why haven't you transported him to Canada with the other Germans? We don't want him here.' She looked up, chin jutting out.

'Even though he's pulled all those turnips for you?' I pointed through the window at the sacks piled up against the barn. 'How many would you have managed if it were just you and the Italians, Mary?'

'Even so—'

I looked at her hands. 'Are those callouses sore?'

The girl scowled and glanced from her hands to mine. 'Unlike some, I haven't got time to put on hand cream and manicure my nails. What's the point when it's dawn till dusk in the muck? We're told we must feed the nation, that it's down to us to prevent people starving. I was going to go to secretarial college, make something of myself—'

I put a hand on her shoulder. 'You work hard. And this prisoner is part of your war effort, watching him for me, helping us interview him.' I opened my satchel and pulled out a card. 'Here's a telephone number.'

The girl took the card, her face still troubled.

'Ring us if anything gives you cause for concern.'

Mary sighed. 'It was hard to get him indoors for your interview. I came up with some story about needing him to fill the stove with logs. The Italians gave me funny looks. Helping you is taking me away from my farm work.'

'Helping us is as important as producing food.'

She looked unconvinced. Mary wouldn't have a clue about our radio broadcasts, how we waged war with Germany by influencing civilian disenchantment, perhaps eventually even opposition.

I remembered something. 'You might want to let Schulte have a look at that tractor. He used to service the motor boats at his family's hotel.'

'Dad loved the tractor,' she said quietly. 'We'd only just got it when he . . .' She swallowed.

'You've had quite a time of it, haven't you?' For a second I experienced my own pain after the fire again, knowing everyone expected me to readapt to the world and do my duty when part of me was still struggling inside a burning church.

Mary gave a fierce shrug.

In the car on the return to Aspley Guise, William and I discussed the interview with Schulte and subsequent conversation with the girl. 'It's going to be harder than we thought to set up interviews with Schulte,' I said.

'I saw a small piece of woodland on the edge of the farm as we drove up the track,' William said. 'They probably kept it for game birds. Any chance our fellow could tidy it up? We could talk to him there, out of sight of the fields.'

'Could work,' I said. 'Otherwise, there's always the tractor. Perhaps it could develop a fault that only Schulte can mend, in an outlying field.'

William scribbled a note to himself on his writing pad. I looked at him enquiringly. 'Schulte will be missing his brother officers,' he said. 'And his men. All those years he's spent with them, by now he'll feel quite isolated. And I don't think the Italians can fill the gap. There's no shared language. We should exploit his feeling of isolation, that sense that he's lost his brothers, his former purpose.' He looked sombre. Was William too still missing his old martial companions and career? We sat together in silence in the close confines of the rear seat, William readjusting his position and wincing as the poorly sprung car bumped over a pothole. No large Austin for us. And no Atkins. I didn't recognise the driver. 'Isolation,' William said softly. 'When you feel that the people who meant so much to you have gone.'

Gone because they'd died or because you'd left them behind. He seemed to be talking about himself rather than Schulte now. 'While they're alive, there's always hope of a reunion.' I was trying to cheer him up, remind him that some of his flying companions were probably still around.

William nodded very slowly to himself.

Mentally I ran over what the prisoner had told us. I'd write up my notes as soon as we were in Mulberry House. Beattie would want to see them and was apt to pounce on me if he felt I'd neglected important questions or failed to properly follow through on prisoner answers. He'd be interested in small details such as the cat lying by the stove while we interrogated Schulte and whether Schulte, like Frau Silberman in Lisbon back in February, had reacted positively to the animal's presence.

William looked pale again. Perhaps the crash landing was still taking its toll. He wouldn't be the only one of us whose body found it hard to forget the past. My face felt itchy this afternoon; I wanted to scratch at the carefully applied pancake make-up. Perhaps the scar tissue was moving again, as the doctor had warned me it might. William was looking out of the car window. I gave my cheek a furtive rub.

I remembered my mother once warning me that physical attractiveness could be a handicap, drawing the wrong kind of men to a woman. Perhaps. But if I could have just another day of being unscarred I'd take the risk. One more day with Patrick, as we'd been before.

Why was I thinking of Patrick now? Something about the interview with the prisoner had unsettled me, made me forget that I was the professional Sergeant Hall, entrusted with important POW interviews. I was just Anna Hall, twenty-three years old, remembering what she'd once had.

'I don't know how you manage to do these interviews and look as cool as a cucumber, Anna,' William said.

'I find them hard at times,' I admitted.

But his recognition that our interview work could be taxing helped to lift some of the tension I'd been feeling this morning. My shoulders suddenly felt lighter.

'You haven't forgotten our team night out on Saturday?' William asked.

I had, in fact. Our research unit didn't broadcast on Saturday, which made it the night we could visit cinemas and theatres. Usually we stuck to nights out in Bedford. Travel to the capital was considered wasteful unless essential, so since I'd started working for Beattie I hadn't returned to London in my time off.

'A film and then dinner at a French restaurant in Wardour Street.' William was reading from his notepad. He blushed. 'I know it's strange writing down the details of a night out, but that way I know it's really happening.'

'Certainly seems like a long time since I've gone up to town.' We were turning into the drive to Mulberry House. When we went inside, Father Becker was alone in the office, reading St Augustine and making notes, running a hand through his hair, looking as though the words on the pages were as fresh for him as they were the first time he'd read them. Perhaps that was what my father meant by having a living faith. I'd be seeing Dad after the meal out, as I was to stay the night in Putney on Saturday.

I'd only just removed my jacket when I heard the crunch of tyres over gravel. Beattie himself, returning with Micki from the local cage. I watched them carefully through the window, having got into the habit of observing my boss ahead of his arrival in our office, trying to assess his mood. His face seemed relaxed. Micki, too, seemed jaunty.

She burst into the room with her usual energy.

'Did it go well?' I asked.

'*Ja!*' She looked at me and grimaced. '*Ach, auf Englisch.*'

We were encouraging her to start conversations in English whenever possible. The Saturday evening trip to the cinema was going to be an incentive to improve her fluency.

She looked at Father Becker meaningfully and turned her back. 'This.' She made a quick obscene gesture with her hands. 'Not just the ratings, either. You should have heard what they said about officers misbehaving at brothels.'

A new medical programme will assure the health of our finest seamen as they relax in ports. Enjoying deserved breaks from active duty has brought with it various risks of infection, but our doctors are now stepping up to the vital task of examining workers in the establishments our sailors visit . . . I could write the news item in my head.

We had no evidence that any such medical programme had started, but it didn't seem unbelievable.

'She did very well,' Beattie said, coming in. 'Sat in the interviews looking like a sweet young thing – some of them were clearly wondering what the hell she was doing there. Then she asked brilliantly obscene questions and they let slip the most wonderful details. The Ali Baba nightclub in Hamburg, the Chat Noir in Saint-Nazaire – all kinds of notables pawing naked girls, nasty diseases, stabbings, wallets stolen.' He rubbed his hands. 'There'll be a couple of bottles of something nice on the table when we have our meal out on Saturday.'

Father Becker was watching Beattie, his face a mask. How could a clergyman bear to listen to the kind of smut we'd been casually throwing around?

10

I'd planned on dressing up for the night out. Taking trouble to do my hair more elaborately, putting on a burgundy silk dress and applying a few drops of the precious scent I'd been saving would put me in the mood. Being a civilian, having a night out in the West End, spending a day at home.

On the Friday night, before we left for the studio, Beattie called me into his office. 'Micki,' he said. 'She's a potential problem.'

I nodded. 'She's not supposed to leave the village, is she?' It was one of the conditions of her working with us.

'It's not technically forbidden for the Germans here to go to London, if they're accompanied by their seniors, but it can create bureaucratic issues if IDs are demanded. Tell her to keep her mouth closed.'

'She'll be discreet. What about Father Becker?'

'He's Swiss, why would he bother any policeman? He's much more likely to trip over the kerb in the blackout and split his head open. You and William both being in uniform will give a reassuring appearance to the group.'

'Uniform? But—' The burgundy dress suited me. The warm colour drew attention to my eyes and hair and away from the burnt cheek. And I could have worn a veiled hat with it.

Beattie was looking at me coldly. 'Anything else, Hall?'

❧

We managed the train journey to Euston without attracting any unwanted attention. When we changed at Bletchley Micki wrinkled her nose up at the stains on her seat and covered it with her handkerchief before sitting down. I remembered Grace being equally fastidious. Father Becker and Micki then pretended to read *The Times* and *Tatler* respectively, showing their tickets to the inspector on the train with brief nods. An elderly couple got on at one of the stations between Bletchley and Euston and made approving clucking noises at William and me. 'Such a fine sight, you young 'uns doing your bit.' The woman peered at my cheek. 'And such a price you pay for it.' The sympathy was kindly meant, but I wished I was wearing my hat and veil tonight.

From Euston we made our way by Underground, the train's windows boarded up, to the cinema in Wardour Street in Soho. Nobody paid us much attention. Perhaps in the city we stood out less obviously.

'We're an odd bunch,' Micki whispered. 'Two in uniform, one in a smart suit, one in a dog collar. And me.' She was wearing a dress and jacket I'd lent her.

'You look lovely,' I told her. 'And give us a much-needed air of normality.'

She grunted but looked pleased.

A black GI stepped out of an alley, a young woman clinging to his arm, arguing with him, her glottal, nasal accent peppering his southern drawl with objections to whatever it was he was proposing. Her thin jacket barely covered the top of her pale chest. Father Becker stopped and stared until the woman scowled at him.

As we entered the cinema Beattie pulled out a large box of violet creams from one of his capacious pockets. 'Don't say I don't spoil you. You won't believe what I had to do to get my hands on these.' I noticed that Micki was careful to position herself next to Beattie. My heart always melted a little when she revealed herself as being little older than a schoolgirl.

William sat next to me, giving a discreet but appreciative sniff.

'It's called *Vol de Nuit*,' I whispered. 'Appropriate that you like it.' It had been named after the pilot and writer Antoine de Saint-Exupéry's *Night Flight*. The glass bottle had a propeller in relief on its surface. I explained these references. William looked puzzled for a second but then gave me a warm smile.

'A present?'

Patrick had given me the scent. 'That's right.' I looked at the screen. 'It's starting.'

Father Becker and Micki seemed to find the comedy playing out on the screen utterly incomprehensible at times. Beattie laughed heartily. For someone with such a sophisticated mind he seemed very fond of humour that verged on the slapstick.

We went on to dinner in a small French restaurant across the road. From the remarks made by the French-Jewish proprietor as he took us to our table I gathered that he owed Beattie his place on one of the last boats out of Bordeaux at the time of the German invasion in 1940. This perhaps explained how the restaurant was able to offer us beef fillet.

When we'd finished our apple tarts and emptied three bottles of claret – one of which was accounted for solely by Beattie – we re-emerged onto the street.

My stomach felt pleasantly full and my head woozy as a result of the claret. I hadn't experienced anything similar since Beattie and I had been in Lisbon. He glanced at me briefly as we set off and gave a half-smile. I wondered if he ever thought about that night.

We walked towards Shaftesbury Avenue two abreast, Micki and I, then Father Becker and William, with Beattie himself striding ahead. I was going on alone to Leicester Square for the Piccadilly Line. The others would catch a taxi to Euston. We approached the gloomy emptiness of St Anne's churchyard. A group of five or six soldiers lurched towards us, absorbed in their own quarrel about a bet.

One of the soldiers, a corporal, tripped on the invisible kerb, regaining his balance by throwing out an arm in the direction of Father Becker. 'Bloody blackout.' He peered at Becker. 'That a dog collar?'

The others in the group stopped. 'So it is,' one of his companions said. 'Bless me, father.'

Father Becker seemed paralysed. 'Walk on,' William told him quietly.

'Hear my confession, father?' another private asked.

'He hasn't got all night,' the first soldier said. His companion glowered at him. Their fists rose and they tumbled into the road, punching at one another. Micki and I passed them, walking faster now. The remaining three jeered at the brawling pair.

The larger of the fighters landed a left hook on his opponent, who fell onto the road, narrowly missing Father Becker, who gave a surprised gasp as he jumped out of the way, more nimbly than I might have anticipated. The three men on the pavement turned their heads at the sound.

'A bit rough for you, are we, father?' one of them asked.

'You'll need to hear my confession now, padre,' the larger man said. 'Look what I've done to him. I'm a sinner.'

The smaller soldier sat up, a hand to his bleeding nose.

'I am afraid that it is not possible,' Father Becker said, sounding distinctly German. Just how drunk were this group? Too far gone to notice?

'Not very Christian, father.'

'Walk on,' I said. Any moment now military police or the ordinary variety might appear and want to check papers.

The larger soldier pulled a torch out of his pocket and shone it at us. His mouth dropped as the beam hit my face. 'Bloody hell.'

The corporal grabbed me by the shoulder, spinning me round. 'Let's have a proper look at you.' I tried to wriggle free but he was strong. 'Did you fall into the stove, darling? I don't mind. Let's have a kiss.'

Father Becker's fist seemed to curve through the dark out of nowhere. The corporal landed on his back on the pavement, his mouth still open in surprise.

'Come on.' William pulled me forward. We moved quickly round the corner into Shaftesbury Avenue, regrouping in a large doorway out of the soldiers' sight while Beattie looked for a taxi.

'That wasn't a very priestly response, father,' Beattie said.

'I boxed as a boy.' Father Becker seemed dazed, brushing down his dark coat even though it was spotless.

'Thank you for helping me,' I told him. He regarded me with eyes that seemed almost resentful.

'I shouldn't have done that,' he said. 'I blame myself for drawing attention. I must cover up my clerical status.' He flicked a final speck of invisible dirt off his coat.

'Yes, you should,' Micki said. 'Can't you keep your eyes open for trouble?'

He looked around, as though expecting to see more enemies coming at him.

I was trembling and tried to hide this from the others. I thought I was used to my face, to the attention it drew, to the fact that random drunks on the street could comment on it. Would they do the same to a man with a similar disfigurement? I doubted it. It was only if you were female that your looks were up for public comment.

Micki pressed my hand gently. I knew she would have come to my aid just as effectively as Father Becker but was observing the need for discretion Beattie had impressed on her. She gazed at William, a slight frown on her face. 'What is it?' I asked quietly.

'William was watching you, Anna. Even when he was walking ahead with Beattie, I saw him look over his shoulder to check you were right behind. Father Becker jumped in before he could do anything about those soldiers, though.'

'Probably just as well. We might have caused a mass brawl in the street. William was keeping an eye on both of us, surely?'

Her brows were knitted. 'Drunks are unpredictable. You need to be a step ahead. I should have expected them at this time of night, and looked down the road for places to run to.'

I imagined she had done this many times in cities across Europe.

'I wanted to tell those men to fu— to go away, but I knew they'd hear my German accent. Like Father Becker when he forgot he wasn't supposed to say anything in public.' She grimaced. 'Idiot. But that left hook of his was something else, I'll give him that.'

I shivered at the thought of the drunken group identifying two German spies apparently at large on the streets of London, meting out what they'd imagine was an appropriate response.

'I have this.' Micki opened her bag and showed me something metallic inside.

I stared at the kitchen knife, which I recognised as belonging to our landlady at Lily Cottage.

'I only borrowed it,' Micki said, mistaking the expression on my face.

I wanted to tell her that she didn't need to arm herself with a knife on the streets of London but knew tonight's events would convince her otherwise. She was still frowning. 'What is it?' I asked.

'Father Becker . . .' She shrugged. 'He seemed almost panicked. Then suddenly he was furious.'

Beattie had managed to hail a taxi and beckoned to Micki, preventing me from asking her more. 'Keep the men safe on the train home,' I said.

She winked.

I waved a farewell to the others and cut through Gerrard Street and the narrow roads and alleys leading to Leicester Square. Almost as soon as I'd turned off, I regretted not staying on Shaftesbury Avenue. It might be spring but the night air had grown chilly and mist was forming. I heard footsteps behind me and turned. I thought I made out a male figure, possibly uniformed, but he vanished before I could be sure. I walked on, faster, certain I could still hear someone behind me. Had one of the soldiers from Wardour Street followed me?

Leicester Square was only a minute away. It had been badly damaged in air raids, but there would be more people milling around. Nobody could hurt me in public.

I reached the square, still keeping up a brisk pace. The station was seconds away. Footsteps sounded out behind me. A group of sailors were singing a song that would have made even Beattie blush. A girl with a high-pitched whine was telling her friend exactly what she'd done for her American boyfriend in exchange for various luxury items.

I found another shop entrance and pressed myself into it, waiting. I heard only the intermittent engines of taxis and buses. When I'd counted to fifty I continued to the station. The ticket office was quiet and the newspaper sellers had gone. I bought my fare down to East Putney, planning on taking the Piccadilly Line and then changing onto the District Line at Earl's Court. Casting a final look over my shoulder I headed through the barrier for the escalator down to the platform. By the time the District Line train crossed the Thames, the carriages would be almost empty. If someone were trailing me, I might be vulnerable. I heard the footsteps again, their uneven pattern.

Turning for a last time before I stepped onto the escalator, I saw a man's silhouette the far side of the barrier, his back to me. Uniformed, impossible to make out the colour in the gloom, but wearing a cap of some kind. The figure moved away from me.

With a sense of relief I let the Underground and its wet-newspaper, bad-drains and stale-clothes odour swallow me up.

11

My father seemed pleased to see me. 'Such a short visit, though. I'm afraid tomorrow morning is busy – we're holding the service at the Methodists' at half-eight.' He gave a slight smile. 'A bit early for you, darling?'

'I'm sure I'll manage.' I tried not to groan. I'd forgotten that the church-sharing necessitated by the incendiary damage to Dad's church meant such a brisk start on Sundays.

'You came alone from the West End?' He looked concerned. 'I hear stories about unruly soldiers. Sometimes civilians, too. It's distressing to hear of people looting bombed houses, making everything even worse.'

The professional voice inside me made a note: was the same thing true in German cities? Could I write a piece about the authorities putting on additional police patrols around bombed premises to reassure citizens?

In the morning I managed to drag myself out of bed, finding a dress in my wardrobe to put on in place of my uniform, and even a pair of stockings I'd forgotten about. I had nothing to wear over my shoulders. The morning was chilly and we'd walk to the Methodist church. I doubted the stand-in would be very warm when we reached it; they'd have turned off the heating for spring. After a moment's thought I went into Grace's bedroom and found a light wool jacket I'd bought for her in 1940, just before the Germans had invaded France.

Would Dad mind me wearing my sister's clothes? I could just tell him it was mine. He was hopeless about remembering who had worn what. In my childhood I would never have dreamt of lying to my father. Now it seemed such an easy thing to do.

As I came downstairs Dad was packing the Gladstone bag he took with him when he travelled for services. 'I hope you don't mind me wearing this,' I told him. 'It was Grace's but I don't have anything else.'

He gave me a brief stare. 'I'd forgotten she had it.'

The jacket was light green, not a shade I'd worn much as it had always felt like Grace's colour, contrasting so well with the copper threads in her hair. Not wearing RAF blue was such a relief I would gladly have worn a banana-yellow or bilious-pink garment.

Dad's service was brief, his sermon cut down to less than ten minutes. The congregation comprised mainly loyal, elderly parishioners.

'Your work continues to be productive?' he asked, as we walked home. 'I don't like to ask too many questions.'

'I'm writing a fair bit,' I said. 'I enjoy it.'

We reached the corner of our avenue. In front of us Dad's church loomed, a large ruined edifice. 'I barely notice it any more,' Dad said.

I said nothing.

He cast a sideways look at me. 'You haven't ever been inside since . . . then, have you?'

I shook my head.

'They're going to condemn it.'

I stopped.

'Knock it down?' I couldn't imagine the street without the church.

'A few years ago I'd have been shocked. But there are worse things than buildings being pulled down. It's not of great architectural note. The Victorian improvements, as they termed them, destroyed many of the medieval features. But I liked to think it was a fitting place of worship.'

'More than that. It was beautiful. Still is.' The church retained a quiet dignity. The tower was almost completely undamaged and seemed to watch over the rest of the damaged building like a sentinel. Dad had brought us up to cherish this place of worship from our infancy.

'I need to go inside,' I said. 'It feels like the right time to do it.' Even so, a coldness filled me at the prospect.

'It's in a sad state,' Dad said.

But he seemed pleased that I wanted to do this. In the kitchen he took the large key off the hook where it had always hung. 'You'll remember how the key sticks in the lock. I must oil it. A man's coming to look at the rood screen this week so I uncovered it. You'll be able to have a good look.'

'They're going to save the screen? Thank goodness.'

I went out through the vicarage back door and up to the gate leading to the graveyard – the private access we'd always used. My mouth tasted metallic and my hand made a nonsense of unlocking the door. I could say I hadn't been able to get inside, abandon the pilgrimage, but then Dad would feel he had to come out and unlock the church for me. I had to do this alone.

The key finally turned and I went inside. The electrics had been switched off and it was hard to see much until I turned into the nave. Where the roof had collapsed, light poured in. I could hear birds outside. Dad had covered the font, pews and pulpit in tarpaulins. Paralysis struck me again. I could still see and smell the black smoke, feel the heat of the flames. I had to do this, had to make myself walk up the nave now.

Put one foot out. Put the other foot out. Repeat. I heard Grace's voice in my head. I kept my eyes on the stone slabs beneath my shoes until I stood by the rood screen. A ringing noise hummed in my ears. I tried to draw in another breath. My lungs still seemed to ache from the stench of the smoke that was no longer here.

The London Blitz had reached its final weeks when I came home for a twenty-four-hour leave. Grace had amazed me – she was so much more confident than she had been. Within the somewhat shabby embrace of the vicarage, she'd found a spurt of energy following our mother's death: cooking, cleaning, helping tend the flock.

'Your WAAF uniform really suits you,' she told me. 'I'm sure this hasn't gone unnoticed, Anna?'

I rolled my eyes. 'The Wrens have a far more attractive uniform than we do, but you know me, never one for vanity.'

'Oh, I'd never call you vain,' she said earnestly. 'You do love beautiful clothes, though. I expect your young man likes you in them.'

'Young man?' I hoped I sounded casual.

She pinched my arm. 'I'm not stupid.' Grace smiled her full, glorious smile at me. 'I'm pleased for you. I say a prayer for him, whoever he is, each night.'

'How did you know that it was . . . ?' I didn't know what to call it.

'Serious?' She laughed. 'I can read you, Anna.'

'I don't think it can be serious, really, not when . . .' When he could be killed each time he flew. But I was lying.

'Give me a hand with these?' She pointed at the carrots in the colander that needed peeling and slicing and watched me critically. 'Try this knife, it's sharper.'

'Isn't it more dangerous?'

She passed me a knife with a short but deadly looking edge. 'Sharper blades are safer than blunter ones.'

'I should get changed,' I said when I'd finished, yawning.

'Too late now,' Grace said, turning to the kitchen clock.

I'd planned on putting on a dress and cardigan, with the brooch Patrick had given me. But she would have noted the new piece of jewellery and questioned me further, so perhaps it was as well.

We sat down. Dad recited the brief grace I remembered from childhood.

'I used to think that you were saying a prayer just for me, Dad,' Grace said. 'Grace before meals. It was years before I stopped feeling smug that we weren't praying for Anna, too.'

'How unkind. I need prayers.' Though I knew, of course, that Dad and Grace both prayed on their knees for me each night before they went to bed.

I told them what I could about my work in the Filter Room, how we organised the tables and responded to new information on incoming Luftwaffe positions and those of our own fighters.

'We're proud,' Dad said. 'You're saving lives, Anna. Or should I say, Sergeant Hall?'

'I hate being a sergeant,' I said. 'I think of someone very bossy, with thick ankles.'

Grace stacked our empty plates. 'You said they might put you forward for officer training? Would that mean a uniform more to your highness's preference? Like the Wrens'?'

'Our skirts are shaped like oblongs. The Wrens just have that something about them.'

'Well I think you look very smart, darling,' Dad said. 'And the shine on those shoes of yours is impressive.'

'It's the years of practice polishing woodwork and silver in the church,' I said.

'I'm afraid your mother and I were hard taskmasters.'

Many of the church's artefacts were very old, some bequeathed centuries ago, long before the Victorian redesign. In my teens I'd raised my eyebrows at the women who'd given up months, years, to embroider the kneelers. But I'd come to love the biblical scenes or religious symbols intricately represented in woollen thread. My own favourite was a kneeler embroidered with the Lamb of God wearing a little chain of flowers round his neck. Dad said the theology behind the image was dubious, but I loved it.

The siren screamed and the three of us started. 'We can't always stop them getting through,' I said, to myself as much as to Dad and Grace. My mind switched to my work friends at Bentley Priory, the RAF's Fighter Command located on the northern edge of London. I felt guilty that I wasn't there with them, though I had been owed leave for months. I thought about Patrick, down in Kent, wondered whether he was scrambling right now, dashing to his Spitfire.

Grace sighed and took off her apron. 'Into the crypt we go.' At the start of the war Dad had adapted the church crypt as a shelter, with a lavatory and running water.

The thought of being crammed in with a small crowd below the ground made me shudder. I wanted to tell them I'd take my chances in the vicarage, but knew we were supposed to set a good example, so followed them to the church, outside which a small queue had formed.

For the first hour it was just a stuffy, dull night sitting on a wooden bench to the accompaniment of bombers rumbling overhead and bursts of anti-aircraft guns. I did my best to smile and help Dad and Grace keep up morale.

'It must be strange,' Grace said. 'Being here on the receiving end rather than doing whatever it is you do to defend us from those bombers.'

I glanced up at the ceiling, suddenly feeling more on edge down here than I did when I was at Bentley Priory.

I was filling the large earthen teapot with boiling water from the urn when something crashed through the nave above us. The pot shook in my hand. I set it down on the table before the water could scald me.

Enamel mugs toppled from the shelves built on one wall. I felt plaster dust sprinkle my hair and face. The warden came down. 'Everyone out.'

We were ushering the parishioners through the door into the grave-yard when someone shouted from across the road. Fire. I looked up and saw the white and yellow flames. Either the explosive had caused it, or a following Heinkel had sprinkled the roof with incendiaries. Bad luck, but not unknown for one building to receive two hits on the same night. One of the elderly women started coughing, doubling over. 'It's her asthma,' her companion said, biting her lip. 'The smoke . . .'

'We need an ambulance,' Dad said. 'Get everyone down into our cellar, girls, it's closer than the public shelter.'

'I'll get the ambulance, you stay here with this lady,' the warden told Dad.

Grace led our group through the side gate into the vicarage garden, moving so smoothly that only a glance down at the brace on her foot would have alerted anyone to her disability.

We walked through the kitchen towards our cellar door.

I stopped. The church was full of the precious artefacts and fixtures that we'd talked about over supper. The candlesticks. The kneelers embroidered by generations of parishioners. All things that our parents had encouraged us to look after.

'I can't leave it all to burn,' I told Grace.

I stood in front of the rood screen willing myself back two years in time, willing my words unspoken. One poor decision of mine; so many consequences for other people.

12

I returned to Bedfordshire on Sunday evening, promising my father that I would visit again soon. The train was cancelled, and I waited for hours in Euston before catching a slow service. After I'd changed at Bletchley, I dozed in my seat, waking with a start. The station signs had been removed and for a moment I panicked that I might have missed my stop. I opened the window to look out as we slowed. The stationmaster's house came into view and with relief I saw we were approaching Aspley Guise.

I felt a sense of homecoming as I walked down the quiet lanes to Lily Cottage. Our strange little team was starting to feel like family.

❧

Micki had already gone to bed when I finally let myself in the front door. We had a busy day ahead of us on the Monday morning and hurried to Mulberry House after a quick breakfast. I was too distracted to remember what had happened after we'd separated on Saturday night.

After lunch we had a quieter moment before the afternoon couriers arrived. Micki and I stood watching William and Father Becker smoke in the garden underneath the flowering cherry.

'So peaceful,' Micki said.

'And seems so safe.' I told her about the man who'd followed me to Leicester Square tube station.

'You think it was one of those soldiers from Wardour Street?'

'Not sure. Think he was wearing a peaked cap, not a side cap.'

'Could be any maniac,' she said. 'We forget what the rest of the world's like. That's what William said, too.' Her brow puckered. 'He was worried about you walking to Leicester Square tube station alone. It seems he was right.' Then she grinned. 'London's certainly a bit livelier than here. Did you see Father Becker's face when he saw the black soldier with the white tart? Those clerics are all the same: sex-deprived.'

'He was certainly shocked.'

Micki considered it. 'Not sure whether it was what they were up to that was shocking him or the fact that she was with someone dark. Probably not many like that GI in Zurich. And certainly not in Germany, walking around with white women, enjoying a night out.'

⚜

Before I returned with William to Waites Farm on the Thursday, I rang ahead – thank God for the farmhouse telephone – to tell Mary to bring the prisoner to the copse.

'My brother used to shoot in there,' she said. 'He'd be pleased to have it looked after, but it's hardly priority food production, is it? And it's the wrong time of year to do very much with the trees.'

'Don't worry about that. Just make it look as though the prisoner's got a legitimate reason to be out there.'

'All right.' Mary sounded more resigned to helping us, if still grudging.

The car parked up in the lane and William remained inside it. We'd agreed that the spark of animosity ignited between Schulte and me at the last interview could be useful.

131

I walked up the track to the copse, glad to be wearing non-uniform wellingtons instead of my black lace-ups. Small clumps of bluebells had sprouted since we'd last been here. A few more sunny days would bring them into flower. Despite the adrenaline flowing through me the prospect of warm weather made me feel cheerful.

I had a clear view of the farmyard. A motorcycle was propped up against the barn wall. My heart sank. We couldn't risk the military policeman overhearing. He sat on a straw bale, back to me, smoke from his cigarette circling him, showing no sign of having heard the motor engine. Good.

I walked on. The prisoner was hacking at brambles and thorns, jacket off, shirt sleeves rolled up. I stopped and watched him at work. He moved methodically, switching from scything to raking offcuts into a neat pile on the side of the path. I thought I'd approached without the crackle of a twig or rustle of dead leaves, but he spoke without turning towards me. 'It's going well, Sergeant Hall.' There was a hint of mockery in Schulte's words. He removed the thick gloves he wore and turned to me.

'As you can see, I am working hard.' He nodded at me. 'But surely there's more essential farm labour, *nein*?'

'You're an agricultural expert now, are you?'

'You don't need to be an expert to see that two women and three prisoners can't possibly produce all the food your ministry tells them they should.' He wiped his brow, the muscles in his arm showing beneath the rolled-up sleeve. 'Poor Mrs Waites is nearly in tears when she receives the latest missives from Whitehall.'

I pointed at the brambles. 'Are you taking them all out?'

'No. Just getting them under control.'

How Germanic.

His gaze took on its watchful expression. 'You haven't driven out here to examine my forestry skills, have you?'

Schulte's tone was bordering on the insolent. He'd forgotten he was a prisoner. 'I do the questioning, not you,' I told him, glad my voice was level and cool.

Food and exercise had filled Schulte out. He was a fit, if lean, young man. Hidden under my jacket was a whistle I could pull out if needed. The MP would hear it, and so would William. But I didn't want to summon William, have a male come to my rescue for the second time in a week. 'So the family are still treating you well?'

He pushed at dead leaves with the tip of his boot, seeming to mull it over. 'Mrs Waites says her son Malcolm is a POW on a farm in Germany.' His voice was less angry. 'She told me she'd treat me as she hoped some German family would treat Malcolm. I told her that farmers near my home use POW labour and they treat the prisoners well.'

Something stirred in my imagination. I kept my expression blank. 'Unless they're Jews?' I wasn't sure why this observation had come to me; perhaps because I'd just left Micki behind at Mulberry House, reading German newspapers with an eye for stories we could embroider for our news broadcast.

Schulte looked down at the leaves he was kicking. 'I don't know why you're asking me about that.'

'But do you know of cases where German farmers discovered that their POWs were Jewish?' I hoped the excitement I felt wasn't showing.

He picked up his saw. I stroked the outline of the chain under the thick wool of my jacket. I could pull the whistle out in a second. But Schulte was looking at the saw's edge, not at me, running a finger over it tentatively. 'When I was home on leave I heard that some farmers who appreciated Jewish prisoners' hard work might forget to tell the authorities. Or pretend they didn't know. Their own sons were away fighting. The animals still needed tending, and the crops harvesting.'

The kernel in my mind continued to grow. 'Tell me about the farms in your area: the crops grown, animals reared, that kind of thing.'

'So much detail?'

'Remember what's at stake for you. That cage?'

His eyes blazed at me in that cold way of theirs. 'Threatening me won't make me want to help you, Sergeant Hall.'

'You're obviously no friend of the regime,' I said, more softly. 'You know the arrangement we made with you: cooperate and you stay here in a good, healthy job. No more questions about Dunkirk. Eventually, when we're satisfied, you can opt for POW camp in Canada as is your right as an officer.'

'My family.' He looked less like a fox and more like a young man again.

'I understand your concerns.'

'Do you, sergeant?' He was staring at the saw again. I wanted to step away but held my ground.

'Tell me what you can,' I said. 'You want the war to end. So do we.' For a few seconds there was silence. He looked at the bramble bush, his expression unreadable. I'd lost him. Beattie would be furious. William would think me incompetent.

Schulte nodded. My heart rate slowed. 'In the afternoon I'll be working on the tractor inside the barn. The engine still isn't firing properly. The other two will be cleaning the cowshed now the cattle are out in the field. If you give me paper and pencil I'll write it all down for you: local farms, animals kept, crops, fruit and vegetables grown. If they have prisoners of war.'

A nice little story about how useful the prisoners of war were proving, with a joke at the end along the lines that some farmers might prefer a hardworking British-Jewish prisoner to the idle son sent to the front. I tried to think of any reason why giving Schulte writing materials might be a security risk but couldn't come up with anything. He had no access to the postbox. There were no other Germans in the area. 'Thank you.' I must have sounded much warmer now because the tension in his shoulders seemed to disappear as he took the sheets I tore from my writing pad.

He folded the sheets carefully and placed them inside his shirt and put the pencil I gave him into a top pocket. 'You will be careful with the information?'

'It's in our interest to keep our sources safe.'

'I'll suggest I do more tidying out here when I finish with the tractor. She'll be pleased I'm so keen.'

She being Mary? He tightened his lips. Miss Waites was obviously still making it clear his presence on the farm was unwelcome. Good. If Schulte felt uneasy with Mary it might make him welcome these meetings with me. Apart from anything else, speaking his own language must be a relief.

'I'll leave the papers under the large log beside the track down there.' He nodded towards the junction with the lane.

'We'll talk again soon when I've read your report,' I told him. He gave me another curt nod, his attention returning to the scythe. As I turned away from him I couldn't help thinking that Schulte could slash my neck open in a second, before I uttered a sound. I told myself to calm down.

The snap of a twig made me stop. Had Schulte come after me?

'Sergeant?' he called. 'Is it your man who comes out here? If he's spying on me, there's no need. I'd be mad to try anything.'

I turned back to him. 'What are you talking about?'

'The man in the long, dark coat who skulks around here at weekends.'

'A local going for a walk, surely?'

Schulte smirked. 'I was in that stinking cage in London with the worst kind of men. I can recognise people who are up to no good.'

'Describe him,' I said, taking out my pad.

'Medium height, dark hair, early thirties. Quite fit, jumps over streams, that kind of thing.'

'I see.'

'Do you know who he is?'

I closed my notepad. 'That's all for today.' I felt Schulte's eyes on me as I walked back towards the farm track.

'How did it go?' William asked when I joined him in the car.

'I think we might be on to something.' I was glad for my drama training, which hopefully meant I could appear relaxed and confident. I closed the glass partition between us and the driver, and quietly filled him in about POWs on the farms easing their way into the affections of the farmers to the detriment of their own sons on the front.

'We say those prisoners are Jewish,' I said.

'Are they?'

I shrugged. 'They might be.'

William frowned.

'What?'

'We'll need to be careful. We don't want German farmers to start ill-treating POWs or handing them in to the authorities for being Jewish just to reassure their sons.'

'Good point.' I liked the way he picked up my ideas, examined them and highlighted any flaws without any of the arrogance men sometimes displayed with women. 'I'll talk it over with Beattie and if he thinks it's not too risky he'll refer it up the chain for clearance.'

William sat beside me in companionable silence, arm resting against the side of the car door, hand to the side of his head, as though thinking. After a while he took his notebook out of his jacket pocket and wrote something.

'Were you all right with Schulte?' he asked.

I gave him a sharp look.

He gave me that grin of his that made him look like an RAF poster boy. 'Oh, ignore me, Anna. You can look after yourself.'

Could I, though? 'Good to know you were sitting in the car,' I told William gruffly.

'Happy to be your fall-back, sergeant,' he said, rubbing his spine. 'I'm about the same size and build as him, but he looks like a fit blighter, despite his time in POW camps.'

'Is your back hurting?'

'A little.' I noticed blueish shadows under his eyes. Sleep must be hard when you had a very painful back injury.

'I don't know much about what happened to you,' I said cautiously. Sometimes people didn't like talking about it.

'I was lucky,' he said. 'The pilot . . .' He paused, seeming to struggle with something, some memory of twisted, acrid, burning metal, perhaps. 'He stayed at the controls, risking his life for the crew. He landed the Halifax in a field, but it started to burn. Then he helped disentangle me. I'm a bit lanky for getting in and out of tight spaces in a hurry, and the flames were spreading.' He shot me an apologetic look.

'I'm fine talking about fire,' I said, not quite honestly. He looked at me without speaking for a moment.

'I can see why you might not like being near it,' he said. 'When I was stuck in the Halifax I could hear the flames crackling, feel the heat on my body. In the hurry to escape I fell out onto the ground and my lower back took the full force. Lucky I didn't land on my neck, the docs say, or I might have paralysed myself. If it hadn't been for . . .' He stopped. I didn't push him to continue.

'Can they treat your back?'

'Not really. At the moment I'm on a mixture of drugs to keep the pain at bay. They work some of the time but as the dose builds up inside me the side effects increase.'

He put a hand to his head, rubbing it. We were silent for a moment. I was remembering the months, the first year, after I'd been in the fire, how pain had snapped at my heels, impossible to throw off. It still lurked now and possibly would for some years to come, the doctors had warned me.

'You told me there was someone you were close to before the fire,' he said. 'But you ended it?' Nobody else had asked me these questions, not even Micki.

'He deserved better than this.' I tapped my cheek. In fact, it occurred to me now, it possibly hadn't been my face as much as my disturbed mind that Patrick hadn't deserved.

William opened his mouth as though to ask another question but shook his head. 'I hope you don't think I'm prying,' he said.

'I haven't talked about what happened with Beattie or Micki. You must be a good listener, William.'

~❧~

In the hospital the doctor had told me no more could be done for my face. I'd have to wait to see whether any kind of surgery might be possible once the facial tissues had calmed down, as he put it. In the meantime I was to stay in hospital until the risk of infection had passed.

I accepted the nurse's hand mirror and looked at myself, examining every inch of my face and burnt arm. This person with the raw, red scab splayed across her right cheek was not me. It was all a mistake. The nurse's expression told me otherwise. I handed her back the mirror silently.

'A young man, a pilot, has been in to see you,' she told me. 'Sister wouldn't let him in because visiting time was over.' From the shake of her head I gathered she thought the sister unduly harsh. 'He's come back several times.'

'I don't want to see anyone apart from my father, regardless of whether it's visiting time or not.' My words sounded like those of an older, harsher person than the girl I'd been.

'He's a lovely-looking young man.'

I shrugged and grimaced as I moved.

'It would cheer you up to see him, wouldn't it?'

'You really think so?' I pointed at my cheek.

She was going to argue the point but stopped. 'I understand, Anna,' she said, using my Christian name for the first time.

'I don't need people to be kind to me.' I closed my eyes. The right one still didn't have many eye lashes and the lid felt stiff. I wanted to pull it over my eye like a blind, shut off the world. 'And I don't need sympathy.'

'He brought the most beautiful flowers for you. Please don't tell me to throw them away.'

'Have them on the nurses' station, then.' I heard her footsteps moving towards the door.

⁂

I shuffled in the car.

'When you survive something awful, you try hard to get back to being the person you were. But sometimes it's as though you're just walking around in a stranger's clothes, pretending to be someone you're not,' William said softly.

I'd felt like that, too, at my sister's funeral, wearing the black dress and shoes I'd worn to my mother's funeral, which now seemed to belong to someone else. I'd become a stranger to my own clothes, my own life, my own self.

I wasn't a stranger any more, I told myself. The new me, with the new job and the new colleagues was the real Anna Hall. I had to concentrate on my work.

'There was something else Schulte said,' I told William. 'Probably nothing; someone enjoying a Sunday stroll.' I described the walker.

William nodded and wrote another note to himself.

When we entered Mulberry House, Father Becker was setting down a tray of cups and saucers on his desk. He'd managed this without spilling more than a few drips of coffee from the cups. 'A fresh bag of coffee beans has been kindly donated by Mr Beattie.'

William and I sniffed in appreciation.

'Just going to take a pill before I have mine,' William said.

'His back's been so bad.' Micki was frowning as he went out. 'We'd only just got into the taxi on the way to Euston on Saturday when he had to get out again to find a chemist.'

'He was very lucky to find one open that late.'

'He said there was a hospital, the Middlesex, almost on the way to Euston. A doctor there has given him a prescription the pharmacy makes up for him as needed. He just made the train.'

'A shame he was in such pain, it was a good night out,' I said. 'Even with the fight.' Micki was still screwing up her eyes, clearly preoccupied with William. Father Becker stood up, carrying his cup and the script he'd been working on.

'I'm going to get some fresh air,' he said.

'William seemed more comfortable on the train,' Micki went on. 'Though he kept muttering about not having noticed, blaming himself for not steering us away from trouble.'

'He's stuck in navigator mode,' I said. 'Thinks he's back in the Halifax.'

She nodded. 'He reminds me of a dog my grandfather once had. He hated anyone coming close to Maxi when he was out in the garden in his pram.'

I looked at her.

She smiled. '*Ach*, you thought my family all lived in some inner-city tenement?'

I blushed. 'I didn't see Beattie's notes on you, I—'

She squeezed my arm. 'I'm teasing. I spent my earlier years in a fashionable modernist apartment.' I'd imagined Micki's life as having been hard. But there'd obviously been an earlier more prosperous, less fearful period. 'Sometimes, if I can't sleep, I imagine I'm back in our old home,' she went on. 'I go up in the lift, through the front door and into all the rooms, one by one.'

'Who do you see in them?'

She paused. I'd gone too far, asked her a question she wasn't ready to answer. 'I see my mother in the kitchen, preparing the lunch: making the little dumplings we all love. My father's playing with the boys outside on the communal lawn. I can just about hear them shouting. Maxi's out there in his pram, too. I go into my bedroom and see my toy circus with the lions and tigers and acrobats and the big top arranged on the rug.' She sounded dreamy. 'I always wondered what the bastards did with that circus. Probably went to some Nazi brat.'

'You were what, eight or nine, when Max was born?'

'I liked having someone younger than me. Before he came along I was always having to prove myself to my older brothers.'

I wanted to say something more and looked at her, trying to see whether it was the right time. 'When we left you and Maxi in Lisbon I kept thinking about the two of you. Was the hospital we found good to him?'

'Nuns ran it,' she said. 'Sometimes very Catholic people aren't good to Jews, but they were kind. They made me up a little trestle bed so I could sleep next to him at night.'

I bowed my head.

'They couldn't bury him in their own cemetery but they found a small patch of garden beside the field where they kept their donkey. Maxi always liked animals.' She cleared her throat. 'Enough of this.' She clasped her hands together and stretched out her arms in what I recognised as part of her warm-up. The arms curled upwards, separated and rotated out at the shoulders. She stretched them behind herself. Next came the shoulder roll. Upper body finished, she kicked off her shoes, lunged one trousered leg forward and straightened it and repeated the movement on the other side. Without the slightest sign of effort she lowered into the splits.

'My hips are stiffening up,' she said with disapproval as she rose. 'Just one quick inversion then back to work.' She flipped upside down into a handstand, feet pointing up towards the biblical quotation. I imagined all the sadness dripping out of her onto the parquet.

'If you had a moment to look at my script,' Father Becker asked, coming back into the office. 'Oh.' He spotted Micki. '*Fräulein*, forgive me, I'll—'

'I'm wearing my slacks so you won't see my knickers,' she told him.

Father Becker blinked. '*Gut.*' He straightened his shoulders and turned to me. 'I think I have created something good for our young radio priest.'

'Excellent.' I took the sheets of paper from him.

'What do you look for when you read my work?' Becker asked, sounding casual, but looking at me intently.

'Anything that might pull a listener out of believing he's listening to a former parish priest rather than a radio actor. Sometimes we can sound too perfect.'

'Too perfect?' He considered me, brow puckered.

'In real life people make slips.'

'Interesting.' He nodded slowly to himself.

'I don't make slips.' Micki came down from her handstand, face slightly pink. 'Slips would have meant a broken leg. Possibly a neck.'

'A good incentive not to fall. Do you feel refreshed now?' Father Becker asked. 'It is good that you have this means of relaxation.'

'More than relaxation,' she said. 'My gymnastics and acrobatics earned me my keep.'

Along with a bit of pickpocketing, I thought, feeling immediately disloyal as I remembered Beattie's stolen wallet.

'I suppose the world will always need entertainers,' Father Becker said.

'You'd be surprised how useful my skills are, even when I'm not performing.' She gave an enigmatic little smile. I pictured her in crowded bars, filching a wallet and skipping away.

13

I went to find Beattie, who was in his study overlooking the flowering cherry trees and banks of daffodils. 'We should really have the whole garden dug up for vegetables,' he said, not lifting his head from his typewriter. 'There has to be some beauty, though, doesn't there? Oh to be in England now that April's there, what we're fighting for and so on.'

'I never really understand people saying they're fighting for landscapes. The Germans didn't intend flooding the Lake District or dynamiting the White Cliffs of Dover if they'd invaded in 1940. Nature doesn't care who wins.'

He grinned. 'So cynical for one so young.'

I wasn't much younger than him, although I had to remind myself of this at times.

'Insightful and so perfectly suited to our works of deception.' Beattie released the catch on his typewriter and pulled out the top sheet and carbons. 'How was Schulte?'

'Very cooperative.' I told him how Schulte had identified a useful cache for storing documents.

'Very foresighted of him.'

'Too much so?'

He shrugged. 'I don't think anyone could have got at him. The two Italians he's with are peasant boys with no axes to grind.' He picked up the fountain pen on his desk and laid it down neatly at the top of the blotting paper.

'What did Schulte tell you, Anna?' He sounded casual, almost indifferent.

I told him about the German farmers and their use of Allied prisoner-of-war labour.

Beattie folded his arms. 'And?'

'The prisoners are so helpful that the sons of farmers away fighting feel redundant.'

'Good as far as it goes.' He yawned. 'I'm sure there's a twist somewhere.' I didn't want to tell him about the Jewish prisoner element I'd discussed with Schulte. Schulte had been so uneasy about it. I'd write up the story without it and see how it flowed.

'And Schulte gave me some good gossip about Party bigwigs enjoying lavish hospitality in his parents' hotel.'

'Nice. We can put that one in after a mention of proposed new German rationing on certain foodstuffs.'

'There's more rationing planned in Germany?'

He let his arms drop outwards. 'Who's to say there mightn't be?' He looked at his wristwatch. 'Anything else, Hall?'

'The prisoner expressed concern that a civilian was paying him too much attention.'

I described the man Schulte had seen. Beattie said nothing, flicking through a pile of papers on his desk.

'I might telephone the farm, ask Mary if she can keep an eye out for this mysterious observer.'

'Is Miss Waites being cooperative?' He stood up and went to the grate with a handful of papers. The top sheet was covered with what looked like squiggles and hieroglyphics. An astrological casting. Beattie still wrote occasional pieces of print propaganda, and sometimes this included horoscopes, created by a woman in a south London suburb who called herself a psychic but obligingly tweaked the readings for various high-ranked Germans as required. 'Do people actually believe that astrology stuff?' I asked. I'd grown up in a household that viewed horoscopes as foolish superstition.

'Some do. We only need a cohort of housewives to believe the stars pointed to an important week for some high-ranking general and he failed to take advantage of it to sow a few seeds of doubt.'

He pulled out his lighter and ignited the sheets, using what looked like a former toasting fork to push them into the fireplace. 'Anyway, you're not supposed to look at my papers, Hall.'

I watched the flames consume the white sheets, heart pumping at the sight. 'Mary Waites is still a bit grudging,' I said. This little fire was no threat to me. The wave of nausea sweeping me was ridiculous.

'Get young Nathanson to sweet-talk her.' Just a week ago it would have bothered me that William was being pushed forward like this, but now I found myself nodding. A young girl like Mary, lugging dung and used straw to the heap, bringing cows in to milk twice a day, rarely visiting a cinema, would be susceptible to William's easy manner and appearance.

'Helping us must be worthwhile for Mary.' Beattie returned to his desk and fed an envelope into the typewriter, his fingers as deft as any professional typist's. 'I know that type of farming stock – if you push them, they dig their heels in. Stubborn folk.' He rattled out an address. 'What might Mary like?' He removed the typed envelope and inserted his letter into it. 'Come on, Anna, you're a woman of the world.'

I could feel the unblemished side of my face blushing as I answered. 'Nylons. Hand cream. Nail polish. Or lipstick.'

He opened his desk drawer and removed a key before nodding at a cabinet on the opposite wall. 'Second shelf down.' Beattie tossed me the key.

The very scent of the shelves' contents took me back to pre-war visits to department stores: perfume, leather goods and the fresh smell of linen and cotton, like a microcosm of Harrod's. I riffled through bottles of scent and lace handkerchiefs, bars of soap, even a packet of silk stockings, almost salivating. Every one of my atoms yearned for fine things: soft, beautiful, pampering clothes and toiletries. For the first time I understood how shoplifters could be tempted. Beattie was seemingly absorbed in the papers he was reading. How easy to slip something into my jacket pocket.

Perhaps that was why he'd asked me to do this. He'd hold a mental inventory of every item here and would love to see me fall into temptation. I forced myself to ignore the senses screaming at me to open a flask of Givenchy scent and apply it to the inside of my wrists.

Paranoia, I told myself. I was no thief and Beattie wasn't testing me. What would Mary like? I found a small tub of Helena Rubinstein face cream, a brand I'd always lusted after even before the war and now wistfully thought might soothe my ruined skin.

'Not that cream, Hall.' Beattie was watching me. 'I'm saving that for someone else. Keep looking.' I moved a crocodile-skin evening bag and a silver cigarette case aside and lingered over a pot of hand cream with a French name on it, unsure it was quite right for Mary. No nail polish, but the former would probably just be a nuisance if it kept chipping when Mary was at work. 'Try the shelf above,' Beattie said. 'There was a Czech lady a few months ago who passed on a few bits and pieces.'

Questions about the Czech lady bubbled unspoken in my head.

'What about this?' I held up a silver tube of lipstick. The colour was a berry pink, perfect for Mary. The silver case alone made it covetable.

He sucked in his own lips. 'That came from a very sophisticated Polish lady I met trying to find a boat in Bordeaux in June 1940.'

I felt something like a pinprick of jealousy – mad because I had no feelings for Beattie.

'All right,' he went on. 'Mary can have the lipstick. Organise a courier – ask for Atkins – to drop it off at the same time she collects the papers from Schulte.'

This was all highly irregular, probably verging on the criminal or black market.

'Perfectly fine to give legally obtained luxuries as presents,' he said. 'You should see what Churchill gets. My cabinet of delights is modest, really.'

'You're not Churchill. Sir.'

He gave me that smug smile of his.

❧

Mary sounded breathless and slightly stunned when I telephoned the farm and told her that she would be receiving a small present. 'To thank you for your efforts,' I said, giving a time roughly an hour after the motorcycle would have retrieved Schulte's report. I didn't want Mary sniffing around the log and seeing what Atkins was collecting. 'Continue to keep an eye on Lieutenant Schulte. Tell us if anything worries you.'

I returned to the front office feeling satisfied with the morning's work, yet unsettled by something I couldn't identify. William stood up, script in hand. 'I'm going to read this to myself outside in the garden,' he said.

'Bad luck.' Micki looked through the window. 'More English spring weather.' Gentle raindrops fell.

'Blast.' He looked rueful. 'I'll go into the hallway and read it to myself.'

His footsteps went up and down the stone-slabbed hall. His was an uneven gait that countered the equally uneven clatter of Father Becker's typing. Perhaps it was the result of the crash-landing. Every now and then the footsteps stopped. I knew he was marking up the script, or perhaps adding something to the list he carried around with him. William was certainly fond of lists. I'd seen him write notes to himself on all manner of things.

Father Becker sighed. The tapping of his keyboard stopped. He rubbed his neck, squinting at what he'd written, and reached for the New Testament he kept on his desk.

'Checking something, father?' Micki asked. She was now lying on the parquet floor, legs up against the wallpapered wall. She carried out this exercise once every couple of hours in between writing up the interviews she carried out with Beattie, saying it was good for her circulation and brain. I was so used to her being inverted I barely noticed any more.

'Best to make sure the quotation is correct,' Becker said.

'Surely you and the whole holy black book are on intimate terms?' she replied.

'My memory isn't as strong as it used to be.'

I noticed shadows beneath his eyes. Perhaps the strain of producing the scripts was starting to take a toll.

'Unfortunate, for a priest,' Micki said. 'Still, at least the faithful know you won't remember all the stuff they blurt out in the confessional.'

He looked thoughtful. 'I've been fortunate in other ways.' Father Becker stared out of the window, perhaps thinking of Switzerland, of the peacetime life he'd forsaken. Of all of us I found him the most commendable. Conscience had led him to Bedfordshire to work for the soul of his country of birth, rather than lack of alternatives, or as was the case for me, the possibility of a fresh start.

Before I'd come here I'd never have imagined doing work like this, with colleagues like these. I'd certainly been extracted from the comfortable but tedious hole I'd dug for myself after the fire.

William came in. 'I'll need to post a letter later. Is there a bag it can go in to be mailed from London?'

'On the console table by the front door,' I told him. 'The couriers pick it up every morning and afternoon. Seems to work pretty efficiently.' We weren't allowed to use the village postboxes for reasons of security.

At lunchtime, instead of returning to his lodgings, I watched William go to the bench in the garden with a writing pad. A girlfriend somewhere? I'd be surprised if there wasn't.

14

Micki's throat had been sore for a few days and was now troublesome. Her face was pale but her eyes were bloodshot. She wasn't talking much. The last symptom worried me more than any of the others.

Beattie ordered her home to Lily Cottage, even summoning Atkins to drive her the short distance through the village. I told Micki about a small pot of honey I kept in my bedside table. Grace had given me the honey a few years ago when she'd kept bees. Dad had passed the hives on to one of his parishioners. There wasn't much honey left in the jar and it was more of a keepsake now.

'I can't take it,' Micki said. She didn't know it had been given to me by my sister, but instinctively she seemed to understand there was something about the honey that made it special.

'It'll just crystallise if it isn't used,' I said, keeping my attention on my writing. 'And I don't want you off sick any longer than possible.'

The office felt too quiet without Micki. William was marking up his script. Father Becker was strolling around the garden. I hoped he wouldn't trip over the rake Mrs Haddon had left out on the lawn while she dead-headed spent daffodils. Father Becker's neck was obviously still stiff; he stopped to roll it one way and then the other. He'd been quiet the last few days, staring at his typewriter for long periods. Perhaps the strain of working in England instead of in peaceful Zurich was starting to take hold. Though his work helping refugees from Germany must have taken a toll. He'd never talked about what he'd done for them.

I took the script I'd produced about fun and games for bigwigs at a lakeside hotel into Beattie's office. *Welcome respite from the rigours of work . . . good food and relaxation. It's certain the public will be pleased their leaders can refresh themselves in the tranquillity of this beautiful spot . . .*

'We'll run it just after the report on air-raid casualties in Munich,' Beattie said. 'And before the new rationing restriction story.' I watched him, knowing that something wasn't quite right.

'You want more?' I asked.

'It's a good story, Hall.' He leant back in his chair.

'But?' I maintained eye contact with him.

'Wasn't there something meatier?'

'I'll have another go when I interview him next week.'

He sucked in his cheeks. I could tell his irritation was mounting. 'Every day counts. Last time we spoke about this you told me Schulte had said something about the sons of farmers feeling resentful that POWs were taking their place on the farm?'

'Oh that . . .' I said.

'Yes, that.'

'It wasn't that exciting.'

'I'll be the judge of that.' He observed me. 'Anna?'

'It wasn't so much what he said as what I inferred. Suggested.'

'Remind me what that was?' His voice was cold now.

'I suggested that farmers' sons away on the front might worry they were being replaced, that they weren't missed.'

Beattie looked over my shoulder. 'I like the sound of that.' He nodded slowly. 'A young farmer lad, away from home for the first time. On the Eastern Front. He hears rumours that his parents have replaced him. Perhaps they never really loved him as much as he thought.' His eyes sharpened. 'But that's not all, is it?'

I wanted to say that it was, but he could always read me.

'I mentioned British POWs who were Jewish. I wondered whether German farmers might keep quiet about this if they worried about losing valuable farmhands.'

'Yes.' Beattie was nodding slowly to himself. 'That's more like it, Hall. I wonder why you didn't remember to include this in your draft?'

I shrugged.

'Perhaps you were saving it for a later date? I'm thinking of German soldiers and submariners,' he continued. 'Sons of the soil who sit in fox holes on the front or in freezing metal tubes, fighting for the Fatherland while Allied Jews find healthy work in the countryside and gorge themselves on fresh vegetables, milk and eggs.'

'Schulte never actually said that.' The air in Beattie's office seemed chillier.

'But we will. Very undermining. Very nice indeed.' He looked at me quizzically. 'What?'

'Schulte grew nervous when the conversation went this way.'

Beattie shrugged.

'He was worried about the consequences for his family. That someone listening might link the story to the hotel and remember that the proprietors had a son who's a prisoner over here.'

'You're not more worried about Schulte and his family than your own people, are you?'

'No, but—'

'Keep the pressure on him. Run this story, Hall.'

'But he'll say—'

'Don't tell him we're using it.' He sighed. 'He's not going to find out, is he? And if something happens to his family as a result, it'll be weeks or months before he's informed. By then we will have extracted even more from him.'

'But that's—'

'Being pragmatic.'

'Suppose there really are Jewish POWs on German farms?' I said, aware I was grasping for reasons why we shouldn't use the story. 'Aren't we putting them at risk by tipping people off that this might be the case?'

'Unlike the Yanks we don't put details of soldiers' religion on their dog tags. There's no way the Germans could officially identify our prisoners as Jewish.'

I picked up a pencil from Beattie's desk and studied it hard to avoid meeting his eyes.

'If we never broadcast anything that might cost a civilian life our broadcasts would be worthless.' His voice was gentle now. 'We send bombers to kill German women and children, Hall. You of all people know this. We're waging total war here, too. I don't even know why we're still discussing this.'

The story we were creating had to be like the point of the pencil I'd picked up: fine and sharp. I stabbed it into my left palm, feeling a release as the lead hurt me.

'We need as much material as we can find,' he continued in a cooler tone. 'I'm pushing for a longer slot. I'm confident we'll get it. Ours is possibly the most successful research unit in Aspley Guise.' His brow puckered. 'No, actually we *are* the best.'

It was all about his self-aggrandisement. Perhaps he read this suspicion in my face.

'We can't afford to squander stories because of unwarranted scruples. Shall I provide you with the exact figures of merchant ships sunk last month, Hall? How many sailors were killed, how much food was lost? If you're worried about innocent civilians, what are you going to tell the British mother who mightn't have enough food for her children?' He hadn't spoken with such passion before. 'Food, or lack of it, is becoming the defining issue in this fight. Do you think that women like Mary Waites and her mother can provide all the lost calories for the nation?' His words echoed Schulte's doubts.

'All right.' My reply sounded defensive, weary. I felt as though he'd physically pummelled me. 'I'll weave in something about Jewish prisoners on German farms.'

'With lots of hearty food.' Beattie smiled. 'Good. Let me have the amended script in . . .' he looked at his watch, 'forty minutes.'

'I need more than that.' I hadn't won this round, but I wasn't going to let him gain every point.

'Forty-five. Or else Atkins will be banging on the door. Oh, and give me back my pencil, please.'

I dropped it onto his desk, picked up my script and returned to the front room, where I sat down to work. The story must have been forming inside my head even while I'd been telling myself I wouldn't write it because I made the additions quickly and fluently, with ten minutes to spare.

I took it into Beattie's office. He looked up, a frown on his face, obviously expecting me to give an excuse. When I put the script on his desk he smiled. 'See? That wasn't so hard, was it? Friend Schulte will never know. His parents will never know. It will all be fine, Anna.'

I couldn't bring myself to answer him so nodded and left the room. The doorbell rang as I walked into the entrance hall. Officially only the landlady was permitted to open the front door because of the risk of us coming across people we weren't supposed to meet. I could hear Mrs Haddon calling to her dog in the garden. I peered through the spy hole. Atkins stood outside. I unlocked the door. 'He barely lets you rest,' I said, letting her in. She grinned but for a second her eyes narrowed a little.

'It's unusual, isn't it?' I said. 'That you're a driver *and* courier? Most people are one or the other.'

Atkins rolled her eyes conspiratorially. 'Is he in his office?' She tapped her dispatch bag. Sometimes we were asked to tweak broadcast scripts or add news items just after Atkins had paid a visit. I suspected she regularly rode her bike up to the cipher people at Bletchley Park before coming here.

'Help yourself,' I said, nodding at Beattie's door.

In our office William was still marking up his script, occasionally stopping to rub the small of his back. Outside Father Becker had managed to negotiate the lawn without tripping up. The landlady stooped down to throw a tennis ball for her terrier. The dog missed the ball. Father Becker caught it and flicked it back at him in a single flowing movement. The dog caught the ball in his jaws. Eyes pinned on Becker, he tensed and lowered his body, backing towards the bushes.

15

'The bluebells are out,' Micki said the next day, in a somewhat husky voice. 'In the woods. Have you seen them, Anna?'

'Hmm?' For a good ten minutes I'd been staring at a paragraph of the latest draft episode of my Clara radio play, trying to make a minor character add more impact to a scene. I became aware that Micki was watching me. William had left the office for lunch at his lodgings.

'I had a look at them yesterday afternoon, when I was feeling a bit better. Perhaps a walk in the woods would help you, too?'

I smiled. It amused me when Micki took on the role of caring for me. She was the refugee and I the person who'd discovered her in Lisbon and now managed her work and kept an eye on her. But really she was in every way better at looking after people than I was. Years of being on the run with her young, sick brother, I supposed. She was not a soft protector; in our lodgings she expressed views on the way I folded my bathroom towel, the correct positioning of my toiletries on my dressing table, and even the way I ate a rare boiled egg.

'The fresh air would do you good.'

'Excuse me.' Father Becker rose. 'I need to use one of the reference books in Mr Beattie's room.'

'All right. Come with me?' I asked Micki.

'Can't. I need to buy some salt in the shop before lunch.' She pointed at her throat. 'Saltwater gargle.'

'Still giving you problems?'

'I feel much better but want to be sure it's gone for good. Your honey helped, though. It was kind of you. There's still a bit left.' She wouldn't meet my eye. I knew she still worried about her time off for sickness. I'd already tried reassuring her that nobody thought she was shirking.

'I'll go for a walk,' I told her. 'On condition that next time you're ill you go to the doctor. We'll pay for it.'

'*Ach.*' But the deal was struck.

'And finish the damn honey.'

She came closer to the desk. 'I noticed a little picture of a bee and a hive on the label. Looks hand-drawn?'

I nodded. Grace had taken such pleasure in writing the labels and drawing the bee and hive.

Instead of sitting down to lunch at Lily Cottage, I asked the landlady if I could make myself a sandwich to take into the woods. She let out a breath. 'You've solved a problem for me. This is all I could buy today.'

I saw two small mackerel sitting on an enamel plate ready for her to fry for Micki and me.

'Miss Rosenbaum needs building up,' I said. 'Give her both those mackerel and anything else you can spare. Use my rations if necessary.'

'You're getting too thin yourself, sergeant,' she told me. The WAAF boxy jacket had once hidden my curves. Patrick had said this was a great pity but perhaps as well for the concentration required of the men working with me in the Filter Room. I didn't seem to have quite as much to hide these days. Like many people at this stage of the war, I'd lost weight.

I wished I could pull on a pair of slacks and a lightweight jumper for my walk, but it would mean returning to Lily Cottage again to change back into uniform.

I walked past Mulberry House, my sandwich wrapped up in grease-proof paper and stowed in my pocket. The grass on the lawns and verges was turning vivid green. I felt an urge to remove my shoes and stockings and plunge my feet into its damp freshness. I caught the spicy scent of viburnum, softened by jasmine: heady, almost lascivious. The entrance to the woods was less than a quarter of a mile from Beattie's front door. He might be standing in his bedroom, where he liked to retreat during the lunch hour for a short, restorative lie-down. He could be watching me now, irritated that I had broken the pattern of taking my sit-down lunch at Lily Cottage with Micki. For all his tolerance of eccentricity, Beattie sometimes reminded me of an elderly retriever who disliked family members breaking the daily routine.

But I wasn't going to spoil the bluebells with thoughts of Beattie. I blinked as they came into view, their blueness almost unnatural, shimmering in midday sun now high enough in the sky to break through the canopy of oak, beech and fir trees. I found an old stump and brushed off the dead leaves so I could sit and eat while I admired the blue carpet. Their scent fell like a light gauze around me, enough to transform my fish-paste lunch into something wondrous. Dad, if he'd been here, might have made some comment about God's benevolence of creation. I did not, could not, believe that the bluebells had sprung from some divine masterplan. But however they'd evolved, they acted as a tonic for an hour.

I finished the sandwich and folded away the paper wrapping into a pocket. Still enough time for a short walk. Birds sang around me. Micki had been right: I needed this time in nature, among the trees. I thought of how Schulte had absorbed himself in his work in the copse.

A crackle behind me made me glance over my shoulder. Perhaps a deer. The sun dropped behind a cloud. I decided to walk up to the pond and then loop back to work.

The path I was on intersected with a track from the right. As I approached, a crow dropped from a bough to caw at me. Another two flopped down to join it. Perhaps they had a store of carrion nearby they feared I'd snatch from them. I'd never liked crows: the way they hopped in such an ungainly manner, as though they were dainty little robins, instead of walking like birds their size ought to. Grace, who'd been fond of birds, had told me that crows were extremely intelligent. To my way of thinking this made them even more sinister. I walked on and the crows fluttered up onto their boughs. A fresh swathe of bluebells caught my attention and I slowed to inhale the scent. Perhaps Beattie was right. This was what we were fighting for: the right for anyone to quietly enjoy woods in springtime, without fear, regardless of their creed or race, if they weren't doing anything wrong.

The crows cawed again. The undergrowth rustled as more of them dropped down from the trees. I heard a more pronounced crackle of dead leaves and turned around. Nobody was behind me, but I thought I made out a shadow between the trees, retreating quickly. *Medium height, dark hair, early thirties. Quite nimble, jumps over streams.* I recalled Schulte's description of the man he claimed spied on him while he worked.

My pulse quickened. I stepped off the track and brushed through the undergrowth to follow the shadow. The person I'd glimpsed had vanished, possibly turning off onto another path that would take them out of the woods and onto the lane. All kinds of people worked in the neighbourhood, many of them engaged in covert activity. I'd heard rumours of people who sounded very like commandos training not far from here. Airfields in the vicinity were rumoured to fly spies and agents to occupied Europe. Was it possible that I had wandered into some daytime exercise? You learned to keep your mouth closed if you saw something you thought you shouldn't. You didn't blab. There was no way I could reassure myself by asking questions.

When I reached the road I looked left and right, my skin feeling clammy. Nobody emerged from the woods.

Micki was standing at the front door of Mulberry House when I reached it. 'You've a rip in your stocking,' she said, looking at my legs. 'And you're very pale for someone who's just had a healthy walk.'

'The bluebells were lovely,' I said, 'but I'm not sure I like the woods very much.'

Micki frowned. Mrs Haddon opened the front door before she could ask me why this was.

For the rest of the afternoon as I read, edited and typed, my mind kept wandering back to the woods. Beattie said it was a quiet day and he wouldn't need me in the studio with him and William, so Micki and I walked back together to Lily Cottage.

'What's up?' she asked as I turned sharply at the sound of footsteps running on the pavement behind us.

'Nothing.' But until I'd seen that it was a schoolboy chasing an errant football, every one of my muscles had been tense.

16

Beattie was meticulous about paying regular visits to returning Allied POWs. Usually these were men who had a chronic or serious illness whom the Germans exchanged for their own equally sick POWs. They often yielded interesting and useful information about what they'd seen in enemy territory. This afternoon he'd gone off to Bedford to interview a returner who'd been held in the south of Germany and exchanged because of a badly broken leg.

When he arrived back at Mulberry House, I watched Beattie get out of the Austin and walk slowly to the front door, tapping a finger against his mouth. Some instinct led me to meet him in the entrance hall.

'What is it?'

He nodded towards his office. Beattie sat down at his desk, gazing out at the lawn, which Mrs Haddon was mowing. I could smell the cut grass and the scent of an early lilac opening its buds through the partly open window. Spring was here, but Beattie's expression was as austere as frost. 'I thought of not telling you, but it wouldn't be right. Schulte's parents and sister were arrested.'

My mouth felt dry. I stared out at the garden, not seeing the blossom. 'Do we know why?'

'We only have what the prisoner I spoke to told me. Until his accident ten days ago, he was on a farm a few miles away from the town.

Then he was treated in the civilian hospital. Word is Schulte's parents were listening to the BBC. Frankly, everyone does, but it's a useful pretext for an arrest.'

My stomach felt cold.

Beattie reached for his cigarette tin. He opened it and offered me one. I shook my head.

A small, cowardly part of me clung to the chance that it might have been the BBC listening that had caused the family's arrest.

'So Schulte's source back home in Germany has dried up,' Beattie said. 'At least we've found out promptly.'

'Dried up? You mean they've probably already been tortured or killed.'

'Very disappointing.' He tapped his unlit cigarette against the lid of the case. 'I can't see how he can help us much now. He won't get any more news from home.'

The professional in me agreed, but a more personal guilt was out-weighing professionalism.

'What about Schulte himself?' I burst out. 'He was helping us, he was anxious about them, and now this – his worst fear – has come to pass.'

'Schulte is German. An enemy.' He lit the cigarette and stared at the glowing end. 'He's given us all he can and now he'll go to Canada.'

Schulte was just an asset, so was his family. A shame when they ran dry, but only for operational reasons.

'Come on, Hall, Schulte's a combatant. He's not someone like Micki, who's never taken up arms against us.' Beattie's voice was icy as he read my thoughts. 'Our priority is the people of this country – preventing as many Allied deaths as we can.'

'I need to get some fresh air,' I muttered, making for the door.

In the garden I sat on the bench, out of sight of Mrs Haddon. The spring flowers reminded me of Schulte's description of the hotel gardens. Too many small details in our broadcasts could have been linked to hotels on that lake: we'd described the carts of produce arriving at lakeside establishments where Party bigwigs enjoyed excessive relaxation. Not hard for someone to find a list of German POWs originating from the Lake Constance area. Not hard to check where those POWs were held in England – the Geneva Convention required making the information available and the Red Cross might know the details. Most of the Germans had now been shipped overseas so there wouldn't be many names to examine. If the Germans tracked Schulte to a camp in Bedfordshire, could that possibly compromise the radio station? The Germans might jam it, or put out announcements condemning it as British propaganda.

I hadn't been to the studio the night we'd broadcast this particular bit of Schulte's intelligence, but I'd written the script, been so careful not to include any details that would identify the hotel. Through the window I saw Beattie stand up and stretch before putting on his jacket. He sometimes walked the short distance to see Sefton Delmer if the weather was fine.

I waited until I heard the front door open and close before going quietly back indoors. I opened Beattie's office door carefully, checking that nobody was coming out into the hall. Beattie kept all the final scripts in his filing cabinet. The key was in his top desk drawer. One ear open for the others, I took the key and unlocked the cabinet. Beattie was good at filing, which had always surprised me somehow. I searched for the dated file slip and pulled it out, riffling through the scripts until I found the little piece about Jews on farms in Baden. I'd described the town as having several lakeside hotels that benefited from the fresh local produce. In the margins Beattie had added an extra phrase: *a charming hotel with its well-known red shutters . . . famous for its sailing boats . . .*

Perhaps there were other hotels with red shutters and boats in the town, but I didn't think so.

I had to be the one to tell Schulte what had happened to his family. The prospect made me want to be sick. Perhaps I didn't really have to do this. He was a combatant, as Beattie said. An enemy, like the Germans who'd dropped the incendiary and deprived me of Grace. The parents and sister might already have been released by now. A busy afternoon stretched ahead of me, with another episode of Clara to complete.

No, I was making excuses. It had to be me who told Schulte. I replaced the script in the cabinet and locked it and went back into my own office. The others were absorbed in their own work and barely looked up. I waited until I heard Beattie come back into the house and return to his room.

I knocked on his door. He looked puzzled to see me. 'May I have the car this afternoon?' He raised an eyebrow. 'Sir.'

'To go out to the farm?'

I nodded.

'You know I can't authorise a vehicle and fuel unless it's for official work.' He returned his attention to his paperwork.

'Surely this counts as official? Sir.'

He kept his eyes on his papers. 'Cycle out there if you really have to make a personal visit to the prisoner in work time.'

Half an hour to get there. Twenty minutes to see Schulte and another half an hour to cycle back here. With the evening deadline hard upon us. And Beattie knew this. He'd also be aware that I remembered all the times he'd taken a car for some purpose of his own that were almost certainly not connected to his official duties. Was he waiting for me to challenge him on the point? Damn him, I wasn't in the mood for an exchange with Beattie. I wouldn't give him what he wanted. I'd cycle.

'Is this wise?' Beattie asked. 'Schulte might take this hard. Even though there's not an ounce of evidence it was our doing.'

What about the red shutters? I wanted to shout. 'You always said Schulte would behave because he didn't want to return to the cage.' But if Schulte did lash out at me, perhaps I deserved it. On the other hand, perhaps it would be wise to take William with me. But William needed to rehearse his script for tonight.

Eliza Graham

'Does it mean the Germans know where the programme is coming from?'

'That's a far more important question. Intelligence doesn't think so. There've been no unusual attempts to jam us. Nobody on the ground in Germany has heard the authorities warning listeners off our broadcasts. It's probably just bad luck that the Schulte family were arrested now.'

'He won't see it like that.'

'Which is why I'm telling you it's best not to be the one who breaks it to him. He'll receive word in due course.'

'I have to be the one to tell him.'

He scowled at me. 'Why are you taking on the role of unit martyr, Hall?'

'Perhaps someone has to.' I closed his door with some force as I went out.

Everything had to be controlled by Beattie, all of it. He liked to play us like puppets, pull our strings, watch us dance for him.

The bicycles belonging to Mulberry House both had flat tyres, costing me another quarter of an hour while I hunted down the pump in the garden shed. I cycled out of the village into an easterly wind, still cool enough in spring to feel like sandpaper on my face. Each of the miles to the farm gates felt as though the weather were reading my mind, trying to prevent me from carrying out what I knew was my duty. When I finally reached the farmyard, Mary came out of the pigsties, wiping her hands on the legs of her breeches. 'I didn't know you were coming. Lieutenant Schulte is out on the tractor in the top field. I'll get him in for you.'

'There wasn't time to contact you, Mary.' A lie, though if he'd forbidden me the car Beattie might also have prohibited a telephone call. The truth was I hadn't wanted Schulte to know I was coming. Perhaps a mistake: telephoning ahead might have given him time to prepare himself for bad news. Another small doubt entered my mind. I brushed it away. This was the right thing to do.

166

'Is he . . .' Mary pushed a lock of hair out of her face, looking rather older than she had before and slightly flushed. 'In trouble? Or being moved?'

'Not that I know of.'

An expression I couldn't read passed over the girl's face. 'I'll get him for you. Why don't you go into the kitchen? Mum'll make you some tea.' She was as terse as ever but seemed fractionally less antagonistic towards me.

Mrs Waites was kneading putty-coloured dough at the table. 'A lumpen old loaf this one'll be,' she said. 'I blame the flour.' She looked up at me. 'No, um, Lieutenant Nathanson with you this afternoon?'

Any other time I'd have been amused by the studiously casual way she mentioned his name and the disappointment when I told her I was here alone.

I heard the tractor engine outside in the yard.

'The prisoner will hear bad news,' I told Mrs Waites.

Her mouth fell open. I wanted to ask her to stay within earshot in case Schulte went for me. My cowardice sickened me.

Before she could say anything Mary came inside with Schulte. Mrs Waites covered the dough with a damp cloth, and she and her daughter retired to the farmyard, Mary casting a curious look over her shoulder.

Schulte looked inquisitive but cheerful. 'They let me out on the tractor now, sergeant, did you see?'

'That's good.'

'And I have a few more snippets for you,' he said in English. 'Is that the right word, "snippet"?' He sat down, looking up at me. The wild tension I'd first seen in him in Kensington had all but gone now, but he must have read something in my expression. 'Have I done something wrong?' He looked out at the farmyard where Mary was returning to the pigs.

I straightened myself in the kitchen chair. 'I'll come straight to the reason for my visit, lieutenant,' I said. 'There are reports that your family have been arrested.'

In an instant his tanned face seemed to fade to the colour of Mrs Waites's bread dough. 'When?'

I told him what Beattie had told me.

'All of them?'

I nodded.

He looked straight at me, silent.

'We haven't heard anything further.' Still he said nothing. The watchfulness in his expression was turning to something harsher.

'It was because of what I told you, wasn't it?'

'We don't know the reasons but—'

'The Gestapo will have lists of POWs who passed through England. They'll know I was interrogated in the London cage – even if there's no official record, another prisoner might have recognised me, informed on me in a coded letter.'

I couldn't deny this might have happened.

'They'll think I've been talking.' He gave a harsh laugh. 'They're right. I'm a traitor.'

The cat that had been sleeping by the range got up and scratched at the closed kitchen door.

'It might not have been anything you gave us for the broadcast. We were careful.' I tried to put the mention of those red shutters in the script out of my mind.

Schulte's eyes had seemed cold the first time I'd seen him outside the London cage but now they were like freezing shards.

'Your parents listened to the BBC, you said—'

'I helped you. And now my family has paid.' He banged a fist on the table. Mrs Waites's rolling pin jumped on the floury wooden surface.

'I really am sorry.' I sounded like a pathetic girl.

He stood up. 'I have work.'

'I'll try to find out more.' I had no idea how I'd do this. Beattie must have contacts; it was worth asking him, risking his displeasure again.

'You have no idea what they're going through. They could be in some cellar, waiting to be shot. Or in a concentration camp. Grete is only a schoolgirl.'

'I'm sorry.'

'Our interview is over.' He flung the kitchen door open. The cat shot out in front of him. I could have called Schulte back, reminded him I was the one who determined when an interview was finished. But as Beattie had pointed out, this was private business, not official work.

Mary came into the kitchen. I wondered how much she'd overheard. There was an expression on her face I was too flustered to interpret. 'He's just found out that his family have been arrested,' I told her.

'That why you cycled out here, was it, to tell him?'

'Yes.'

Mary folded her arms. 'Very kind of you.'

I looked at my watch. Damn, time was tight. At least the wind would be in the right direction for me on my return. I'd have to map out the last bit of my script in my mind as I cycled. A little voice inside me whispered that I could use some of this afternoon's events as material. Clara had had to tell one of the family retainers – make it an old man, not a young male prisoner – that a family member had been arrested because of something she'd let slip. Clara would feel like I did now, unworthy of what she liked to think she stood for.

Mary still watched me with that curious, triumphant look on her face.

'Will you be coming here again, Sergeant Hall?'

'Not as often.'

'Wrung him dry, have you?'

Schulte's hands had been calloused: he'd obviously been putting in hours of labour. And he'd got the tractor working again. This girl had no need to treat him so contemptuously.

'Goodbye, Mary.' I walked out into the farmyard, hoping I wouldn't see her again. She followed me outside.

Mrs Waites came to join her daughter, a small basket of eggs in her arms.

'No car, sergeant?' she asked.

'Couldn't be spared this afternoon.'

'Oh.' It was only one word. It implied that she thought my trips to the farm were no longer considered important work, that consequently I was less important to them. I might not return here. If I uncovered anything more about Schulte's family I could visit him in the evening at the POW camp.

'Be gentle with him,' I told Mrs Waites.

The two women watched as I swung myself into the bicycle saddle. I glanced back at them. The pair stood close to one another, shoulders almost touching, silent.

I cycled off, feeling their gaze on the back of my neck. I needed to push this encounter with Schulte and the Waites women out of my mind. My attention needed to be on my script, on using the imparting of bad news storyline to finish it. I stopped at the junction with the lane, still feeling eyes on me. I looked over my shoulder. The women had gone indoors. Beside me the trees in the copse rustled. Something metallic caught the sunlight and flashed. 'Hello?' I called. 'Who's there?'

Was Schulte watching me, armed perhaps with the scythe? His fury might have driven him to run out here to wait for me. I pushed down hard on my pedal, turning into the lane and accelerating away from the farm.

When I'd put half a mile between myself and Waites Farm, I dropped my pace. The wind was now propelling me back to where I belonged: with the liars and deceivers. I was twenty-three, fully adult, but I felt an urge to cycle past Mulberry House and make for the railway station. Go to earth in the vicarage. Bury myself in some virtuous duties: knitting socks and jumpers, helping to rehome people, visiting elderly parishioners. Dad would be pleased to see me showing an interest in parish work.

As the first houses met me I again had a sense of being watched, but the pavements were empty. Except for a horse and wagon there was no traffic on the lane to Mulberry House. I dismounted in the drive and threw the bicycle against the side wall, no time to put it away in the garage.

When I walked through the office door Father Becker glanced up at me, his gaze keen. 'Sergeant. Have some water.' He poured me a glass from the jug kept on his desk and got up to hand it to me.

'Where're the others?'

'The lieutenant went to the village shop. Micki is in the stationery office asking for typewriter ribbons.' As Becker handed me the water I caught the scent of something on his breath. Whisky? He didn't seem the worse for it, his hands were steady. Perhaps this clumsy man worked the better for a relaxing tot.

William himself came in as I was working on Clara. He looked brighter this afternoon, colour in his cheeks, but his pupils were red, I noticed, a little bloodshot. 'Went to look for peppermints in the shop,' he said. 'Then back to my lodgings to take my medicine.' He straightened his tie and sat down, opening his folio case. 'I think I'm getting there.'

I took another gulp of water; my mouth still dry from the long cycle. 'We're going to be very tight for tonight's broadcast,' I said. 'I'll make the last changes to the Clara script and then I'll look at your pieces.'

Clara. I needed to pin down what I'd created in my head as I cycled back here. I closed my eyes briefly and heard the story playing out again in my imagination.

Clara tells the old man about his son's arrest by the King's guard . . .
'But my son did nothing wrong. It was me, wasn't it, my lady? I told you
what my son said about the King and the King found out.' The blood leaves
his face. She's stabbing him with a deadly poison dart that can never be
removed.

'It was my fault.'

The old man's daughter comes out of the cottage. 'Got what you wanted?
Wrung us dry, have you?'

It still needed formatting as a play, of course. I could do that almost automatically, now the episode was complete in my imagination. Not much time for rehearsing, but the Jewish actress from Vienna reading Clara's part was well used to the character now, and would pick up tonight's storyline easily.

'That was quick,' Father Becker said as I pulled the sheets out of my typewriter.

'Just as well.' I glanced at my watch.

'Must be a good episode, Anna,' William said, 'if the words are flowing so smoothly.' Much as it sickened me to admit it, the script *was* probably one of my stronger episodes. 'Are you all right?'

'I'm fine.' I met his concerned blue-eyed gaze and longed to confide in him. 'I had to tell Schulte . . .' Father Becker was typing away. He knew about our use of Schulte, of course, but hadn't been privy to the discussions about how we deployed the information Schulte gave us. 'I had to go out to the farm unexpectedly,' I said.

The door to the room burst open. Beattie. God, I hated the man so much I could have thrown my typewriter at him. He came to my desk and picked up the script, scanning it quickly, pretending to wince. 'Do I see real life percolating into the play?'

'Guilt is a powerful emotion.' I gave him a frosty smile. 'If people empathise with Clara's feelings of remorse, they may examine their own behaviour more objectively.'

'Sins of omission and commission.' Father Becker bent his head. He'd never said much about his work in Germany or about what he'd done for refugees in Switzerland. I'd assumed there were lives at risk. He too might have personal regrets for a past failure.

Beattie nodded. 'You're certainly our expert on how to examine our consciences, padre.'

Father Becker lifted his head, something indecipherable written on his features. 'I have done my best for my country.'

He felt a responsibility for Germany itself, I thought, for its lost soul; that was why he was here, working among its enemies.

William stood up and straightened his back, grimacing. 'We all have to look out for one another, don't we?'

My mind floated back in time, to my previous job plotting aircraft. A wave of longing to be working on calculations again swept me. Trigonometry. The purity and certainty of numbers. That was how you could look after people. William must have felt the same when he'd been a navigator. You took bearings, found positions. Charted a course. I'd failed to look after people.

Schulte.

Grace. The sister I'd been told to look after as a child, even though she was older than me. I'd failed Grace.

❧

I can't leave it all to burn.

'Dad said to go down to the cellar, Anna,' Grace said.

'I have to try to save some of it.'

'It's too dangerous.'

I looked at Grace, cheeks rosy. She was stronger now, fit from digging in her vegetable garden. 'If we both went we'd bring out the important things in no time at all.' I was pulling a scarf off the hook on the kitchen door, wetting it under the tap, winding it round my mouth.

This was Grace's chance to show herself she was as fit and strong as anyone. 'Come on,' I urged her.

∽✦↝

'Hall?' Beattie was staring at me.

I gave a start. 'Sorry. I was, um . . .'

'Reflecting on something?' Father Becker said gently.

'I suppose I was,' I said. 'Something that happened a while ago.' I blinked. 'Sorry.'

'Hmmmn.' Beattie stood. 'We'll need a couch like Dr Freud's in here soon. Back to the job in hand.' He looked at me. 'Come with me to the studio?' He didn't always invite me to go over to Milton Bryan in the evening. Micki had only been a few times. Father Becker was forbidden access as on his only outing to the studio he'd tripped over almost every cable in the place. Eventually, Beattie said, all the research units would operate from Milton Bryan. He knew I was looking forward to the move, that I loved visits to the studio.

'I have a headache,' I said, picking up my satchel. 'I need an early night. I can go through tomorrow's scripts at home.'

'Hope you're not catching Micki's lurgy.' He might have been a kindly old uncle. My loathing of him was so strong I was surprised he could stand there talking to me without flinching from the waves I emitted. William bent over the writing pad in front of him and Father Becker frowned at his typewriter. On this occasion I didn't think it was a problem with jammed keys that was causing his concern.

I longed to talk to someone about what had taken place today with Schulte. William was the only person I could confide in but I wouldn't see him alone before he left for the studio. Micki would ask me what was up when we were together in Lily Cottage this evening; she'd see something in my eyes. I'd have to find a way of avoiding her.

As I picked up my satchel and made for the front door, someone rang the bell. I stood back to let Mrs Haddon answer it. She thanked the caller and came in with a neatly pressed men's handkerchief. 'That was the postmistress's girl,' she said. 'Lieutenant Nathanson dropped his hanky in the post office when he was filling out a form.'

'I'll give it to him.'

Mrs Haddon rolled her eyes. 'He's got a bit of a following among girls in the village. Maisy was very disgruntled that I wouldn't bring him to the door.'

I laughed, feeling a little better, and took the handkerchief into William. He thanked me and replaced it in his pocket. 'My mother told me never to go out without one. Imagine if I started sniffing in the studio. Must have lost it when I bought my peppermints.'

I was about to tell him he'd actually been filling in a form, but stopped myself. What kind of form would he complete at the village post office? One for a telegram? We weren't allowed to send telegrams from the local post office for the same reason as our letters were taken to London for mailing: so that nothing could link us to the village. Had William forgotten this? On the other hand, he might have been filling in a postal order form or something else completely innocent.

I thought of asking him, but my rage at Beattie was still like hot paraffin inside my veins. William was Beattie's responsibility, not mine.

17

Micki came back to Lily Cottage at the usual time that evening. She ate her supper and announced she was having an early night to throw off the remnants of her sore throat once and for all. I gave her an hour and went up to check on her, finding her already asleep. I touched her brow gently. It was warm underneath my fingers. She'd thrown off her sheet and blanket, but I pulled them up over her chest and checked that the window was open an inch. In repose she looked younger, more like her little brother. I shivered, remembering Maxi lying on that pallet. I looked at the photograph on the bedside table, the group of six. Micki and Maxi, as the smallest of the four children, sat on the laps of their father and mother respectively, their older brothers framing the group, leaning in, eyes crinkled. It wasn't impossible, was it, that one of the older brothers at least might be able to survive whatever it was the family was enduring? If the boys were as tough as their younger sister, there had to be some hope for them. Did Micki still feel any optimism about their prospects?

Uncertain what to do with myself now, I washed a few pieces of underwear and a silk blouse that wouldn't survive the local laundry and hung them on a clothes horse by the open bathroom window. From the garden came the scent of new grass and leaves. I could take my writing pad and pen outside and make notes on the bench.

I walked quietly through the empty kitchen and out of the back door. A last blackbird was singing. Dusk hung around, scented with hyacinths. I sat down, placing pad and pen beside me on the bench, pulled my cigarettes out of my pocket and lit one, careful to hold the lighter flame away from me. On an impulse I moved the flame towards myself. Was my fear of fire growing just a little less powerful? Out in the lane a car slowed, idled and then drove on. I drew once on my cigarette, placed it on the arm of the bench and started to write. It was really growing too dark to work. The pen's nib made uneven strokes on the paper. I peered at it. Damn. It really did need replacing now. I didn't have much free time for finding a stationer's that might sell me a spare.

'It's worn out,' a voice behind me said.

I jumped.

Beattie.

'Did everything go all right with the evening broadcast?' I wanted to ask him what he was doing here but something made me hold my tongue.

'Splendidly. Father Becker's script for William benefited from your edits. And tonight's Clara episode was a cracker.'

I hoped he couldn't see me blushing. But I was still angry with him. He held out a hand.

'Give me that poor pen. I might have a spare nib that'll fit until you have time to buy a replacement.'

I gave him my pen and he put it in his inside pocket.

'Our work sometimes seems like shovelling dung but it's worthwhile, Anna.'

'I know.'

'I understand how you feel about Schulte. He's not a bad man.'

'So you don't think he might have shot those British soldiers?'

'I wanted him to think I doubted his innocence so he felt vulnerable with us, keen to cooperate. I don't actually think he was involved. Unless he's a very convincing liar.'

'Like us.'

He winced. 'You've done so well with Schulte, got him to open up. It wasn't an easy task. He was suspicious at first.'

Rightly so.

'And you manage the team well. Micki, Father Becker, Nathanson: they'd do anything for you. I pulled off a bit of a coup getting you to work here with me.'

I frowned.

'Anna Hall,' he said musingly. 'Most beautiful girl at Somerville, possibly in the whole of Oxford. Clever and talented.'

'Not so beautiful these days.'

Mistake. You should never throw a self-denigrating comment at Beattie; he'd always use it against you. But tonight he seemed more mellow.

'When I first knew you at Oxford I assumed you'd be the kind of girl who'd be swooped up by someone wealthy. Perhaps you'd work for a few months, but he wouldn't like it. All your drive would go into organising charity bazaars.'

'That's what happens to a lot of women.'

'You're not like a lot of women. Bringing you here has proved that.'

'Most women don't get the chance to show what they can do.'

'You like flux, Anna. Change. Problems to solve. If you'd stayed on in Suffolk you'd have ended up married to some dull chap.'

I scowled at him. 'Perhaps I would have liked that.'

He shrugged. 'I just hope I haven't spoilt you for peacetime in some semi-detached house in Surrey, with whist and tennis as your only diversions as you fret over meat rations.'

'You think I won't make a decent housewife?' I didn't know if I felt flattered or the opposite.

He was lighting a cigar. 'You will if you just lie to yourself.'

'Lie?'

'Tell yourself you only ever wanted to fuss over your husband's suits.'

I'd never had the chance to find myself bored with married life. Nor would I ever have to persuade myself that food shopping and housework was completely satisfying. The incendiary bomb had taken it all away from me. No, I'd taken it away from myself.

❦

After Grace's funeral I'd returned to hospital for a few more days so they could check my burn for infection and bathe it with saline. The same nurse I'd had last time intervened again on Patrick's behalf at visiting time. 'He says he has to go back tomorrow, his leave's up. This is your last chance to see him, Anna.'

'I don't want to see him.'

'Or you don't want him to see you?' She put a hand gently on mine. 'You haven't given him a chance.'

'Haven't you got anything better to do than act Cupid?' I closed my eyes. 'I want to sleep.'

'You can't sleep through the rest of your life, Anna. You're young.'

'You're right, I don't want him to see me. He's nothing to me.'

❦

Beattie puffed out smoke, the aroma breaking into the train of memories. 'I make up stories about my life, too. The early parts in particular.'

'How old were you when you left Berlin?' I asked, curiosity distracting me away from my recollections.

'About ten. My memories are fond ones. Swimming in a lake. Trips to the Tiergarten. Playing in the garden.'

'Lilacs in bloom?'

'There were lilacs, yes. But now when I think about my parents' friends – the affable baker who'd give me an extra cake with the bread order, the woman who cleaned the house – the memories are tainted. I wonder how much they all closed their eyes.' He eyed the cigar. 'And then I wonder about myself. Would I have told myself the same lies they did?'

'None of us know just how honest we'd be with ourselves,' I said. Actually, I did know this. I hadn't even been able to face Patrick one last time. I'd written to him to save myself the pain of letting him see my wrecked looks, to spare myself the anguish of telling him it was over in person. The coward's way out. I couldn't place myself in judgement over anyone else. Not even Beattie.

It was growing cooler; the smoke from my cigarette and Beattie's cigar turned to vapour in the evening air.

'If I'd stayed in Berlin I know I'd probably have exceeded my own lowest expectations,' he said. 'I have no illusions.' The scent of Beattie's cigar was weaving its way between me and the hyacinths' perfume.

'I have to tell you something. You'll probably want to fire me.'

He narrowed his eyes.

'I went through your filing cabinet, found the script where you'd added the details about the red hotel shutters.'

Silence. Something flapped overhead – a bat.

'Go to bed now, Hall. Long day. And I need you on top form tomorrow.'

'Is that all you're going to say?'

'Thought you were going to tell me you'd been at my whisky.'

He must have walked away after that without me hearing. The garden gate clicked.

'Don't go,' I said. I heard him take a breath.

'Anna?' He sounded startled.

'I want you to stay.'

For a moment there wasn't a sound. He'd ignored me. I heard the gate click again, his footsteps returning to me.

I didn't know what I was doing, what I was asking. He'd shown me those chinks, made me feel empathy for him as he'd described his childhood, softened me. But I couldn't afford to feel soft towards him. I needed to harden myself, embrace the worst in myself, show myself that I could survive in its depths. And a bit of me still wanted to take revenge on Beattie for what had happened today. I'd told him about searching his filing cabinet, something that should have brought about disciplinary action, but he hadn't responded.

'Are you sure?'

'Yes.' The word sounded more certain than I felt.

He put a hand round my waist. 'Micki—'

'Dead to the world with her fever and the landlady is probably knitting in bed with the wireless on.'

'I don't want to take advantage of you, I—' He sounded breathless.

'You're not,' I said coldly.

I shook off his hand and led him inside. He removed his shoes at the kitchen door and crept inside in his socks, holding the shoes as he followed me upstairs. I could hear the gentle snoring of the landlady through her door. In my room I switched on the lamp. He gazed at me silently. I stood over him, knowing that for the next hour he was my creature, would do what I wanted, how I wanted. 'Take off my shirt,' I told him.

He pulled at it.

'Carefully, I don't want any buttons ripped off.' When he'd removed the shirt, I realised that the blackout was still up and attended to this.

I made him remove my skirt, my thick RAF stockings and my underwear. The latter wasn't regulation issue, as the surprised expression in his eyes made clear. He put a hand out to touch my breast and I pushed him away again. 'Not yet.' I removed my hairpins and shook out my hair, watching him all the time.

'Anna . . .'

'Wait,' I told him. Usually before bed I would have removed my pancake make-up with Ponds cream. I didn't want Beattie to see me without the pancake. Instead I picked up the little bottle of *Vol de Nuit* and sprayed myself with a few drops.

He let out a groan. I bent forward and undid his tie. My face might be mangled but my body – apart from that small patch on my upper arm – was as it had been before the fire. It remembered that night in Lisbon.

He tried again to touch me but I brushed him away. Beattie wasn't going to do anything tonight without my permission. Maintaining my eye contact with him I lay beside him on the bed, running my hands up and down my body, taking time to enjoy the feeling of my own skin around my breasts and between my legs, down to my feet and back up to the sensitive sides of my torso. He made another attempt to grab me. 'Not yet,' I told him.

When I'd extracted as much pleasure from myself as I desired I told him to remove his clothes, telling him the exact order in which this was to happen. He obeyed me. I looked at him. His body didn't have Patrick's loose-limbed grace, but it was powerful across the shoulders and chest, and trimmer across the waist than I had remembered. In Lisbon I'd been too shy to look at Beattie. Now I made him into an object, my object. His breaths were coming in gasps, but I pushed him down onto the pillow.

'May I kiss you?' he asked.

I thought about it. If he kissed me it would make this, whatever it was, intimate and I wasn't sure I could bear that. I shook my head and straddled him.

The first time didn't do it for me. The last of my anger still gripped my body. And when I looked down at him I still had the sense that I was staring at the wrong man.

I let him rest briefly and then I taunted him into another, very willing, frenzy. I knew him better by then. The cool air turned the perspiration on my skin to little beads. Anger was blunting into curiosity. I looked up at Beattie and saw him watching me, curious, too, and willing, oh very willing, to continue the exploration.

I looked away.

At the climax I felt my body, my sense of who I was, dissolve. He sank down beside me and kissed me on each eyelid, so softly I could hardly feel his lips. He murmured something under his breath and I could only just make out my name, said over and over again, in a note of wonder. 'May I kiss you properly now?'

I nodded. The kiss wasn't a deep one, it was tender, almost protective.

My head sank onto his chest, his heart beating under my scarred cheek. I wanted to move, to push him out of the bed, tell him that I'd finished with him. He was still the wrong man, and I had brought him into my room for the wrong reasons. And yet I found I couldn't do without that rhythmic heartbeat which seemed to be pulsing its energy into the dead tissues of my face. He kissed me again, this time on the top of my head, and did the same to the scar on my upper arm. I found my lips touching his chest, just once. 'Sorry,' I said. 'About going through your filing cabinet.'

'I don't know what you're talking about,' he said. 'Just lie here quietly with me.'

I'd failed at what I'd hoped to do with Beattie. I'd wanted to show him I could control him. And to show myself that I was strong. In fact I'd been exposed for what I was. Everything I'd tried to hide was lying in the open. Not just my burnt skin, but the innermost parts of myself, the parts I had hated so much. Beattie had seen me. I'd seen him. We knew one another. The realisation ought to have horrified me, but I could lie here with him completely at peace.

'My wonderful Anna,' he said.

Out of habit my mouth opened to tell him he was wrong. The words fell away before I could speak them. My hand reached for his. And then I slept, deeply, peacefully.

18

Morning. Beattie was gone. A slight scent of him lingered on the pillowcase and sheet: bay and lime. I pulled back the curtains and pushed the window fully open to air the room. As I raised an arm to my face I smelled Beattie on my skin. It wasn't my morning for a bath so in the bathroom I filled the basin with warm water and washed myself with my sponge and bar of soap. My mind was somewhere it hadn't been for almost two years: a watchful yet peaceful place. The tissues of my body felt sated, relaxed, but my skin seemed to glow with energy as I rubbed it with the sponge, as though the blood was flowing through me fully for the first time.

Serene as I felt, I didn't want to face Micki over the breakfast table. I could hear her getting out of bed, whistling, the floorboards creaking as she carried out her morning stretches.

I crept downstairs to make myself a slice of toast and wrote her a quick note, saying I'd gone for another look at the bluebells and would meet her in the office.

Mulberry House was peaceful when Mrs Haddon let me in. 'Mr Beattie's sleeping in this morning,' she said. 'Must have forgotten to set his alarm clock.' I managed not to blush.

Micki joined me in our office at nine.

'How's the throat?'

'How are the bluebells?' she asked, eyes like flints.

'Micki—'

Someone knocked on the door. Mrs Haddon was standing outside. 'Excuse me, sergeant, but Mr Beattie's coffee and toast are getting cold. I wondered whether he'd come in here?'

'No. He must be in the garden.' I looked out of the window but the garden was empty.

'Perhaps he's still sleeping in?' Micki gave an angelic smile. 'Had a sleepless night, maybe?'

'He's not in his room – I've just been up and knocked on the door and popped my head round in case he was poorly,' Mrs Haddon said.

Someone rang the front doorbell. 'That'll be Beattie. He'll have lost his key,' I said, watching through the office door as Mrs Haddon went to let him in.

But it was William and Father Becker arriving for work. William gave me his usual smile, stopping to check the postbag.

'Is Mr Beattie in his office?' Father Becker asked. 'I would like to use a reference book.'

'Don't worry about disturbing him, he's not here yet,' I said.

'Not like him.' Micki eyed me coolly.

Becker muttered some German endearment at the terrier, who emitted a yap.

'It's your dog collar.' Mrs Haddon laughed. 'Ironic, isn't it, father? I think it makes Freddy nervous, though he's fine with the vicar here in the village. Perhaps he's not used to Catholics.'

William was still checking the postbag. I knew there was nothing in it apart from a letter for Beattie, which Mrs Haddon would take into his office. A girl, I thought. William definitely had a girl he was desperate to hear from.

We prepared for the usual team meeting at ten, sitting at our desks, writing pads open. 'He's not coming,' Micki said, at quarter past.

William looked at her. 'What do you mean?'

'He must be held up somewhere.'

'Held up?' William blinked.

I went into Beattie's office and telephoned Sefton Delmer, hands shaking as I feared I was exceeding my brief. Beattie would be furious if I'd put the wind up those in charge of us for no good reason. I was put through to Sefton Delmer's secretary. 'Leave this with us, Sergeant Hall. We'll make the necessary calls.' Something in her voice implied concern.

Within twenty minutes a black Triumph motorcycle crunched up the drive. Atkins. Once again disobeying the rule about not opening the door, I went to let her in. 'I need to search his desk,' Atkins said with a nod.

'How . . .' How was she involved with this? She showed me an ID card. I blinked at it. Atkins wasn't just a driver and courier, she worked for a special intelligence unit.

'My boss will be along in a moment and he'll clear everything with you. There are special constables searching for Mr Beattie. Just try to get on with your work in the meantime.' She gave me a quick smile. 'He can't be far away. We know he didn't catch a train this morning and none of the drivers have taken him anywhere.'

I returned to our office. When a civilian car drew up and disgorged a man in a grey suit, a cold boulder sank inside me at the sight of his stony expression. Mrs Haddon let the man in. I heard him ask her questions. She knocked on the door. 'Can you come out now, please, sergeant?'

He shook my hand and showed me his ID. Special intelligence, a photograph. 'Sergeant Hall.' He led me into Beattie's office and sat down behind Beattie's desk. I didn't like to sit until he waved me to my normal chair. 'When did you last see Mr Beattie?'

'He came to see me in my lodgings last night.'

'Was that usual?'

'No.' I looked down at my hands and told the man in the grey suit an abbreviated version of what had happened between Beattie and me.

'I see.' His voice was neutral. 'And you recall Mr Beattie leaving your bedroom?'

'No. He was gone when I woke up at seven thirty.' I stared out of the window, not seeing anything.

'The landlady says Mr Beattie never returned to the house.'

'Oh.' It was a pathetic riposte, but I couldn't think of a reason why Beattie wouldn't have returned to Mulberry House.

'Was this the first time you and Mr Beattie had been close, sergeant?'

I shuffled on my chair. I wanted to lie but had no way of being sure what this man might know. 'Once before, a few months ago when we were abroad, we . . .' I couldn't think of how to finish the sentence.

'In another country, as the saying goes.' The grey-suited man gave me a dry smile. I knew the rest of that line. He rose. 'Carry on with your work, Sergeant Hall. Atkins will bring you anything Beattie would see in his absence.'

'Me?'

'I don't think there's anyone else suitable as a deputy, do you?' He handed me a card, blank except for a telephone number. 'If you have security concerns, ask to be put through to this number. Failing that, Atkins can get hold of us. Don't talk to anyone else. Don't tell your colleagues anything more than that Beattie is AWOL.'

'I can't . . .'

He turned at the door, an eyebrow raised.

'Nothing.' I'd been about to say I couldn't manage things here. He nodded and was gone.

I went back to our office. Father Becker typed away, seeming calm. William had his writing pad out. He pushed it away. 'What's happening?' he asked.

'I'm going to look for Beattie myself.' I remembered something. 'The bluebells,' I said. 'Perhaps he went out there to look at them.'

'The bluebells?' William's face showed puzzlement.

'You're right, it doesn't sound like Beattie, but perhaps he heard Micki and me talking about them.'

Micki looked at me. Was she thinking that Beattie might have made a change to his normal morning schedule, not because of the bluebells but because of what she'd overheard last night?

'We can be there in fifteen minutes if we step out.' Micki stood up.

'The broadcast—' William said.

'There's plenty of time. I just need to look for myself.' I grabbed my jacket and cap.

'But Anna—'

'We won't be long,' I told him over my shoulder as I opened the office door.

Micki and I walked as briskly as we could without running until we turned off into the footpath leading into the woods. 'Last night,' I said. 'I don't know what to say.'

'Then don't say anything.'

I felt as I had that night in London, walking down to Leicester Square, and yesterday afternoon, cycling back from the farm: a sense that there was someone behind me. I wasn't going to give in to this neurosis when there was something much more important at stake.

We hurried on into the trees, the footpath taking us into the shadows. The track reached a crossing. As we approached, the crows flapped and cawed, landing in the lowest branches of the trees, but not fleeing from us. I remembered the collective noun for them and wished I hadn't. I shivered, a cold and metallic taste filling my mouth, my stomach rolling. The trees blocked off the morning sun. Even the bluebells seemed cowed by the gloom. Beattie might have chosen a brighter morning walk. A cool, sour taste was filling my mouth and my fast walk was turning into a run. We turned right, onto a smaller footpath.

At first it looked as though a very large crow had toppled beak down into the dark waters of the pond. 'Oh no.' I put a hand to my mouth, closed my eyes and opened them again. But the same black object was still floating in the water.

Micki splashed in, up to her knees, pulling at his suit jacket. Even now I noted just how strong she was for her small size. I waded in and grabbed Beattie's arm. Between us we lifted him onto the bank. Micki turned him over.

His face was a chalky white. Micki felt for the pulse in his neck and then each of his wrists. 'He's gone,' she said.

'We have to try.' I rolled him onto his chest again and slapped him on the back, hoping that some of the water in his lungs would run out, that he would cough. 'Come on,' I shouted.

Micki took my hands in hers. 'Leave him, Anna,' she said. 'He's been in the water too long. Go for help. I'll stay here.'

'No.' I realised that my cheeks were wet and it wasn't water from the pond. 'I have to stay with him.' I rolled Beattie onto his back. The weight of him was almost too much for me.

'All right.' Micki was already running off down the track.

I sandwiched Beattie's hands between mine. They felt like a marble statue's. His fingernails were manicured; Beattie had been vain about his hands. He wore a signet ring on his left ring finger. I must have seen it a thousand times without really bothering to look at it. I'd now never know the significance, family or otherwise, of the little crest that looked like some kind of griffin. He must have worn it last night in bed, too, but that already seemed like an age ago. On his wrist the Longines watch appeared to have stopped at half-eight, presumably at the time of its immersion. Would the police use this as evidence? I was falling into amateur sleuth territory again, trying to protect myself from my own emotions. I found myself rubbing Beattie's hands, attempting to warm them. I forced myself to stop and tried to sit still. But I couldn't. I straightened Beattie's navy-and-green tie and tugged down his jacket. He'd always hated being less than perfectly presented.

I wanted to roll his head forward so his mouth would close but didn't dare. 'What happened to you, Alexander?' I whispered. I had never used his Christian name before, not even last night. But nothing before had seemed as intimate as my being here with him now.

I felt I was protecting him from those crows, still cawing. A murder of crows, that was the collective noun. Carrion crows. Beattie shouldn't be lying out here on last year's leaves and the scrubby undergrowth around the pond, soaked and cold, with those black, ungainly birds mocking him. I looked at the footprints going up to the water's edge: mine and Micki's, and two larger sets. Beattie's and someone else's?

'Who was here with you?' I asked the dead man. 'You wouldn't have risked falling in, would you?' Death by water, said to be kinder than death by fire. But Beattie had feared water, he'd told me so on the flight over the Bay of Biscay to Lisbon. 'Was it me? Something about last night?' He looked up at me, silently. 'I wasn't kind to you at first. But then we found a way of being together, didn't we?'

Beattie continued to stare up at me. 'It was all right between us, wasn't it?' I whispered. I remembered the old superstition about the last thing a dying person saw being imprinted on the eyes. I peered at his brown irises but saw only my own reflection. Had I wreaked internal calamity on him? Disastrous for Beattie himself, and for this country which needed Beattie and the labyrinthine folds of his mind. Once again I felt the sense of somebody watching me. The crows gave another burst of cawing. I turned my head to survey the woods but saw nobody there.

I must have sat there with him for half an hour before Micki returned. With her was Atkins and the man who'd come into Beattie's office and given me his card. 'Move away from the body, sergeant,' he called. 'Leave this to us.'

I stooped so they couldn't hear and whispered to Beattie, 'I won't let you down.'

When I stood up Atkins nodded at me. 'Go home and change.' She glanced at my soaked shoes and stockings. 'Get your housekeeper to make you some hot, sweet tea.'

'There's no time,' I said. 'Tonight's broadcast—'

'Will be all the better for you not sitting around in wet clothes.' She gave me a brief smile. 'Find something stronger for your nerves, too. Beattie doubtless has a bottle somewhere in Mulberry House.'

'He does,' Micki said. 'But he told me someone seems to have been drinking his whisky.'

I'd spent so much of the last hour in my own emotional storm I'd failed to look at her. She appeared small, uncertain, as she stood among the bluebells, her stockings and skirt soaked too. Once the initial shock of Beattie's death passed, she would worry that her own status would become insecure. It had been Beattie who'd brought her here to safety. If my job ended I had the refuge of my father's vicarage and other employment options. Micki wasn't a naturalised alien. Beattie had been the one who'd pushed through all the paperwork, shouted at officials on the telephone, even gone up to Liverpool to extract her from the holding camp.

I stood up and approached her, placing my arms on her shoulders. 'It'll be all right,' I said.

She tensed up. 'How can it be all right? He's gone. There was nobody else like him. Nobody.'

I looked at her more closely and saw something in her face that I hadn't noticed before. 'You . . . ?'

Micki nodded. 'Yes, I was in love with him. Probably just some silly fancy of mine. I knew there wasn't a hope of him feeling the same way about me. He's only ever had eyes for you. But you didn't love him.' She shook her head.

I remembered how she'd made sure to sit next to him in the cinema. It hadn't just been on account of the box of chocolates he'd brought with him.

'I'm sorry,' I whispered. 'I've really mucked everything up, haven't I?'

She swallowed and pushed her shoulders back. 'It's none of my business what Beattie and you got up to.'

'Yesterday was a bad day,' I whispered. 'I felt, well, I don't know what I felt.' I shouldn't have called him back last night when he went to leave me.

'This has nothing to do with you.' She was sounding more like the Micki I knew. 'But the consequences for all of us are going to be severe.'

'We will manage this,' I told her. 'Even if we lose our jobs here, I'll make sure you get something else. You've been such an asset to our unit. Other people will want you.'

I couldn't let Beattie or his team down. She let her head droop momentarily onto my shoulder. When she raised it, her eyes were a little less accusing, though damp. I'd never seen her weep before. 'I know,' she said. 'You'll manage it, Anna. You always do. And we'll find the bastard who did this to him.'

We walked back towards the village. The splashes of pond water and my perspiration had washed away my pancake make-up. Two boys on their way to the village shop stared at me and one of them muttered something about my face. I didn't care.

Beattie was dead.

19

The coroner decided that Beattie had not intended to take his own life. The other set of footprints at the pond could not be proved to have anything to do with the incident and might have been there before the drowning – the woods were, after all, a popular local destination.

He wasn't a suicide so Beattie could be buried in consecrated ground. But where?

Grey-suit Man's secretary telephoned me. 'He's a civilian who didn't leave a will and seems to have no family. You knew him . . . before, Sergeant Hall. Do you have any suggestions?'

I felt a wave of sorrow for Beattie, who had done so much but left nobody behind close enough to know his final wishes.

'The service needs to be discreet,' the secretary said. 'We don't want to draw attention to Beattie and his work.'

I pursed my lips.

'On the other hand, we want to give him a good send-off.' She sighed down the telephone line. 'A conundrum.'

'I know where we can go.'

I rang my father. Dad spoke to the bishop. Permission was granted to allow the funeral and burial at the church, despite its planned deconsecration. A mid-morning service, Dad said in a telegram. I put him in touch with Grey-suit Man's secretary. The same woman told me that the catering bill for refreshments following the service would be covered.

A three-minute telephone call wouldn't have been long enough to sum up Beattie's life, so I wrote to Dad with a version that was as honest as I could make it. I had to borrow a pen from the landlady as Beattie had taken mine, I remembered. Had my pen been in his jacket pocket when we'd pulled him out of the pond? Thinking about this made me feel peculiar.

'I can't say much about his work,' I explained in my letter. *'But it was important and he was very good at it. He was kind to those who worked for him.'*

Writing it all down made me realise how much this was true. Beattie had been many other things to me, especially on that last night, but now I was clear that he had been my friend. He'd given me this job, pushed me to make a success of it, helped me forget the past.

Dad wrote back saying that I'd remember the state of the church interior.

But it's clear Mr Beattie was very well regarded. Some anonymous official has provided funds to pay for cleaners and basic repairs to the pews and pulpit and to buy flowers, and refreshments for after the service. I hope you're managing to carry on with your work. Your team must miss him terribly, he said.

My team. At least for now, until Sefton Delmer could reorganise us into another research unit or units. I'd always been Beattie's second in command, his lieutenant, though he had never called me any such thing. I'd probably been paid less than William because I was a woman, a sergeant rather than an officer. I looked at the three of them as they sat at their desks. They'd been so silent, working away on their scripts and POW interviews. Even Micki. Especially Micki. Sudden death, so common a companion in war, had shaken us.

I had made arrangements for refreshments to be served after the service at a pub near the vicarage. When I telephoned to confirm the details, they told me that a side of smoked salmon had already been anonymously delivered.

I was given an extra day off to travel ahead to the vicarage to make sure everything was in hand. Sefton Delmer himself would supervise the evening's broadcast. The other team members were to travel down first thing on the morning of the funeral. 'What happens about Micki Rosenbaum?' I asked Grey-suit Man's secretary. 'She's only ever been allowed outside the village if Mr Beattie was present.'

'We'll send a special pass for her.'

William made notes of all the arrangements, replacing the note-book in his breast pocket and patting it. He caught me watching him and gave me a gentle smile.

I wondered whether Father Becker would be bothered by attending a service in a Protestant church. When I put this to him, he looked over my shoulder, as though seeking guidance from the heavens. 'I've heard stories of soldiers fighting far from home with one padre, who attends to both Protestants and Catholics. I would be honoured to see your father's church, Sergeant Hall.'

'It's not at its best now and will be deconsecrated at some point.'

'*Ach*. And this was the site of your sister's death, no?' He sighed. 'Such a heavy price we pay in war.' Something else was conveyed in his glance now, something appraising. Perhaps this was what Catholic priests did: looked into your soul.

'I will pay the price until my own death,' I told him. 'It was my fault. This,' I pointed at my cheek, 'feels almost like the mark Cain received for killing his brother.'

He looked at me, eyebrows raised.

'My father told us to stay in the cellar in our house after the bomb fell. But I didn't listen, thought I could save some of the things in the church. And what's worse . . .'

What was worse was that I had dragged Grace with me.

ം

'Come on,' I urged her. 'Help me take things out.' She stared at me for a moment with those large, innocent eyes of hers, uncertain, before taking a wicker shopping basket off the table and shoving it into my arms. She ran a drying-up cloth under the tap and tied it over her face and wrapped an apron round her waist, hoiking it up to form a bag.

Smoke had colonised the church in the ten minutes we'd been gone. It swirled through the pews, stinging my eyes. Glass splintered above us, the boards put up at the start of the war preventing the windows from falling in. I ran down the aisle through the nave, turning left into the vestry. Unlocked. Thank God. Inside I opened the tall cupboard storing chalices and candlesticks. I grabbed an armful and ran back down the aisle, passing Grace, who was collecting prayer books from the pews. I tipped out my load onto the grass outside the church door, praying looters wouldn't snatch them.

Grace came out with an apron full of books and unloaded them onto the ground. The pages flicked open in the breeze. 'Hurry,' a fireman shouted as I ran back. The wind must be fanning the fire.

Grace followed me, moving in her jolting, faster, gait. I tossed the basket away and grabbed armfuls of the kneelers, running back out to throw them onto the grass. With relief I saw the Lamb of God tumble safely towards the candlesticks.

Grace came out, yelling something inaudible through the damp facemask.

'Just one more load,' I shouted to her through my own wet scarf. By now the flagstones were wet from the firemen's hoses. I was thankful for my rubber-soled WAAF-issued shoes. I heard my sister behind me. 'Here.' I handed Grace a silver bible stand.

'Hurry,' she shouted, panic in her voice.

The smoke was thick now, obscuring the door, choking and acrid. I abandoned the chalice and candlestick I carried and put out a hand to reach for a pew, disoriented, coughing, eyes stinging.

'The porch's in front of you, keep going.' Grace sounded calmer now, the older sister reassuring the younger. I took one step and then another, continuing until I could make out the door. Something thumped. I turned. Grace must have slipped on water from a hose, that weaker foot in its brace perhaps unable to help her regain balance. She lay seemingly dazed on the stone floor.

I dropped to my knees and tugged down my scarf so she could hear me above the roar and immediately choked on the smoke. 'Can you get up?' She moved her right arm and gasped.

I unwound my scarf. 'I'll strap it up so you can move.'

She murmured something I couldn't hear; the smoke was making me dizzy. Overhead the Heinkels and Dorniers rumbled on, accompanied by gunfire from the ground.

Something flashed above us; burning timbers falling from the roof. I jerked to the side reflexively. The timbers crashed onto the flagstones inches away from us, their heat blazing against me. Grace was still lying where she'd fallen. A corner of her jacket had ignited. I removed my own jacket and batted at the flames. 'Get out, Anna,' Grace muttered. 'Leave me . . . firemen, they've . . . helmets.'

Another slab of burning timber crashed down the wall beside us. It missed me but caught a thick velvet curtain attached to a wooden rail on the wall, hiding an alcove that, centuries ago, housed the confessional box. 'Go!' Grace screamed the word at me with a vehemence I'd never heard before.

'I'm not leaving you.' But now the curtain and I had become one being; flames from the velvet leaping onto my jacket, spreading to the sleeves, licking up the collar towards my face. The world shrank to the fire trying to devour me, and our dance together. Grace shouted out. I was lost to everything, throat full of smoke, eyes blinded. Death by fire, a martyr's end. I heard a scream – mine? Grace's?

❧

'So it was my fault she died,' I told Becker.

'Perhaps. Perhaps not. But even if it was, you seem to have punished yourself harshly.' He sounded less like a priest and more like any other colleague now.

'I'm not sure my father would agree.' To my annoyance, my voice trembled. I'd seen the blankness in Dad's eyes when he looked at me. I couldn't bring myself to tell him that Grace wouldn't have returned to the blazing church if I hadn't persuaded her. Perhaps he'd guessed, but I'd never confessed.

'We can never really see what's in people's hearts,' Becker said with a quiet intensity.

'Priests must have more of an insight than most people,' I said. 'Your parishioners talk to you in the confessional, don't they?' His expression changed to one I couldn't decipher. I blinked, remembering that I didn't have time to indulge myself like this.

William had been observing us, one hand fiddling with the knot of his tie. 'We'll see you tomorrow, Anna,' he said. He'd been quiet since Beattie's death, his back seeming more troublesome than usual. The shadows beneath his eyes had returned. I hadn't slept much, either. When Grace had died I'd retreated into sleep, but now I couldn't seem to release myself from my own mind even at night. My dreams always turned to that dark track through the woods, the crows, the dank pool where Beattie floated.

'We'll all be together as a team to say farewell to Beattie,' William said, his pupils large. He lit a cigarette, hand shaking. Was he feeling that yet again he'd inflicted bad luck on a team?

'I hope we'll do your Mr Beattie proud,' Dad told me, when I reached the vicarage. 'I don't know what we'll do if the weather's bad, though.'

'He wasn't really my Mr Beattie,' I said automatically. 'Don't worry about it raining, Dad. It won't.'

Beattie would already have ordered a clear day. I smiled for the first time in days.

Dad had organised a pair of local women to polish the woodwork, and sweep and mop the flagstones. That afternoon a taxi delivered a dozen bunches of violets with no sender's information on them. It was Lent – Dad didn't want flowers on the altar, so we arranged them in small vases at the main entrance and along the windowsills beneath the shattered coloured glass, with a single bunch to be placed on the coffin. I recalled Beattie gazing at the garden at Mulberry House and seeming to enjoy the spring flowers.

I was glad Beattie would be laid to rest here, my father's gentle but steady voice reading the centuries-old words from the King James Bible, commending him to the eternal.

Dad did his best with a supper of fried-up corned beef and a few potatoes but my stomach still felt empty when I went to bed. I dreamt that someone served me up a big pie with a puff-pastry lid, oozing fragrant juices. I cut into it and saw it was full of black crows. They flapped out of the pastry to peck my eyes.

On the morning of the service the church looked more welcoming than I could have hoped for. I sat near the front but couldn't resist turning around to see who was filing in. I noted Grey-suit Man, now in a black version, with a woman who might have been the secretary I'd spoken to. Sefton Delmer sat at the back in a long, dark coat and nodded at me as our eyes met.

A group of girls who worked as telephonists at the studio came in with a couple of technicians. I smiled at them, remembering how Beattie had brought them bars of Fry's chocolate.

Atkins walked in and went to sit with the telephonists. I beckoned her over to us. 'You were Beattie's favourite driver and courier,' I told her.

She smiled. 'I gave him a racing tip or two. There aren't many meetings these days, but he did well.'

Dad read the words I'd produced for him and passed up to Sefton Delmer for approval. Less nervous than I expected when it was my turn, I read from the beginning of St John's Gospel: *In the beginning was the Word, and the Word was with God, and the Word was God . . .* We couldn't talk about Beattie's work, but we could acknowledge that words had been his delight.

The cords lowered the coffin into the ground. I had to prevent myself from yelling at the men to stop so I could check that he was really inside. Beside me Micki shifted from foot to foot. The earth was sprinkled on top of the casket. Beattie really wasn't going to open the lid and enquire indignantly why we weren't getting on with the evening's broadcast.

When the service was over I saw Atkins, hands in pockets, striding away, probably making for the tube station. 'Come with us to the pub,' I said. 'You're part of the team.' Her eyes narrowed, but she nodded.

The five of us huddled together in a corner drinking the brandy supplied for the occasion.

'Top-ups?' Atkins asked. She took our glasses and headed for the bar.

'I still can't work out what happened,' Micki said, looking down.

'Forgive me, but perhaps Mr Beattie was still intoxicated in the morning and fell into that pond,' Father Becker said. But I'd seen Beattie drink a bottle of wine and two brandies and sit down to write a perfectly formed script all the while. And I knew he hadn't been drunk that night but couldn't tell the priest why I knew this.

'The waste,' William said. 'So much work still to be done.' He hunched over, grimacing. Atkins returned with our refills.

William excused himself and headed for the gents.

'The back is really bad today,' Micki said, watching him as he walked away. 'He goes that pale colour. But I'm not sure the drugs are helping his state of mind.' She took another sip and replaced the glass on the table.

'What do you mean?'

'Benzedrine tablets. Aspirin. I've seen a phial of morphine in his desk drawer, too.'

'Sometimes morphine's the only thing that can get rid of the pain.' I remembered lying in my hospital bed, watching the clock hands move around to the time the nurse would give me my next dose.

'God knows what he keeps in his lodgings,' Micki went on. 'I wouldn't be surprised if he took barbiturates at night.'

'I'd no idea.' It wasn't uncommon for RAF pilots to take Benzedrine to keep them alert. Patrick had told me that many of his friends kept a bottle in their lockers. I hadn't considered what they might take to help them sleep. Something stirred in my memory: a conversation?

'Often William says he's just taking aspirin, but there are all kinds of pills in that box of his.' Micki shrugged. 'Who can blame him if it's the only way he can do his work? But he shows *verworrenes Benehmen.* Confused behaviour?'

'What do you mean?' Atkins asked.

'As we came into the church he muttered something about Beattie I didn't understand. And he relies heavily on that notebook of his to remind himself what's happening.' Micki frowned. 'Where is he? He's been ages in the gents.'

Just then William came back through the saloon. He stepped aside to let a young girl pass. She was clear skinned, rosy cheeked, her fair hair falling in a cloud onto her shoulders. She looked at William through her eyelashes as she walked past, and smiled. He returned the smile.

At Mulberry House there'd been whole days when I'd forgotten my ruined face. Beattie had enabled me to be clever Anna Hall: doing important and secret work. And he'd shown me I was desirable. The reality was that girls like this one were the ones most men wanted, even the kind ones, like William. I'd probably be starting again in a new work place soon. I wasn't a native German speaker, unlike William, Micki and Father Becker. They could write scripts in the language. William and Micki could interview prisoners and search German-language newspapers for material, analyse code-broken signals for the little nugget that could be twisted and presented to the German public. As for me, I'd probably have to face the pitying stares of those interviewing me for a new job. My face would matter again.

Father Becker was looking at the girl, too. He saw me observe this, blushed slightly and looked down at his drink. The priest was a man of flesh and blood, as Beattie had told me. We all played roles but sometimes we showed ourselves for what we were.

Something nagged at me, telling me to pay attention. I had to be alone to concentrate, to work out what it was. The pub was filling as lunchtime continued, growing noisier.

I looked at my watch.

Micki put down her glass. 'We don't need to go to Euston yet, do we, Anna?'

'I said I'd help my father close up the church again.' The lie came quickly to my lips, but that was no surprise. 'You're all up to date with your scripts. I'll be back in good time for the car to the studio.'

'Are you all right?' Micki asked me.

I picked up my handbag.

'Please look after yourself, Anna,' William said, his face creased with concern. 'You can rely on us.'

Atkins watched me, expressionlessly.

⁕

Dad returned to the vicarage to find me sitting at the kitchen table. 'Anna? I didn't expect you to still be here.' He gave me a peck on the cheek.

'Just finishing up a few things.' I hadn't actually done anything, except sit staring out of the window.

'It'll be sad for you, returning to work with your boss so sadly absent.'

'I'm not sure whether they'll redeploy me or whether I'll be out of a job.'

'Someone like you will never be out of work for long, my dear.'

'I need to think,' I blurted out. 'To work out what has happened.'

'Sometimes a change of scene gives objectivity, doesn't it?' he said, looking at me with particular intensity. He opened the larder door and pulled out a bottle of sherry. 'Someone gave me this last Christmas. I find a small glass now and then helps.'

'I could have told you that.' I found two glasses and Dad poured the sherry.

'I don't know what the bishop would say.' He looked out at the garden. Grace had replaced some of the flowerbeds with her vegetable plots, but enough of the tulip bulbs my mother had planted years ago had survived to make a splash of red and yellow.

'You and Grace loved growing up here with such a big garden to play in. Your old swing's still up, though the ropes probably need replacing.'

I swallowed. 'There's something I need to say.'

He looked at me enquiringly.

'It's about that night.'

Dad sat down at the table, shoulders slumping, looking older.

'It was my fault. I persuaded Grace to go back into the church with me to save what we could. She wanted to stay in the cellar.'

His face went very pale. I'd spoilt the moment of closeness between us. 'You couldn't regret your actions that night any more than I regret mine,' he said, in a harsh tone I'd rarely heard him use before. 'What was I thinking, not checking you were both safe in the cellar?' He shook his head. 'We all cared too much for that church, that *building*. That was my fault, too. I encouraged you to cherish it, Anna.'

As children Grace and I had polished the silver chalices and candlesticks and the wooden pews. At Christmas we'd arranged the crib figures and cut laurel branches to make the stable.

'They're just objects, aren't they?' I said. 'The kneelers, the chalices, the bibles. The church itself, too.'

'They held such memories. But they weren't the church.' Turning to me, he touched his chest. 'The real church is the love of God we carry inside us, not in bricks and mortar.'

'I'm glad we've had this conversation,' I said. 'For so long Grace has been between us.'

He nodded. 'I'm glad, too.'

Companionable silence fell between us as we gazed out at the garden. I could imagine a woman weeding the beds, children playing on the swing.

'Anna?' Dad was looking at me gently. 'There's something else. Just before you came home that terrible night, Grace told me she thought you were serious about a young man.'

I stared down at the table.

'The nurse on your ward told me he came to the hospital many times, but you'd never see him?'

'I wasn't kind to him,' I whispered.

I had read all the letters Patrick sent me in hospital, but I did not weaken. When I was discharged, I placed them in the desk in my bedroom at home and took to my bed. Whenever I woke I'd remember Grace was dead all over again.

I accepted the thick pancake make-up that friends in the theatrical world found for me and wore a veiled hat outside when I wasn't in uniform. At my request the WAAF found me the job in East Anglia. Patrick might have been able to trace me if he'd really wanted to, but it wouldn't have been easy for him to come and see me in person.

Not that he would have done. Not after he'd read the last sentence I'd written to him: *I don't love you any more.* What a lie that had been; the biggest of my life.

My father squeezed my arm gently. 'Have you . . . ?'

'No. I haven't seen Patrick.' Saying his name aloud made me shiver. 'Hopefully he's safe and found some nice girl.'

With a smooth face and no demons inside her.

Dad looked as though he wanted to ask me more but I left him to his sermon writing and went upstairs to my bedroom. I sat on the bed in which I'd slept from infancy, every sinew and tendon relaxing into the old sags in the mattress. A wave of feeling swept me, so powerful that I clutched the edge of the bed. People didn't show too much emotion for loss these days, not in public and sometimes not even in private. In wartime there was always someone else who'd made a bigger sacrifice, lost more. And if you fell apart you might not be able to continue. Had I even wept much for Grace when she died? Or for the end of my relationship with Patrick? After the fire I'd told everyone I was fine and carried on, following the accepted script.

The night with Beattie and the discovery of his body had released something buried deep inside me. I rocked on the bed, hands over my face. I was safe from being overheard in this room. I had time. The first noises I made seemed to come from a stricken animal, hurting my chest as I let the loss overwhelm me. Beattie and I had found a kind of peace together that night. I hadn't loved him, but there had been something between us: an understanding, an acceptance. I was weeping for Beattie, but also for the death of Grace and of the relationship with Patrick.

Eventually I lay back on the pillow and looked at the cracks in the ceiling. The blast from the church bomb in 1941 had damaged the plaster. I could trace out new cracks, like roads or pathways, some of which led to other paths, others that faded out.

Buck up, Hall.

I needed to return to Aspley Guise and find out who had killed Beattie.

First I had to patch up my face. I examined it in the dressing-table mirror. The left side was still a young woman's, with a clear complexion and only a few lines around the eyes. I smiled and the left corner of my mouth curled up. I peered at my right side. The smile pulled up that corner of my mouth more than it had before; the muscles or tendons seemed to be slowly recovering. But the skin above my mouth still appeared incapable of fluid movement. I put more exertion into my smile and the scarred tissue shifted like a layer of rubber. It wasn't hurting as much these days. I couldn't remember the last time I'd taken anything for it. I let the muscles relax and patted my face with pancake and powder and applied lipstick. My eyes still bore the puzzled, weary expression of someone who'd lost a person they cared about. I knew from experience that they might stay like this for some time.

I turned my back on my reflection and went to the wardrobe. The clothes left inside were years out of fashion, but had been expensive when I'd bought them. I wondered if Micki might like some of the dresses for summer but worried about offending her again. I folded a few into my suitcase anyway.

I went to my writing desk. I hadn't opened it in two years. I pulled down the flap and found the letters in the little drawer at the top. Patrick's handwriting – clear, slightly hesitant – reproached me. I should throw them away – not fair to hang on to a former lover's letters like this. He was probably long-since married. Or dead. I knew the last letter off by heart. *Give me a chance to show you how much I love you . . . You are everything to me and I want to help . . .*

I'd put a little jeweller's box in the drawer with his letters. Inside the box lay the small four-leafed clover brooch. I hadn't been wearing it the night of the raid because I hadn't had time to change out of my uniform.

I hadn't sent the brooch back to Patrick when I'd ended things between us. He'd told me it wasn't valuable, but he'd thought I'd like it. *It brings out the green in your eyes,* he'd said. Returning it to him would have been giving him another slap in the face. So it had stayed here, in the dark, ever since.

When I went downstairs my father was making notes for the parish newsletter. I wanted to confide in him, tell him my fears about Beattie. I'd signed the Official Secrets Act and never told him anything of my wartime work. But I could tell him that—

'Goodness me.' Dad was looking at the clock above the stove. 'Tonight's bible class is almost upon me. I must go, child, I'm afraid.'

I said goodbye to him but decided to give myself ten minutes to say farewell to the garden, to look at the shrubs and bushes my mother had nurtured.

Beside the gate leading into the church's graveyard a small rhododendron's buds were bursting into cream and pink flowers. I opened the gate and entered the graveyard, stopping briefly at my mother's and Grace's graves.

Beattie's resting place was now filled in with earth. 'I'm still not sure what happened to you,' I told him.

If you had half the wits I thought you possessed, Hall, you'd have worked it out by now.

I looked at my watch. Time to leave for the station. I was cutting it fine and if a train were delayed or cancelled, as frequently happened, I'd be late for the studio.

20

The following morning found us attempting to recover our routine at Mulberry House. All of us listened for Beattie's footsteps in the corridor outside, the flinging open of the door to our office. 'That telephone of his seems so quiet.' Micki sighed. 'It feels so wrong.'

William stood up and bent over, breaths coming in short rasps, grimacing. 'We can do this,' he said, standing straight again. 'Anna has everything under control. We're a team.'

Father Becker regarded him from behind his typewriter with an impassive stare. He must have known of far worse situations than this when he'd helped refugees fleeing Germany. Perhaps he was considering his own position, wondering if he could ask to be returned to Zurich now Beattie was dead. He worked hard for us but I recalled his struggles with the typewriter, his obvious discomfort with the liberal atmosphere we worked in and the more salacious stories we fed to his compatriots. Becker lit another cigarette.

The scripts and news items for this evening I'd sent over for Sefton Delmer to approve reappeared in the bag delivered by a courier none of us recognised. I found myself longing to see Atkins, for the reassurance of those blue eyes, that ramrod-straight back. Micki had thought to take the remaining smoked salmon sandwiches when they'd left the pub for Euston. I ate one at my desk, not liking to leave the office unattended over the lunch hour.

At half past three William retired to his lodgings to take his medication and freshen up. Minutes later Father Becker pulled his sheets out of his typewriter. 'This afternoon I shall finish a little early,' he said. 'It is my feast day, my patron saint's day. I have completed my script for tomorrow. William has read it over.' He flicked off another invisible speck on his jacket. 'I'd like to spend some time quietly in my room.' Of course a man of God would want to spend time praying in a situation like this one. Becker looked drained. Perhaps my suspicion that he'd had enough of working for us was correct. I couldn't blame him. He didn't have to be here. Or perhaps he couldn't adjust to being managed by a woman, even temporarily. You didn't have to be a Roman Catholic priest to find this an unusual arrangement; most men would find it strange.

I didn't have time to dwell on Father Becker's state of mind. This evening I would go to the studio as programme editor in Beattie's place as I had every evening since his death, except for the night before his funeral. I would be the one who checked that everything was in order. I hadn't got used to the responsibility. Half of me still felt sick, half excited. I knew this state of affairs could not continue. Our research unit would be redeployed or given to someone else – not a sergeant, not female – to direct. For the moment, there was a kind of solace in carrying out the work as Beattie would have wished. But even as I sorted through papers and wrote myself notes something niggled at my mind. I watched Father Becker tidy his desk with his usual meticulousness, wishing us a good afternoon. Something he'd said was bothering me, but I couldn't put my finger on it.

As he left the room he nodded at me with solemnity. 'Thank you, Anna,' he said, 'for letting me go early.' The relationship between us certainly was shifting, perhaps because of my changed role. But he'd used my Christian name for the first time. The moment of solemnity was lost when the corner of his jacket caught the script on William's desk, sending pages fluttering over the floor. '*Ach*, how can I always be so clumsy?' he said, falling to his hands and knees to recover the pages and replace them on William's desk. '*Entschuldigung.*'

'It's reassuring,' Micki said. 'Some things never change, father.'

With a parting nod he left us. I watched the door close behind him, heard him stride across the gravel drive.

I sat for a moment, thinking, trying to make sense of the contradictory thoughts and memories pulsing through my mind, before standing and going into Beattie's office. The desk was empty. Sefton Delmer or the Grey-suit Man must have had someone clear it while we were away at the funeral. To my relief the library of reference books remained on the shelves. I wondered whether Beattie's cabinet of delights had already been emptied but didn't have time to look now. It took me five minutes to find the book I needed. I read the relevant pages carefully and several times.

I sat for a moment, eyeing Beattie's black telephone. I picked up the receiver and asked the operator to put me through to Grey-suit Man. His secretary transferred me to him immediately and I told him what I suspected.

'I'll send the usual contact,' he said. I assumed he meant Atkins.

'When?' I asked. 'We're due in the studio shortly.'

'Don't worry, Sergeant Hall.'

Grey-suit Man had perhaps not believed I had anything important to tell him. Maybe he knew that my days here were numbered.

I returned to our own office, sat down at my desk and folded my arms across my chest, feeling cold, heavy.

William went into the garden for a last breath of fresh air before the car arrived to take us to the studio. From the window I watched him throw the ball for the terrier, looking almost like a schoolboy. In turn Micki watched me. 'Anna? Can you talk about it?'

I shook my head.

She folded the POW interview transcription she had been marking up. 'You have to go to Milton Bryan, Anna. I do not. I can try to find him.'

What a fool I'd been to think Micki hadn't guessed what I was suspecting.

'What did Father Becker do to – what's the English expression – tip you off, Anna?'

'His Christian name is Paul. St Paul's feast day isn't today. I checked in one of Beattie's reference books.'

'Are there not lots of saints with the same name? Or is there a middle name he uses for this religious stuff?'

'I checked them all.'

'What made you suspicious?'

'My father's church is St Paul's. We're not Catholics and we don't celebrate saints, but I vaguely remembered Dad mentioning St Paul's feast day being in June.'

'That wasn't all, though, was it?'

I looked at Micki sharply.

She shrugged. 'A priest who freezes when someone asks him to hear their confession?'

'Even the pope himself might baulk at doing that in Wardour Street on a Saturday night.'

'Becker didn't look frightened when he dealt that hook.'

I recalled the expression in the priest's eyes when he'd hit the soldier. 'Just because he's in holy orders doesn't mean he's not a man. He might have been quite a bruiser before he was ordained.' I sighed. 'That's what I told myself.'

'We wanted to believe in him.' She took a breath. 'He was a good colleague. I argued with him but I liked him.'

'He must have fooled the people he boarded with, too,' I said. 'They didn't suspect he wasn't a priest.'

'A bunch of Jews like me? What would they know?'

'That wasn't all,' I said, my arms still wrapped around myself, the world seeming to slow down as I thought back.

'A fit and agile man who pretends to be clumsy?' she said.

'A blunt knife.'

She stared at me.

'My sister once told me that blunt knives were more dangerous than sharp blades. Father Becker's been acting as our very own blunt knife. I wonder who he really is?' A writer by trade, possibly a script-writer? A German military intelligence agent or someone employed by the Gestapo? There were God knows how many different Nazi security services operating overseas. The scar tissue on my cheek seemed to tighten, igniting my nervous system; I felt an impulse to scratch the cheek raw, feel it bleed. Perhaps hurting myself would release some of the feelings sweeping me.

Control yourself, Hall.

'And how the hell did he get here? Ah.' Micki nodded slowly. 'Beattie didn't actually interview Father Becker in Switzerland himself, did he?'

He'd been busy with the new studio, with interviewing German POWs over here. Intelligence had carried out the interview.

'Becker was swapped?' I thought about it. 'The Germans sent someone else? Someone who looked enough like him to be convincing?' I remembered Beattie telling me how initially reluctant Becker had been to leave Zurich. Then he'd changed his mind. What had happened in the intervening days?

'I've heard of people being blackmailed into letting someone take their identity,' Micki said. 'Perhaps the real Becker had family in Germany who were threatened.'

Like damp seeping through a wall I felt the full horror of the situation slowly wash over me. I wanted to run away, to creep back to the vicarage, to tell everyone that I couldn't do this any more.

'Anna?' Micki said my name sharply. 'You've reported this. It's not for us to dwell on the how and why Becker deceived us.'

'More than deceived us – killed one of us.'

'Even so, we must concentrate on what we can control now: tonight's broadcast.' She was just a girl of eighteen, stateless, almost without possessions, but I sat up straighter and checked my watch as she spoke to me. Our audience must not be left without the programme. That family of listeners I'd created in my mind's eye – the mother with her knitting, the father returning late from fire-watch duties, the daughter doing her homework – they'd be waiting, wireless switched on.

William was still outside playing with the dog in the garden. 'Should we tell him?' I asked Micki. What would Beattie have done?

Micki shook her head. 'You know how highly strung he is.'

William always found the lead-up to his broadcasts nerve-wracking. 'You know, I was almost starting to suspect him of something. I don't even know what,' I said, 'because he filled in a form at the post office. I thought it was for a telegram but it might have been for a postal order.'

'I can't think of a more unlikely traitor than William,' she said. 'He's devoted to the team. Even if he was sending a telegram it would have been completely innocent – some girl, perhaps. People here do break the rules, you know. Like you going to the pub. It doesn't mean anything sinister.'

I shuffled. 'It's just that he's so jumpy sometimes.'

'It's the medication. I told you, he takes too many pills.' Her expression darkened. 'Unless he's communicating with someone who sends him drugs?'

'If he runs out, he can't exactly jump on the train and go to that hospital pharmacy in London for more supplies. You may be right.' Relief flooded me. Suspecting William of a drugs problem was better than the nebulous suspicions that had started to form in my mind, ones I couldn't even articulate to myself.

'There's nothing we can do about it now. Go to the studio as normal, Anna. Keep William calm.'

'Suppose . . .' I trailed off, not sure I could even imagine my worst fear taking shape: Becker gaining access to the studio, disrupting the broadcast. But he couldn't get in, I reminded myself, because he didn't have a pass.

'Beattie always said those guard dogs would snap the necks off anyone trying to poke around.' Micki seemed to know what I feared. 'It won't be dark for ages. I'll take a bicycle and have a scout around.' She sat up. 'You know one of them's missing?'

I shook my head. 'You can't go cycling around the countryside alone.' Micki was an alien, even though her ID showed she worked for a government ministry. A suspicious policeman might arrest her. Without Beattie to advocate for her, it might be difficult to have her released.

Micki made a scoffing noise. 'Everyone knows me by sight. It'll save time if I can find out where the sainted priest is heading.'

'If Father Becker's done what we suspect, he's a dangerous man.'

'He's no *Father* Becker,' she almost spat. 'And I can be dangerous too.'

I recalled the knife she'd pulled out in Lisbon and smiled involuntarily. Then I imagined the reaction if the police caught her cycling around with a blade in her possession. Or worse, witnessed her apparently attacking a cleric.

'Wait here until Atkins arrives, Micki.'

'What's so great about Atkins? She's just a posh girl who likes motorcycles and horses.' There was an edge to her voice.

I walked over to her desk and touched Micki's shoulder. 'Don't take personal risks. I can't . . .' I heard a door open, William's uneven footsteps on the parquet. 'I can't lose you, too.' My voice trembled on the last words. She raised a hand and placed it over mine. The vitality of the girl pulsed through her warm skin. I felt as though I might be able to manage the situation after all.

William was opening the office door. I swept my papers into the satchel.

'The car'll be here any moment.' I glanced up as he came in, giving him a brief smile. I was employing every ounce of my acting skills to keep my shoulders relaxed, my voice busy but not over-worried, just as they would be on any working afternoon as the adrenaline built up towards the broadcast.

'Where's Father Becker?' William looked at the priest's empty desk. 'There's a Latin pronunciation I'd like to go over with him.'

'Left early,' Micki said. 'His feast day, apparently.'

William looked at me, his eyes narrowed. I was suddenly reminded of Schulte's intensity the first time I met him.

Schulte. That was where Father Becker, or the pretender, was going: to the farm. To hush the traitor before he could impart any more useful information to the enemy.

William was packing his script into his folio case, looking away from me. I mouthed, 'Tell Atkins he might be at the farm,' at Micki as I left the room.

Should I telephone Mary Waites? Warn her to bring Schulte inside, lock the door and not admit anyone? She'd want to know why. I'd have to tell her who and what we suspected. I couldn't do this without permission.

The car pulled up outside the house, breaking into these thoughts.

Pay attention, Hall. What's most important right now?

William held open the car door for me.

The driver this evening was a Liverpudlian I'd seen once or twice before. 'No Atkins?' William asked brightly.

'Tonsils, apparently.' The driver shrugged. 'Very sudden. She was fine at breakfast, but these infections go around like wildfire.' She spoke in a way that didn't encourage further conversation. Drivers weren't supposed to talk to us nor us to them. I should have noticed that Beattie had broken this convention with Atkins. But then, he'd broken so many of them.

'Poor old Atkins,' William said. I looked at his open face, feeling the familiar sense of comfort in his presence. I wanted to tell him the role Atkins had played the morning of Beattie's death, and about Father Becker betraying us and doing even worse. I still had Micki and William; the three of us were still a team, could cope with whatever was going on.

What would Beattie be doing now? Even now – especially now, nauseous with nerves – I felt his loss.

You know damn well what I'd be doing, Hall.

Preparing to go over every detail, double-, triple-checking that we had a flawless programme.

An image of Grace flicked through my mind. Grace was no theologian but had believed in Providence. She'd have been flustered if questioned about doctrine but would probably have said that God put you in situations where He intended you to be. Then it was up to you. I didn't share her faith, but this seemed like a good way of looking at life.

The exasperated voice of my dead boss spoke to me again.

Stop having a fit of the vapours like some sixteen-year-old about to step onto the stage in the school play.

Even from the grave, it seemed Beattie could simultaneously annoy and inspire me.

I opened my satchel and reread the evening's broadcast schedule. We slowed, about to turn into the drive leading up to the studio. As usual we halted at the guard post. I felt an urge to open the car door, to run into the guards' hut and tell them to find Father Becker. But it was better to wait for Grey-suit Man or Atkins.

They let us through. Outside the main door stood another armed guard. He nodded at me. 'Evening, Sergeant Hall.'

'Go inside and set up,' I told William. 'I'll catch up in a moment.'

'Of course.' He gave me a quick appraising glance but didn't say anything. It was right not to tell him, I reminded myself. He needed to be calm, undistracted for his performance. I waited for him to disappear. 'If anyone arrives for me, please let me know at once.'

The guard's face lost its relaxed smile and tightened. 'What's that?'

'I'm expecting a visitor.'

'No visitors to the studio, sergeant.' He folded his arms. 'Not without prior authorisation.'

'This man or woman will have vetting.'

'Ah.' The guard gave me a reassuring smile. 'I'm sure Lieutenant Nathanson has organised everything.'

A riposte was on my lips but the purr of a motorcycle engine distracted me. The door opened.

'Sergeant Hall?'

A crystalline, authoritative voice.

Atkins herself stood behind me in the doorway, those baby-blue eyes of hers now colder than polar ice. She wore her dispatch rider's uniform: black breeches, shining boots, cap on head, messenger bag slung over her shoulder. She handed some kind of signed authorisation to the guard. He stood up straighter. 'I'm authorised to deal with this situation,' she said to us both. 'Others in my team have also been deployed.'

Who exactly are you? I wanted to ask.

She looked at her watch. A frown creased her smooth brow. 'Do you absolutely need to be here for the whole broadcast, sergeant?'

'Yes.' The word came out crisply. No matter what was happening outside, I knew Beattie would have wanted me here. I'd be the one given the scrambled telephone messages about bombing raids on Germany to insert into my news script. The one who might need to pull the censor switch and stop the broadcast if anything went wrong. Our eyes locked. I held my gaze.

Atkins addressed the guard. 'Set up a patrol of the studio perimeter fence.'

'Nobody can get in here, it's—'

'One pair patrolling the fences and another between the gates and lane,' she told him. 'Quickly as you can.'

'I've got to go.' William would be in the studio, adjusting the microphone, moving his chair into position. I headed for the control room. Only there did I remove my scripts from my satchel. Beattie had made it clear that nobody unauthorised should see any of the material, not even here.

Was I certain that nothing in tonight's broadcast was compromising? Had Father Becker inserted anything into it that might alert the German authorities to what was going on in this quiet part of England? I scoured each line: a sermon about rendering unto Caesar what was Caesar's. Becker had outlined this script with Beattie at their usual weekly meeting before writing it in full and it had been signed off by Sefton Delmer. The twist lay in the last thirty seconds when the radio character Father Friedrich reminded his audience that rendering to Caesar meant giving the state what the state was owed. A coin. Loyalty. Work. But not your soul. Your soul belonged to God. The state could never claim it.

William would surely have spotted anything out of the ordinary, any words that didn't belong, a tone that was unusual, a reference that seemed off. By now he knew his radio character inside out.

The light switched on. The opening news broadcast was delivered by the announcer. He finished. Now it was William's turn. Yet again I marvelled at his complete transformation into the role. Father Becker's swan-song had done us proud.

William stiffened. He was still reading his script but I could see him frowning. Only a very attentive listener would be able to make out the slight tightness in his voice now. Only someone watching would see the furrow appearing on his brow. He was scanning ahead for the next line. Whatever he saw was troubling him.

I stood up. The announcer sitting beside William turned his head and raised his eyebrows at us. William was still speaking but more slowly, his hands falling open on the table, his face white. He pushed the script aside. It fell to the floor.

The last sheet, representing the final thirty seconds of broadcast and containing the essential twist, was blank.

21

William glanced towards me. For a moment neither of us could move, but he continued to address his audience, his radio flock.

He'd have some memory of the lines on the missing page, I told myself. He'd read the draft several times earlier in the day. William was a professional. But his words were coming out more slowly. Any second he would freeze. Would he have the nous to jump forward to the final Latin blessing? The audience might notice that the homily had ended without its usual style of conclusion. There'd be a missing half-minute to fill with pre-recorded music, but beside me the technician was already moving towards the turntable.

If William froze so completely that he didn't go to the Latin benediction, we'd have to pull the switch on him. There'd be less than a second to decide. Silence on air was forbidden; that was how frequencies were taken over, was probably how we'd done it ourselves at times. Even if this didn't happen to our station, the German audience would know something was wrong, some doubt would enter their subconscious.

I looked at the clock. Less than twenty seconds to decide. I'd never used the censor switch or even seen it deployed before. I'd thought it would only happen in extremis, if German paratroopers stormed the gates and tried to shoot their way into a studio during a broadcast.

This was an emergency.

What's that in your hand? Beattie's voice asked me silently.

My own copy of the script. I flicked to the last page and saw the typed paragraphs I remembered. I removed my headphones and waved at the announcer, pointing to the door between us. William now had his eyes closed, obviously pulling words from his memory.

The announcer stood up and unlocked the door. Our eyes locked momentarily. I handed him the last page of the script and closed the door silently, grabbing my headphones and returning to the window to watch and listen.

William was still word perfect, but his face was the colour of the paper and sweat ran down his cheeks.

The announcer touched William's hand lightly. The last page of my copy of the script was in front of him now. William's eyes opened. He sat straighter. The colour seemed to rush back into his cheeks. His voice relaxed into Father Friedrich's again. The announcer flopped back in his chair. The broadcast was secure.

Three seconds, two seconds, one second. William finished his final benediction as Father Friedrich and took a gulp from the glass of water. He waited until the next item, a pre-recorded Rhineland folk song, had commenced, before pushing back his chair and standing. He and the announcer quietly slapped one another's shoulders. If Beattie'd been here he'd have known where to track down a filing cabinet with something strong filed under 'Emergency'. Even now, I could smile at the thought.

William slipped out of the studio door. I wanted to embrace him but that was out of the question in such a public place. I contented myself with clasping his hand, only releasing it when he winced.

Atkins appeared and looked from one of us to the other.

William frowned. 'I know that last page was in place at Mulberry House before we left. At least, I thought I did.'

Atkins and I exchanged glances. William's hand went to his back. 'Bad again?' I asked.

'Just a spasm. My tablets will sort me out.' He patted his pocket.

'You're one of a kind.' Beattie would have been so proud. Not that he would have expressed this pride. A particularly good bottle of something would have been opened. Beattie would then have been particularly rude to William for a few days afterwards, in case he got above himself.

'I'm just part of a good crew,' William said. 'You looked after me in there, Anna.' There was something solemn in his words that made me look at him more closely. 'And I hope I do the same thing in return.'

I wanted to say more, but there wasn't time to talk right now. Half an hour to go before our schedule finished. After the folk songs there'd be a final news programme. I was assuming that any details of air raids on German cities I needed to add to my news items would have been given to me by now.

Assumptions are the kiss of death, Hall, I heard Beattie tell me.

I knocked on the door of Sefton Delmer's office, feeling perspiration on my forehead. A woman's voice told me to come in. Without my needing to ask her she checked the out-tray and a message pad. I waited for an explosion, for Delmer himself to ask why the hell there'd been such a slip-up with the script.

'Nothing for you, sergeant.'

'I can close down as normal?'

She nodded. I shut the door. They must know about Father Becker; Grey-suit Man must have telephoned the studio. Not that they would tell me. We were each confined to our own little squares on some complicated grid. Probably only a few people in the whole country knew how all the squares connected.

'Go home and rest,' I told William. 'Have an early night.'

'I . . .' He blinked, looking dazed. 'Yes, an early night. Good idea.'

I returned to the control room, watching as the announcer switched to the music studio, where the live dance band waited. Our music was irresistible enough to make my leg jig up and down as we listened and I forgot that our leader was dead and that one of our team was a traitor, on the run. The technician smiled as he noticed. 'It's going well,' he said. 'Mr Beattie would be pleased.'

The announcer took over. In front of him sat my news script. He flicked through the pages, double-checking. My own copy was now dog-eared from being read. He looked up and gave me a thumbs-up.

I sat perspiring as the music came to an end and we switched back to the studio. The announcer read the news items. There was a nice little lie about the end of a shortage of anaesthetic drugs for civilians. Soon even non-combatants undergoing minor operations might benefit from pain relief again. I hoped that some Nazi official was sweating as he feared he'd be on the operating table fully conscious while his bunions were cut off. The anaesthetics idea had been Beattie's last story. I remembered him agonising as to whether piles would work better.

The news was over. A final blast of Beethoven. The light switched off. We were off-air. The announcer slumped in his chair, wiping a handkerchief over his face. 'What a night.'

Atkins was waiting for me outside in the corridor. 'Can you come now?'

'I have to get final sign-off.' I went back to Sefton Delmer's office. The woman inside told me I was free to leave. 'We'll be in touch shortly, but for now, carry on as normal,' she said.

'Does *he* know what happened earlier?' I meant Delmer himself.

She nodded. 'We were a second away from intervening.' Her face softened. 'Alexander Beattie said you had a cool head, sergeant.'

To my horror I felt my eyes pricking and left the room quickly. 'I need to see the telephonists,' I told Atkins, but to my relief the girls told me that no calls had come in. I'd been half-expecting an irate senior military officer or minister to have rung in to complain that I'd missed off an essential item or used something that hadn't been properly approved. I handed the girls the bars of Fry's chocolate I'd found in the cabinet of delights.

'Nothing going on outside?' Atkins asked the guard as we left the building.

'Nothing.'

'Keep it that way,' she said. 'High alert, all night.'

William was getting into the car that would take him back to his lodgings. His face was drained of colour. I slowed down.

'I need to make sure he's all right,' I said.

'No time.' She pointed towards the motorcycle. I'd imagined we'd go wherever it was she was taking me by car. I'd never sat on a motorcycle before and eyed it with a mixture of excitement and distrust.

'It's quicker than a car,' she said. 'I'll get on first, then you jump on behind me. See the pegs?' She pointed to the one on our side. 'Put your feet up on them. Arms around my waist, but don't crush me. Or put one hand behind yourself on the rack, if you prefer. Alexander used to do that.'

Alexander? Beattie on a motorbike? Even now my eyes widened at the thought.

'He had better balance than you might imagine.' She sprang onto the motorcycle.

'Are we going to Waites Farm?'

She nodded.

'We'll be there in less than ten minutes. This has a 500cc engine, more powerful than the other couriers' bikes.' I detected a note of pride. 'Hold on tight.' The engine ignited and the motorcycle roared into life. Atkins nodded at the guards and they let us through the gate. We turned left into the lane, accelerating rapidly.

'Schulte won't be there this late,' I said, above the engine. I thought of something else. 'Won't Becker go to the camp? He could say he was there to minister to Schulte's soul or something.' I raised my voice as our speed increased.

'I rang the camp. If Becker turns up, they'll throw him in a cell. Franz Schulte is safely locked up in his hut there.'

'Who do you work for?' I said, raising my voice as Atkins accelerated.

'Lean with the bike,' she said. We took a corner at a speed that made my muscles clench.

Ahead of us a boy was herding cows into a field after milking. Atkins would surely slow and wait . . . She shot to the opposite side of the road. The boy's mouth widened into an O. Atkins was heading for a gap between the cows and the hedge. Too small. I closed my eyes. When I opened them it was to concentrate fixedly on the back of her dark jacket.

Atkins turned into the track leading up to the farm. As we bumped along, I scanned the fields, could see nobody outside. We pulled up outside the farmhouse. 'You get off first,' she said.

'What am I going to do here?' I hadn't even thought to ask before, had just blindly followed instructions.

'It's your German,' she said. 'We might need to speak to Becker in haste and without ambiguity. When we find him.' Father Becker spoke some English but had never been entirely fluent. 'My German's not good enough.'

I felt a brief, unworthy relief that there was something I was better at than Atkins. But I was still only a substitute, a stand-in for Beattie who'd been born and raised in Berlin. I couldn't be regarded as that vital in tonight's pursuit of Becker, or they wouldn't have let me stay at the studio until the end of the broadcast. Or perhaps it was the other way round; they thought the broadcast mattered too much to disrupt. That thought made me feel better.

Atkins ushered me into the farmhouse. Mrs Waites stood inside the kitchen, her face blank, wrists clenched together.

'Where's Mary?' I asked. The woman seemed to slump down into herself. I wasn't surprised at the response.

I steered her to a chair.

'Did the milking and never came in for her tea.'

I looked at Atkins but her perfectly symmetrical features showed no sign of consternation.

'May I use your telephone, Mrs Waites?' Atkins asked, poised as a debutante at a tea party. Mrs Waites nodded.

'That German you sent us has taken my girl as a hostage, hasn't he?'

'The lieutenant's safely locked up in camp.' I stopped before I could mention Father Becker. From the hallway I half-heard Atkins murmur down the line.

'We should never have had him here,' Mrs Waites continued. 'You said it was our duty, but it was too risky. Look at your Mr Beattie, drowned by German spies.'

Despite all the efforts to keep it quiet, the nature of Beattie's death had obviously spread through the neighbourhood.

'What do we do now?' I asked Atkins when she returned.

'We wait,' she said, picking up the kettle from the range and filling it with water. 'The police are watching railway stations and buses.' From her inside jacket pocket she produced a hip flask. 'Whisky,' she said. The smell reminded me of Becker. Mrs Waites demurred at first but agreed after Atkins looked at her more pointedly. The edge of my anxiety seemed to soften as I drank the fortified tea. Mrs Waites retired upstairs to wait for her daughter.

Atkins and I sat in the kitchen. The cat came in and lay by the range.

I opened my satchel. Tomorrow's Clara script was inside. I'd hoped to have time to check it over one last time. 'Would you mind turning away from what I'm reading?' I asked. 'I'm not supposed to let anyone else catch sight of it. I just need a few minutes to read it through.'

I thought Atkins might be annoyed by the request but approval flashed briefly over her face. She sat cross-legged on the floor in front of the stove, flexible as a schoolgirl, back to me, stroking the cat.

At first glimpse it appeared to be the script I had typed. A reference to Aesop's Fables made me sit up. In my version Clara had referred to the story of the frogs and the king. The frogs requested Jove give them a king. At first he dropped a large log into their pond. When they asked a second time he sent a heron, who ate them up – a useful metaphor. I'd discussed the use of the fable with Beattie. 'Deftly inserted if not a strikingly original parallel with the election of Hitler,' he'd told me. 'Beta plus. Alpha minus, if I'm being generous.'

In the version of the script I had in front of me now the frogs had been replaced with the fable of the dog and the shadow. The dog drops the meat he carries securely in his mouth to snatch at the piece of meat in his shadow's mouth.

I must have gasped out loud. Atkins looked at me. 'More tinkering by the unholy priest,' I said.

'I'm sure you'll sort it out, Sergeant Hall.'

Becker's substitution was the same length as the text it replaced – making the change hard to spot at a glance. But surely he'd know the script would be reviewed before I handed it to the actors? I reminded myself that William's script had been checked, yet Becker had somehow managed to exchange the original last page with the blank sheet just before we'd left for the studio this evening.

Atkins was still observing me. 'I think the good father intended carrying out several low-level acts of sabotage. Cumulatively it might mean your unit's broadcasts being discredited by those in charge,' she said, reading my mind. 'Even if the altered scripts never got as far as causing havoc on air.'

'One of them nearly did.'

Our eyes locked.

'Who is Becker really?' I asked, replacing Clara in my satchel and fastening it.

Someone moved outside in the darkness. Atkins was at the window in a single bound, her hand reaching inside her jacket. She'd carry a handgun, I realised. Of course. Her elegant shoulders stiffened and then relaxed. An object bumped against the farmhouse wall. 'Just a bicycle,' Atkins said from the window. 'I do believe it's your colleague, Miss Rosenbaum.'

It always took me a moment to recall that Miss Rosenbaum was Micki. I went to let her in. Her cheeks were pink from exertion.

'I saw William after the broadcast. He wouldn't say much but I gather there was trouble at the studio?' she whispered.

I beckoned her inside. 'You shouldn't be here. How did you know I'd come here?'

She rolled her eyes. 'Two women on a dispatch bike flying out of Milton Bryan at diabolical speed? They'll be talking about it for weeks.' She followed me into the kitchen, which seemed to fill with oxygen as she entered.

Atkins frowned but didn't reprimand Micki. The three of us sat at the table, the blackouts pulled down again. Atkins sat very upright, but seemingly without tension. I could imagine her on her hunter outside some copse, waiting for the hounds to flush out a fox. Micki looked as though she might burst into acrobatics at any moment. As for me, I probably looked like a woman who hadn't slept well for days and needed fresh clothes and a square meal. The make-up would be sliding off my damaged cheek. In my satchel I carried my powder compact, but I didn't want to move away from the others to touch up my face.

Atkins stood up, a finger to her lips. I hadn't heard anything but as I strained, I made out voices. Mary, I thought. And a male voice.

German accent. Becker.

'Go upstairs to Mrs Waites and tell her to stay in her room,' Atkins told me.

I moved towards the staircase. I hadn't been upstairs before. The ground floor of the farmhouse was almost a working premises. Upstairs there were paintings on walls, rugs on floors, photographs on shelves and dressing tables. The oak furniture looked old and polished. I'd regarded the Waites family as a means to an end: they'd provided cover work for Schulte. Seeing their possessions on display reminded me that they were people in their own right, not just cogs in our wheel of operation.

I didn't know which was Mrs Waites's room and walked along the landing, past a room with a dressing table in it on which I spotted the lipstick we'd sent Mary. On the top of the mirror she'd hung rosettes from pre-war gymkhanas. A row of dolls sat on the bottom shelf of her bookcase.

Another open door revealed shelves with small model soldiers and sports trophies arranged on it. Her brother's bedroom.

The door at the end of the landing was closed. I knocked on it. 'It's only me – Anna.' I hoped that using my Christian name would reassure her.

'Come in,' Mrs Waites said. She was sitting in darkness, the curtains not drawn over the window. As I came closer I saw she clutched something woollen in her lap – a piece of darning? 'I'm trying to distract myself,' she went on. 'Thought I'd finish mending this sock, but I haven't made a single stitch.' She was the kind of woman who'd been brought up not to flap, to take her mind off things by doing something useful, but it wouldn't work tonight.

I drew the curtains – thick, black velvet lengths – and turned on the oil lamp beside her bed. This was a feminine bedroom belonging to a wife and mother who'd cooked, looked after the hens and tended the vegetable garden rather than carrying out heavy, dirty farm work as she did now. Yet Mrs Waites seemed to have accepted her change in role and that of her daughter – the pretty girl who might have made something of her life as a secretary instead of ruining her skin outdoors in the mud and cold.

'That's my Mary outside, isn't it?' Mrs Waites asked.

The one child she still had at home. The one who ought to have been safe here.

'There are people down there taking care of everything.' I tried for a soothing tone. It had gone quiet again outside.

'I thought Lieutenant Schulte was a decent type. For a German. But there are other Germans round here, in the village, and who knows what they're capable of?'

I was tempted to tell her that one of these Germans, Micki, was now sitting downstairs, having cycled out here to help. Something else occurred to me, not relevant to tonight's events, but which would need managing later on.

Mrs Waites put down her darning.

'Who's got Mary? Is he dangerous?'

I put a finger to my lips, listening. The back door leading to the yard creaked. Atkins was on the move. I heard her boots tread across the farmyard.

'Why did it take you so long to come out here?' Mrs Waites asked. I couldn't tell her that I'd delayed Atkins at the studio because the programme was the priority, more important than her seventeen-year-old daughter's safety. I strained my ears to hear what was happening down below. Footsteps came towards the farmhouse – two or three sets of them, I estimated. Mrs Waites lunged for the window, pulling open the curtains before I could prevent her. We were looking down at the farmyard.

'What's the plan? Make for one of the ports to Ireland?' Atkins addressed one of the figures in front of her.

'Why not, sweetheart?' Becker spoke in English, sounding more fluent and less the kindly, considerate priest. He was a fugitive now, but even in the dark I could see how he stood taller.

'Without ID or money for train tickets or a vehicle?' Atkins asked.

Mary was shaking in Becker's grip. Her chest rose and fell in short jerks.

'He's got a gun pointed at her.'

Where'd Becker got the weapon? Perhaps he'd smuggled it into the country from Switzerland. Maybe Swiss priests weren't subjected to body searches on entry to the UK.

I saw something else. Micki had emerged along the side of the house, having, I guessed, crept out of the front door, treading silently on those gymnast's feet of hers. She now stood behind Becker, her eyes on him, assessing the situation. In her right hand she carried what looked like a rake. She could hit him with it, but that gun held on Mary's temple might fire a bullet as the rake struck. Mary now looked as though it was only Becker's grip on her that stopped her from collapsing; her legs shook.

'I thought I might take that rather wonderful motorcycle of yours,' Becker told Atkins. 'It'll put some miles between me and you.'

'We have police watching every ferry. Let her go.'

I heard the safety catch click off.

22

'Don't make a sound,' I whispered to Mrs Waites, grabbing her arm. Atkins must have seen Micki standing behind Becker by now. Micki sprang up onto the top of a milk churn, silent as a panther, and from there climbed onto a stack of straw bales.

'All right,' Atkins said. 'Release the girl and we'll let you go.' Atkins moved a few steps forward and to her right, forcing Becker to reposition himself, Mary still in his grip. I saw that Atkins was manoeuvring him so the bales were at his back, close enough that Micki must be able to see every knitted stitch in Mary's violet cardigan. I couldn't see Mary's face clearly in the gloom but could make out the rigid outline of her body as Becker held on to her.

'She's staying with me for a bit longer.' Becker's arm tensed around Mary.

Micki's rake swiped down at the hand holding the revolver. The gun fired and crashed to the ground. After a second's silence the chickens squawked. As Becker's grip on her relaxed, Mary pulled herself free. Micki hit Becker again with the rake, this time on his arm, preventing him from retrieving the revolver. Atkins jumped forward and stuffed the gun into her belt before grabbing Becker. As he struggled to release himself, showing far more coordination than he'd ever exhibited in Mulberry House, Becker swore at her in German. Micki jumped down, muttering equally fierce German curses, brandishing the rake. 'I'll blind you if you move,' she hissed. 'Not so brave now without a gun against a kid's head, are you?'

He stood still. 'I would not have hurt the girl.' Perhaps Micki believed him. She lowered the rake, but the set of her shoulders threatened further violence if required.

I heard a car bumping up the farm track. Mrs Waites was pulling away from me. I let her go and we both ran downstairs.

The men in the truck that pulled up looked like regular soldiers. Atkins stepped towards the officer accompanying them, saying something I couldn't hear. Becker was hauled into the truck. I swerved past Atkins to the rear door before it could be closed. One of the soldiers made an attempt to hold me back but I elbowed him aside. 'We trusted you,' I said to the prisoner.

For a moment Becker looked at me as he had when I'd admitted feeling responsible for my sister's death: as though my words were touching him somewhere. As though he'd liked me. I'd certainly liked him – admired him, even.

Then his face hardened. 'Trust? Those people in Germany who listened to your broadcasts trusted you, Anna,' he said. 'You made them into your friends over the wireless, but you manipulated them for your own ends, encouraging them to surrender or put themselves into danger or making them fearful of things that weren't going to happen. Women. Children. Old people. Doesn't that bother you?'

'Not as much as the fact you betrayed us.' The other aspects did bother me at times, but I wasn't going to admit it to him.

'I didn't betray you. I don't care about you. People like Schulte and Miss Rosenbaum here are the ones who have betrayed their own country.'

Micki's chin jutted forward. She looked as though she might spit at him. For a moment I wanted to cover him with spittle, too.

'That's enough.' One of the guards was pulling me away.

'You killed Beattie,' I shouted at Becker.

He started to say something but stopped.

'I know he didn't fall into that pond,' I said, watching him. No sign of guilt appeared on his face. We could have used him as an actor after all – he'd done a good enough job of pretending to be someone else all this time.

The guard tugged at my arm.

'Where are you taking him?' I asked. Nobody answered. Becker was perhaps bound for a place I'd heard of just outside Richmond Park in south-west London, where agents were interrogated prior to execution, sometimes in the Tower of London. I hoped that was where this murderer was heading.

Atkins plucked at my sleeve. 'Come away now, Hall.' I stepped back.

'We thought he was one of us,' I said. We'd drunk coffee with him, joked with him, gone to the cinema with him. He'd even commented on Micki's gymnastics in the office with what had seemed like genuine friendliness.

'He was never one of you.' She said it with the neutral coldness of the professional. Atkins must regard me as a fool, incapable of spotting that I was working with a spy.

'How long have you known?' I watched the truck pull out of the yard. Mrs Waites had come into the farmyard and clung to her daughter. Atkins was quiet. 'I can't see that would be telling us very much,' I said.

'Beattie thought something was up fairly soon after William Nathanson arrived.' She spoke the words guardedly.

'Why?'

She shook her head and went to talk to Mary.

William had been planted by Atkins's team to keep an eye on us? On me? On Micki? I revisited the comment he'd made earlier this evening about looking out for me. I remembered Schulte's accounts of a black-coated man spying on him. An active-sounding man. That hadn't been William, but Becker, an apparently blunt knife who was really something far sharper than he pretended. Only Mrs Haddon's terrier had been worried by the gap between appearance and reality. Did spies emit some kind of electric signal that dogs could pick up?

Atkins was asking Mary questions in an authoritative but kindly tone. I heard Mary reply that Becker had come across her after she'd returned the cows to their pasture and was inspecting a crop in a neighbouring field.

'Your Father what's-his-name came looking for Franz— Lieutenant Schulte. He'd returned to camp. The prisoners were all collected early because the officer in charge there needs them to dig out a new drain for the shower block.'

I thought of the proud Lieutenant Schulte digging drains.

'Franz – the lieutenant – didn't have to dig, but he had to get a lift back to the camp with the others. I was alone when that priest appeared out of the trees.' She shivered.

I remembered the times I'd thought I was being watched.

'He grabbed me,' Mary continued. 'Said he'd bargain me for a motorcycle or car.'

'He didn't . . . ?' For the first time Atkins seemed to lose a little of her composure.

'No,' Mary said emphatically. 'He didn't do anything to me.'

Atkins let out a breath. 'There'll be more questions at some point. But for tonight, I suggest you all get some rest. You're safe now.' With a nod to us all, she moved away in the direction of her motorcycle.

'Will I see you again?' I asked, following her to the house, feeling like a girl whose favourite prefect was about to leave the school.

Atkins paused and turned back, some warmth in those pale-blue eyes of hers. 'I can't really say.'

'It's strange not having you drive us in the Austin.'

She smiled. 'I won't miss that clunky gearbox.' Her expression became more serious again. 'Alexander could never say much about your work, Sergeant Hall, but it was clear he had great faith in you.'

At the mention of his name emotion swept me again. I folded my arms as though to contain myself. 'I feel . . .'

'Lost without him? Uncertain? Of course.' Her voice was sympathetic now. 'I will miss him, too. But you're not alone. Lieutenant Nathanson and Miss Rosenbaum would obviously do anything for you.'

Despite this, some man would eventually be placed in charge of me.

Perhaps Atkins knew what I was thinking. 'For now, it's your show, Anna Hall. Throw your heart into it.' She placed a hand on my arm briefly before she walked off. I heard her jump onto her motorcycle. The engine gave its throaty purr. *500cc . . .*

As she drove down the track to the lane, her hair was a pale punctuation mark against the black of her cap and jacket. I could hear the motorcycle for a few seconds after it passed out of view.

Micki came to stand beside me. 'You can see why some men would pant over that girl, can't you?' she said. 'And some women, too. It's the black breeches and boots. There's this bar in Hamburg where girls—'

I put up a hand to prevent her saying anything more. 'Let's go to The Blue Anchor.'

Her eyes widened. 'I thought—'

'The pub was out of bounds? Officially, yes. But tonight you and I are going to sit in a corner quietly and have a drink.'

'I'd like that.'

'You were wonderful this evening,' I told her. 'Thank God for your circus training.'

She was silent.

'The way you leapt up onto that hay bale without a sound.'

'I have to tell you something.' She sounded younger, quieter.

I looked at her.

'I never actually performed in a circus. Well, not as an acrobat. I cleaned the tents and caravans. Counted the takings.'

'I thought . . .' What had I thought?

'The family remembered me – my father took me to see the show every time it was in town. Until, well, until Jews weren't allowed to go to performances.'

'So how did you . . . ?' I shook my head. 'You don't have to tell me. It's not my business.'

'I want to. It feels right.'

We stood by ourselves in the dark.

'When the police came for my family, Maxi and I were out of the apartment, playing hide and seek in the garden.' Words were falling out of Micki now. 'We lived in this modernist block, quite famous architecturally, with landscaped grounds. We weren't allowed to play outside. No Jews in public spaces. But we used to sneak out if nobody else was there. I saw the four of them leaving with a few suitcases.' She put a hand to her mouth. 'I just knew not to . . .'

I waited.

'There was a hollow that dipped towards a pond, out of sight of the apartment entrance. We hid there when we were playing. Maxi and I crawled down and lay on our stomachs among the reeds, very still. When the police brought them out of the block we could hear my mother – she was hysterical. My father told the police he had no idea where we were. We heard them slap him round the face. But they drove off without us.' Micki shivered.

In the background I could hear Mary talking to her mother, her voice as low as Micki's.

'The circus was set up three or four miles away. When it was dark we walked there. I had to carry Maxi for some of it. I begged them to take us in. No way would they have let me perform in public: a new girl with no training and Jewish. But they sheltered us for as long as they could, until it became dangerous for them.' She gulped. 'I should have told you the truth before.'

'Nobody else does.' I squeezed her arm. 'Not all the time. Perhaps you needed a story that made the past a little more bearable?'

She blinked hard and made a dismissive gesture with her hand. 'Beattie would say you needed that psychoanalyst's couch again, Anna.'

I wanted to say more to her about Beattie, about how awful I felt about not noticing her feelings for him. I could tell by the way she stuck her jaw out that this wasn't the moment.

'How do we get to the pub?' she asked. 'Before closing time, on foot?'

I heard a motor engine. A car, a small one, was bumping up the drive. I recognised the Liverpudlian driver. 'Atkins must have arranged transport for us,' I said.

'Come on.' Micki moved towards the car. 'I'll stick the bicycle in the boot, even if we can't close it. One of the bikes is still missing, by the way.'

'We need to find it. We won't have cars driving us everywhere from now on,' I said. 'Beattie was given the Austin so he could talk to Atkins in private.'

'The weather's getting warmer by the day,' Micki said. 'Good for us to get the exercise. Let's say goodbye to the Waiteses now, make sure they're all right.'

The women looked steadier when we walked across to them. Mary was no longer clinging to her mother. It was too dark to be certain, but I thought the rosiness had returned to her cheeks.

Again, a suspicion crossed my mind, but it wasn't anything that needed acting on tonight. The prospect of a quiet corner in The Blue Anchor and a glass of whatever alcohol it might provide was now overwhelmingly inviting.

23

'Tell me about you and Lieutenant Schulte or I'm going inside to talk to your mother about what I suspect.'

It was just before eight the following morning. I had cycled out to the farm on Micki's bicycle while she was still sleeping. I found Mary by herself behind the farmhouse, moving chicken runs so the hens could peck at fresh grass.

She tried to slip past me, but I caught her sleeve.

'Have you gone mad?' She shook herself free. 'You've been listening to gossip.'

'I haven't listened to anything at all.'

She opened her mouth to resume her denials but sighed. 'My mother trusted me and I've let her down.'

'I thought you hated him.'

'I did.'

'You meet him in the fields before the truck comes for him in the evenings, don't you? Out of sight.'

Mary nodded. 'Not last night, though, as he was taken back to the camp early.'

The change in plan had probably saved him from Becker's gun. 'Has it gone far?' I felt some responsibility for the girl. We'd insisted on the prisoner coming to the farm, after all.

'Not yet.' Her eyes met mine.

'Don't let it, Mary. It could result in . . . complications.'

It would be impossible for Mary and Schulte to pull away from one another once a certain point had been reached, though. I remembered how it had been with Patrick and me: balancing on a high bar, knowing you'd topple off, that the fall was unavoidable, but unable to climb down. Nobody could have stopped me sleeping with Patrick. Daughter of the vicar I might have been; it had made no difference. The fear that I might lose him had added to the passion.

'Be careful,' I said. 'You know what people are like. And it won't be good for Lieutenant Schulte if people think he's taking advantage of you.'

'He's not.' But her voice was less strident now.

'Look after yourself.' I hoped I sounded concerned rather than judgemental. 'You've done good work for us by having him here on the farm and enabling us to see him discreetly. Mr Beattie . . . was so pleased.'

'You hear all kinds of stories,' Mary said. 'About what they're like, the Germans. You see those Pathé news programmes at the pictures. But Franz, he's just a boy like my brother.' She shook her head. 'I think they tell us lies about the enemy. I know a lot of them are cruel to civilians and persecute Jews, but they're not all evil.' She kicked at a stray boulder in the field. 'It's all bad enough, what's going on in the world. Why do we need more false stories?'

'You have a point,' I said softly. I looked at the hens with their chicks, at the green on the hedgerows starting to ripple white with blossom. Something flipped inside me, as though someone had turned on a switch. My feelings of paranoia, guilt and anger seemed to ebb away. This girl, this young woman I'd regarded as a nuisance who had to be bribed with cosmetics into helping us, whom I'd suspected of all kinds of things – she was just worried about upsetting her mother because she'd fallen in love with a prisoner of war. Mary and Schulte ought by nature's laws to be left in peace. But in wartime it was fraternisation.

'Don't let it go too far.' I knew my warning was futile. I'd make arrangements for Schulte to be moved. Much as I felt for him and Mary, it really was time he went to Canada with the rest of the German prisoners.

Mary raised a hand in farewell as I stepped through the gate. I knew she was watching me as I ran across the farmyard to jump onto the bicycle before Mrs Waites spotted me or the truck bringing Schulte here for work pulled up.

At the junction with the lane I stopped, remembering how before someone had seemed to watch me from the copse. If it had been Becker cycling out here, we'd missed his absence. He'd always seemed to be present in the office. No doubt someone was currently extracting the practical details of his espionage from him now. I shivered and cycled on.

Passing the turning to Mulberry House I continued to the square so I could quickly shop in the village store before work. I didn't have a cabinet of delights like Beattie but perhaps I could find biscuits or even chocolate to cheer up the depleted team. My ration card held enough vouchers for some small treat.

As I walked across the road, I felt a strong urge to turn around; the same feeling I'd had before that someone was just behind me, watching me. I told myself there was no need to be neurotic now.

I propped the bicycle up against the shop front, glimpsing my reflection in the window. I blinked, halted.

There, behind me, was the blurred image of a man. The events of the last weeks rushed through my mind: the fear and guilt, the doubting of my own mind. And there he was, my pursuer, features indeterminable in the smeared reflection, but so close.

I pivoted round to look at him.

24

'William.' I let my breath out, feeling like an idiot. 'You made me jump. I thought you were someone else.' I couldn't tell him what I'd feared, and grinned at him inanely.

'Sorry, Anna.' He gave me his quick grin. 'Didn't mean to startle you. Are you going inside?'

I told him about the plan to buy biscuits.

'I was after another packet of peppermints myself.'

'You must almost be through your sweet ration. How are you this morning?' I remembered his drained face last night.

'I'm fine.' He met my gaze and held it.

'I felt bad at having to dash away like that. We caught Becker with Mary Waites, holding her hostage,' I said. 'It was him.'

'Him?'

'Becker. Who sabotaged your script. Who . . .' I looked over my shoulder. We were alone. 'Who drowned Beattie,' I whispered.

'Drowned Beattie?' William blinked hard. 'Father Becker? Could he really do something like that?'

'You're making the mistake of thinking he's who he said he was. He's not a priest at all.'

'It's a lot to take in.' Shadows passed over his face. Then he seemed to shake them away. 'Let's go inside, shall we?'

He persuaded the shopkeeper to liberate a packet of Garibaldis from the stock room, pulling out his ration book and insisting on covering the purchase. I remembered my suspicion that he'd sent a telegram. I'd have to remind him to be careful to follow the rules in future. If there were a future for our unit. He opened the door for a woman with a large pram, and helped her toddler climb the step up into the shop.

'It's just the two of us this morning,' he told me as we exited. 'Sefton Delmer's secretary telephoned as I was leaving for the shop and asked Micki to interview a prisoner of war with him.'

Our personnel and broadcast schedule would probably be grabbed by other teams now. I supposed it was inevitable but something in me still rebelled. Why should other people benefit from Beattie's work in building up this team? William and I turned into the drive to Mulberry House.

'Strange about the bike,' I said out loud.

William was striding towards the entrance. He rubbed his neck. 'The bike?'

'One of them's missing.'

'Must be somewhere,' he said, knocking on the front door.

As we went into our office I told myself to concentrate on the work in hand: tonight's programme. William would have to write the script for his own broadcast. 'Can you do it?' I asked him. 'I'll help as much as I can.'

'Becker and I talked about what he'd be covering over the next week,' William said. 'I think he made some notes.'

We searched Becker's desk and found his notepad, which included an outline for the evening's script.

'There are enough old scripts around for me to use as guides as to language and speech patterns,' William said. 'I feel I know my radio persona quite well now.'

'He was a good writer,' I said grudgingly, as I reread some of the older scripts filed neatly in Becker's desk. 'I wonder if he worked in newspapers or something similar in the past?'

'I'm confident our listeners won't notice any change,' William said, picking up Becker's German typewriter and placing it on his own desk. He wound a sheet of paper into its carriage and typed a few words. 'Not much wrong with the keys, either. That was all part of his pretence, wasn't it? Not being able to handle machines.'

I watched William as he typed, occasionally stopping to rub his back while he read Becker's notes.

'Are you still in pain?'

'Pretty much all the time.' He stopped typing. His face was knotted, the colour of putty. 'I just can't seem to manage the pain relief.' He shook his head. 'Forgive the moaning. I either feel mentally alert, like I do now, but my back's on fire, or I'm not in pain but my mind's clouded.'

'I'm so sorry,' I said. 'Constant pain is exhausting.'

'I know you understand.' He gave me his old William smile, gentle, kind. 'But I'm alive and I owe the pilot who dragged me out my life.' Was he telling me that I too should be grateful I'd survived? That my injury, and all the upheaval we had experienced here, was nothing in comparison to losing your life? The memory of Beattie floating in the pond returned to me. I hugged myself, feeling cold and heavy.

William took his silver pillbox from his inside jacket pocket and took two of the tablets with a sip of water. He closed his eyes briefly. 'Sometimes it feels as though there's a kind of partition through my mind. There's the old me, functioning in the way it always has. And then there's the new me, which operates differently. I can't always remember what it's done.' The pills seemed to act fast on the pain; he was regaining his colour. 'Sometimes I'll go out carrying an object I can't remember picking up. Yesterday it was the blotter from my desk.' He gave a mocking half-laugh. 'When we were in the shop just now I knew I'd been there a few days ago but I couldn't remember what for. I keep thinking I've made a mistake and forgotten about it.'

Now would be the time to ask him if he'd been sending telegrams. But I looked at the furrows on his brow that seemed to belong to an older man's face. Had they been there at the time of Beattie's funeral?

'If it's work you're worried about, you needn't be. You're a complete professional,' I told him.

He raised a hand and rested his head briefly against the palm. 'The drugs give me strange dreams. They feel so real. Last night I had a nightmare about . . .' He stopped himself. 'But nothing more boring than telling people about your dreams.'

I remembered my own dream on the eve of Beattie's funeral about the pie filled with black crows.

'I must try to manage on fewer tablets. If I can walk and stretch out occasionally I can manage. It's when I'm sitting for too long that my back goes into spasm.'

'There must be something else they can do for you?'

He nodded. 'I'll make another appointment. But enough about me. You're good to listen to me and my problems, Anna. But I don't matter.'

'What?'

He leant forward. 'It's you who's important.'

'You've always been such a good friend to me.' A thought occurred to me – did he want more than friendship? Not with a woman with a face like mine, surely. William wasn't looking at me like a lover would, anyway.

His face brightened. 'You just can't be sure what people are really like. I hope we can stay working together.'

'So do I.'

'I dread being sent to a whole new team. You get used to people and then they're gone.'

Beattie. Father Becker. And this had happened to William before, each time he'd switched Halifax crew, and then when his flying career had finally ended.

'I have this nightmare of being seconded to write smut for *Der Chef*,' he went on, seeming to brighten. 'What a fate that would be.'

Der Chef – The Chief – was one of Sefton Delmer's fake broadcasts, ostensibly from a filthy-mouthed disillusioned military officer. Past programmes had described orgies and accounts of women being arrested for urinating in military helmets.

'What are you like at drawing?' I asked. 'They always need people to do those smutty little pictures on the leaflets.'

A team of people designed and created drawings that seemed innocuous until flaps opened to reveal naked blond women welcoming the aroused attention of non-Aryan invaders. The RAF dropped the leaflets anywhere German fighting men might get hold of them.

William laughed and for a moment his expression was his cheerful old one. 'I'm not sure my artistic efforts would cause the Germans much concern.'

'I'm probably safe from having my morals compromised, too,' I said. 'Pornography might be a step too far for us delicate women.' Manipulating fears of venereal disease and impotence was all right for us females, but the sexual act itself . . . ?

'Even Beattie wouldn't make you do that.' William flushed and looked away. The atmosphere in the office seemed heavier again. Did he know about the nights Beattie and I had spent together? About that last night in particular?

The telephone in Beattie's office rang, sparing my embarrassment. I went to answer it. The caller was a wine merchant. 'No further deliveries will be required for Mr Beattie.' I put down the receiver, feeling the loss all over again, sitting for a moment at his desk, which was now empty apart from the same pencil I'd fiddled with.

When I returned to our office, William had his head down over his work. I concentrated on my own script, finding some relief in the task. How much longer could I keep Clara going? The enemy were now close enough to the castle to be visible from the tower. In real life the Allies still weren't showing much sign of invading Occupied Europe, but Beattie had liked the idea of sending Germans a warning.

Half-twelve came. Mrs Haddon brought us in a tray of corned beef sandwiches. 'As it's just the two of you. It'll save you going back for lunch.' She appeared subdued.

'How are you?' I asked. 'It must be so strange, not having Mr Beattie here.'

She bit her lip. 'He had his funny ways, but he was a good lodger. Always finding little presents for me. Kept strange hours and wanted me to cook some very fancy food, mind you.' I smiled, remembering the live lobster that had arrived one quiet morning.

She left us to eat. I returned the trays to the kitchen when we'd finished, coming back in with cups of tea. The coffee beans seemed to have dried up now that Beattie was gone. I placed a cup on William's desk and he thanked me, lifting his head to gaze at me with those boyish eyes of his. He said something.

'What was that?' I turned to him.

'Patrick.' He said the name quietly and at first I wasn't sure I'd heard him correctly.

My mouth moved. No words came out.

A moment passed. 'Patrick?' I asked. It couldn't be the person I was thinking of. I'd never mentioned Patrick's name to William. Nor to anyone in Aspley Guise, not even Micki. Beattie had guessed there'd been a pilot in my life before the fire, but I'd never referred to him by name. Beattie had his sources; he might have found out Patrick's identity. But would he have talked about him to William? Somehow I didn't think so. 'What do you mean?'

'Patrick Matthews,' he said. 'I knew him.'

My skin tingled. I reached inside my pocket for my cigarette case. 'I didn't know you'd come across Patrick.' Saying his name out loud made me blink. My hand shook as I pulled out a cigarette.

He nodded. 'He was our captain. Captain Matthews, sometimes Mat when we were off duty together. He called me Nat – for Nathanson. Mat and Nat, we were.'

'Patrick was in Fighters, not Bombers.' There'd been a mistake. There were two pilots with the same name, in different commands. I stared at the cigarette lighter on my desk. I still held the cigarette, unlit, in my hand.

'He retrained for Bomber Command.'

Because of me? Because, not knowing I'd made the switch myself, he was worried our paths might cross? No. Patrick was a fighting man, he wouldn't have given up his job for a love affair gone wrong. He must have believed that switching from combat to bombing raids over Germany was the best way to take the fight to the enemy.

The burnt side of my face hurt. I rubbed it distractedly.

'How did you know I . . . knew Patrick?'

William stared down at his hands. 'You fly in crews with people, you become close.' He seemed to be saying it as much to himself as to me. 'Even people like me are eventually accepted. I wasn't a bad navigator. I tried to do my bit, to look after everyone.'

'People like you?'

'Not entirely British.'

'You always sound so English,' I said. He looked pleased.

'I worked on it. I always just wanted to be part of the team. We were all only together for months, until we crashed.' I could hear the despondency in his voice.

'Did he . . . ? Is he . . . ?'

'Oh yes, Patrick's alive.'

I felt the perspiration forming on my forehead. The air around me seemed to be crushing me.

'Patrick talked about me?' Airmen weren't inclined to discuss their girls, unless it was in light, often crude, terms. Sometimes they'd open up to WAAFs about a serious relationship, but not often to another male.

'He told me his girl had finished with him after she'd had a serious bomb injury. That was all he said, but I could see he'd taken it hard.' He looked up at me. 'It was when you and I talked after my first broadcast that I was sure.' He tapped the side of his head lightly. 'Sergeant Anna Hall. WAAF. Badly hurt in a fire.'

The coldness running down my spine felt like a stalactite. I put the cigarette into the ashtray. Patrick was alive. A thousand questions swarmed my mind, but I couldn't articulate any of them.

'Does Patrick know you and I work together?' I asked.

'He didn't at first.'

'But now?'

'He was in a bad way after we crashed, Anna. He—' He stopped. 'You still care about him, though, don't you?'

'It's been two years.'

'You still wear the scent he gave you. I asked him if he'd given it to you.'

My mouth opened and closed. 'I can't talk, William. Not now.' I managed to light the cigarette.

'But—'

'Please, let's just get on with our work.' But the words on the page I was typing seemed to jump across the sheet as I looked at them.

'I've been keeping an eye on you, Anna,' he said. 'It's not safe here. It looks like such a peaceful place, but it's not really.'

Keeping an eye on me? Following me? Had it been William, not Father Becker, following me that day in the bluebell wood? And before, after our night out, when I'd walked from Shaftesbury Avenue to Leicester Square tube station? I'd heard those uneven footsteps of his. Had William also watched me from the copse at Waites Farm as I cycled away? He might have taken the missing bicycle.

A cold fury pulsed through my head. Why on earth would William follow me? Was he adopting the role of my protector? Saving me for Patrick, keeping at bay any men who might supplant him?

'I'm going to check something in the encyclopaedia in Beattie's office.' I needed to be alone.

I sat with my cigarette at Beattie's desk, wishing Micki was back. I wanted those sharp eyes of hers to look at William for me.

The tapping of William's typewriter reached me through the wall between the offices. I was certain he didn't know what was going through my mind. Mrs Haddon was in the kitchen; I was not alone with this man I'd liked so much, had regarded almost as a brother as well as a colleague and friend.

I heard the front door open. Mrs Haddon called the terrier. His paws tapped over the tiles as he raced after her. The door closed behind them. I could join them, walk round to the call box and telephone Grey-suit Man.

William stopped typing. Was he reading through his script? I heard his footsteps creak across to the door. He was coming in here. I sprang up and grabbed at random at the books on Beattie's bookshelf, pulling out a world atlas. I rushed to sit down again with it as William knocked on the door. He came into the room without waiting for a response.

'Found what you're looking for?'

I looked down and saw I'd opened the atlas at a map of the West Indies. 'Got a bit distracted.' I managed a smile.

He looked at the opened page. 'Are you sending Clara to the Caribbean?' He said it in the same old bantering tone that he and I had fallen into from the earliest days of his arrival here.

'Clara would like that. I know I would.' The last words came out with more force than I'd intended. I would have given anything to transport myself to some warm, secluded beach.

'I wish you could go to a tropical island, Anna. You'd be safe. The cities are full of dangerous types these days. It's not good for women to be in those places.'

I remembered the brawl on Wardour Street.

He moved in closer. 'You didn't mind me talking to you about Patrick, did you?'

'Just a bit of a surprise.' I breathed out slowly, doing my best not to show alarm.

'You and I always find it so easy to talk to one another.' He was perspiring, swaying slightly. 'You don't know how much that means to me when everything else seems so . . . confused.'

'You're not well.' I said it softly. 'If you're happy with the script, why don't you go home now and rest until it's time to go to the studio?' I could telephone Grey-suit Man and tell him what I'd found out, say he couldn't do anything until after William had broadcast.

'Oh, I'll stay and keep you company,' William said.

A sense of isolation overcame me. Micki was out. I couldn't risk making a telephone call with William in the house. *The programme comes first. Always.* When he'd finished, I'd find a way to pass on what I knew. Until then I had to put on a mask with William, pretend I had no suspicions, that I was happy to talk about Patrick.

'I'll take one of my tablets,' he said.

Should he take another one so soon? I smiled at William, trying to appear unflustered. 'I'll make some more tea, shall I? Perhaps you'll feel better for a cup.'

He followed me through to the kitchen, finding cups and saucers for me while I filled the kettle and put it on to boil. The script I'd been working on wasn't quite finished. It was for tomorrow, but I'd promised to hand it over to the actors at the studio tonight when they were there recording another broadcast. In addition, I still had the news bulletin to complete. Memos had arrived during the day, telling me what I needed to include and the weight to be given to each piece. Fortunately nothing urgent seemed to have cropped up this afternoon.

The kettle was refusing to boil. 'Do the drugs take long to work?' I asked.

'Ten or fifteen minutes.' He took the cup of tea I gave him. 'I must write down what time it is and the dose. I've accidentally taken too many in the past. It can make me feel a bit peculiar.'

'Peculiar?'

He frowned. 'As though I'm not really present. I see myself doing things, taking the blotter off my desk, like I told you, but it's as though it's someone else doing it. Then I come to again.'

I repressed a shiver. 'Must be hard carrying on when you feel so rough.'

'Work helps.'

'Yes,' I said.

'It's the rest of life that's harder. I can walk through the bluebells and know intellectually that they're beautiful, but when I look at them, they're just plants that will eventually wither, rot and die.' I stiffened at the mention of the bluebells.

The perspiration still gleamed on his brow. Perhaps William was too ill to broadcast. But who else could I find to fill the slot at such short notice? Mentally I ran through a list of all the native German-speaking actors and broadcasters in the village. Nobody sounded close enough to William. His was a warm voice, young but curiously avuncular at the same time, perfect for the character he played. William was irreplaceable. If he left we'd have to pretend that he, like his predecessor, had been arrested. We'd have to create a new radio priest character. It was impossible to do all this within a few hours. And if we dropped the religious slot we'd have to fill the slot with something else, which would mean another emergency telephone call to Sefton Delmer.

No, William had to do his broadcast. My cup shook on the saucer. I placed it on the draining board. 'Must get back to Clara.'

'You haven't drunk your tea.'

'So I haven't. I'll take it with me.' I picked up the cup.

His nostrils widened. I looked at him.

'My sense of smell. It's much stronger since the crash,' he said. 'I pick up scents I could barely notice before. This tea – it's not even a scented one like Earl Grey, but I can pick out every note. The bluebell scent in the woods was so strong it almost felled me. And I notice which brand of soap people use, their toothpaste. It's strange.'

He'd smelled my *Vol de Nuit* on Beattie that morning? That had been how he'd known Beattie and I had spent the previous night together?

The courier knocked on the door, wanting William's script so it could be approved. I resisted the temptation to write a note and slip it between the sheets, asking for help. William followed me into our office. We sat opposite one another. I knew I had to finish my episode, but my brain wasn't firing the necessary signals to my fingers. William would notice if I stopped typing. I had to carry on.

Clara was in the castle with her father. Food was running short. The enemy was inching closer. Her brother and lover were far away. I wanted Clara to jump onto her horse and gallop to the safety of the neighbouring state, a neutral power. But Beattie and I had agreed she had to stay in the fortress, looking after her dependants, right up until the last minute. Her attempt to defend them was to be shown as futile.

I closed my eyes for a moment. The wretched girl was supposed to be a personification of the enemy, but somehow she'd become someone I liked. I'd taken some traits from Micki: Clara was handy with a dagger and light on her feet. She was loyal but had a sharp sense of humour. She felt genuine. *You're probably the only honest thing I've written*, I told her silently. *I wish you were real so we could talk.* What would Clara do in my position? How would she deal with this new revelation about William?

She'd feel what I felt now.

Confusion, doubt, nausea, shakiness. My fingers moved more rapidly as I wrote about a mysterious knight whom Clara had taken into the castle when he'd appeared wounded, claiming to know her fiancé. He was charming and helpful, but now this newcomer was arousing Clara's suspicions, appearing on the stone staircases late at night when she climbed the steps to her chamber, telling her he was watching over her. Making her feel if not scared, then very close to it.

'That's the car outside,' William said.

I jolted back into reality. My fingers clenched.

'You were really wrapped up in that script, Anna. The typewriter looked as if it was about to jump off your desk.'

I forced myself to smile. 'You know what it's like when the words start flowing.' I stood up and pulled the sheet of paper out of the typewriter.

The courier was reappearing in the drive with William's script. She knocked on the door and Mrs Haddon brought in the envelope. When I opened it I could see it had been signed and approved. Not a word changed. I felt a small flush of pride for our depleted team.

'Shall we check it ourselves one last time?'

William handed me one of the carbon copies. I spread it out on the desk and William did the same with his approved top copy.

'Exactly the same,' William said. 'Nobody can tamper with them now.' He placed his copy in his folio case. 'You can rely on me, Anna.'

'I know,' I said.

I didn't recognise the driver in the small car waiting outside. A pang of loss for Atkins and Beattie's favourite black Austin swept me.

At the guard post I once again felt a temptation to blurt everything out, tell them that something was wrong. I looked down at my knees so

I couldn't. We entered the studio as usual and I managed to exchange the normal pleasantries with the studio manager before William and I sat down. He took out his script. I looked at the studio clock: still time to fill before the announcer arrived. To distract myself I opened my satchel and took out the Clara script, careful not to open it past the second page so that William couldn't see the bit about the mysterious knight.

I glanced at him. His face was clammy again. 'Would you like some water?' I leant forward to pour him some from the carafe on the desk. As I did, my sleeve caught on the Clara script. The sheets fluttered to the ground. I bent to pick them up.

'Let me.' William scooped them up and put them on the desk between us.

The last page lay on the top. I reached out a hand towards the sheets. As I did, the door opened and the announcer arrived, the usual middle-aged man from Saxony we'd worked with for months. He was an old hand at radio.

The clock's minute hand approached seven. I stood up, opening my satchel to hide the script safely away.

'I'd like you to stay, Anna,' William said. 'If you don't mind. I know it's not usual, but in case my back . . .'

'Of course.' I sat down again, legs shaking, the Clara script still on the desk between us. The announcer adjusted the microphones, pushing the sheets of paper just out of my reach. He groaned, placing a hand on his stomach.

'The whale meat in the canteen last night . . .'

The light went on. The announcer introduced the programme and ran through the news items we'd given him, masking any sign of abdominal difficulty, but wincing from time to time.

Even now, feeling my heart flutter, I was proud of the item saying a temporary shortage of champagne following a warehouse fire had now been redressed, guaranteeing supplies for important Party events. The RAF had actually reported a raid over Occupied France resulting in a warehouse fire, but machine parts rather than champagne bottles had been pulverised. I imagined German families muttering about coping with meagre rations while those in power fretted about losing luxuries.

The announcer concluded and introduced Father Friedrich.

As he did every time, William seemed to transform himself into the part. I'd seen him, listened to him, so many times, but this evening, I once again became one of his audience, finding it hard not to fall for the trick, not to believe him a kindly man of the church rather than a wounded British airman. Perhaps I'd been wrong about him. He couldn't have harmed Beattie.

William gave the final blessing. The announcer presented the live dance band in the music studio. We looked towards the control room. A thumbs-up from the technician as they switched over.

'Another solid performance,' the announcer told William. 'Well done, my boy.' He grasped his abdomen again. 'Keep an eye on things here, I need to make a dash.'

I looked at the control room. The producer frowned at me. We were on air – if something went wrong with the live music broadcast, someone would need to announce a change in programme. William could do it at a push.

I went to pick up the Clara script. William's hand reached it first. 'Was that a new character I saw on the last page?' He flicked through the script, as easily as we had always done in the office, passing pages to one another for comment. 'A knight? I love the way you bring in the medieval aspects.'

He read the page without a word and replaced it on the desk. 'So,' he said. 'The knight with the mysterious past who follows Clara around.' He gave me his gentle smile. I looked at the clock. How much longer until the announcer returned?

William reached inside his pocket for his cigarette lighter and case. 'Like one?'

I shook my head. His hand trembled as he lit it. I looked again at the studio clock. Seconds before the news, I estimated. 'If he's not back before the swing band finishes, you'll have to read the news and wind the programme up,' I told William, trying to sound matter of fact. The news sheet was on the desk, in front of the microphone, with the shorter summary read at the schedule's end.

William coughed on his cigarette. 'But I haven't rehearsed . . .'

'It's all here,' I showed him. 'You just have to read it.'

His hand trembled. Ash from the cigarette tip dropped onto the script. He moved his left hand to brush it off. As he did, he knocked the hand holding the cigarette, which dropped from his fingers. 'Damn.' Small flames creased the edges of the sheet. Their warmth glowed on the scarred part of my cheek. The paper was blazing, flames lapping other sheets, igniting them. *Fire.*

I made for the door. The alarm started to clang outside in the corridor.

'I can't . . . Sorry.' I reached for the door handle. As the door opened the announcer ran in. 'The sand bucket?' He nodded at the aluminium bucket each room here contained in case of air raids.

My legs trembled. It would be like last time. The flames would consume the desk, the studio, the whole building, all of us. Timbers would crash to the ground, knocking people down, setting them alight, burning them. I had to get out.

Smoke was billowing out of the door, people were running towards the studio. The broadcast was at risk.

Get a grip, Hall.

This was my responsibility. I stepped back into the studio and grabbed the bucket of sand. By now the fire had consumed all the script. The announcer was moving microphones out of its way. The bucket handle was in my hand. Images filled my mind: the church,

Grace falling, the smoke. I threw the contents of the bucket over the burning script.

And the fire was gone. I blinked. The smoke dispersed. The alarm stopped.

'I'm so sorry,' William said. 'I was careless.'

The announcer glanced at the clock. 'We're just in time.' He gave the producer a thumbs-up, pulled the microphone towards himself and sat down.

I grabbed my satchel from my chair, opened the door again and left the studio, vaguely aware of William behind me. I needed to carry out the usual sign-off, but first I needed air. After that I had to tell the police or Grey-suit Man, Sefton Delmer or *someone* about William. I had to rewrite my Clara script before I forgot what I'd written today. I couldn't let the fire shake all thoughts of action from my head, returning me to the traumatised person I'd been two years ago. I couldn't be that woman again.

William was still following me, but then he had been for weeks now. I opened the main door and walked onto the grassed compound outside. 'Why did you do that to Beattie?' I asked, the fire having unleashed my fears and suspicions.

He flinched and started to say something. I cut him off. 'Did you think he was somehow standing in Patrick's way?'

'Beattie corrupted people.'

'He did not corrupt me.'

William turned white. 'But I saw him pestering you.'

'What?'

'He was in your bedroom that night. Pulling at your clothes.' He blushed.

William had been in the garden watching us in my room before I'd pulled down the blackout.

'I wasn't playing peeping Tom, Anna. I saw Beattie go with you into the house. I was worried.' He grasped for the word. 'Shocked. Couldn't believe it.' He touched my hand. 'Don't worry, I knew it couldn't be what you wanted.'

I stared at him. 'How could you possibly know that?'

The guards had noticed our raised voices. They were interested, watching us, but not alarmed enough to do anything about it. Not yet.

William stared at me. 'I owed it to Mat.'

'Owed what to him?'

'I felt I should help get him back with you.'

'You thought Beattie deserved to die for the sake of your personal debt to Patrick? That it didn't matter about him? About me?'

'I thought he was forcing himself on you, Anna.' Again he rubbed his temple. 'But . . . I didn't touch Beattie.'

His voice was quieter now. He trembled. I wondered whether it was pain or the drugs.

'Then how did it happen? You were there, weren't you?'

I hadn't thought it possible that William could turn any whiter, but he did. 'I just wanted to talk to him. He went to the edge of the pond.'

'Beattie hated water, he wouldn't do that.'

William dropped his head. 'That was my fault. I was angry.'

'You had no right to be angry if it was about me.'

One of the dogs standing with its handler by the gate looked at me, ears pricked.

'He was holding something of yours.'

I frowned. 'My fountain pen?' Was Beattie remembering he'd promised to put a nib on the pen for me? 'I don't understand.'

'I grabbed it from him, told him he couldn't have it. He came towards me. I threw it away from him, thought it would land in the bushes and I could pick it up for you after. But I didn't seem to know my own strength and the pen landed in the water.' He shook his head. 'He ran to the pond, perhaps he thought it would float. I went after him and shouted at him to leave you alone.' He stared down at the grass. 'I must have startled him. It was muddy. He lost his balance.'

'You didn't help him out? You left him to drown?'

'I thought he'd get out by himself. I didn't know the pond was so deep. His clothes must have dragged him down.'

'Beattie couldn't swim,' I said. 'He had a fear of water. That pond's so deep locals warn their children to keep away.'

'Oh God, I didn't know that.' William's voice shook. 'I walked away . . .' He put a hand to his brow, covering his eyes. 'It just felt like a kind of waking dream. A nightmare. I came back to Mulberry House and Mrs Haddon let me in with Father Becker. Just like the start of any other work day. And I thought I must have imagined what had happened in the woods.'

William stood, arms wrapped around himself, rocking slightly.

I pictured Beattie's muscles tensing as he fell into the water, the panicked breath he'd taken, his feet scrabbling to find a hold on the muddy bottom, his clothes heavy. Perhaps he'd slipped again as he struggled, inhaling the brackish water into his lungs. Or banged his head on some hidden rock, stunning himself. It only took a few inches of liquid to drown. 'I thought Beattie'd be sitting in his office,' William whispered. 'At his desk. But he wasn't. Then I thought he might have gone out to buy something from the shop, or perhaps gone over to see Sefton Delmer. But he didn't come back. And I couldn't remember what I'd really done and what was just my mind tricking me.' He patted his jacket pocket. 'I have my notepad. I write down important things because I know I get confused. But I hadn't written anything in it about Beattie that morning.'

I turned my back on William. 'I don't want to talk about this any more,' I said, shivering, too, as though I was also floundering in dark, cold water. 'Go back to your lodgings. I'm going to report this. I think you need help.'

'I just wanted to clear the path for Mat.' He was talking softly, almost to himself. 'I was the navigator, I made sure we reached our target, then got us home the safest way I could. That's all I wanted to do for Mat, make sure he found his way to you.'

I became aware of a commotion the other side of the gate. A small female figure was arguing with the guards, hands lifting in exasperation. Micki. A man stood behind her.

25

William was still talking, but I wasn't paying attention because I was running towards the guard post.

'They won't let me in.' Micki sounded breathless. 'I haven't got the right pass, but you need to talk to this man, Anna. He says he knows you.'

The man stepped forward. His right arm was missing from the elbow down, the jacket sleeve folded up and pinned. He was young, though the lines around his eyes – perhaps caused by the pain of his injury – gave what had once been a carefree face a more serious expression than I had known before.

'Patrick,' I said. He was looking at me, at the burnt side of my face that I'd kept away from him two years ago. Now he knew.

But there wasn't time for this. 'William,' I said. 'He needs help. He's not . . . right in his mind.'

Patrick and Micki looked at one another. 'It's just as you said,' he told her.

'I have to finish up here,' I said. 'I'm going to bring William out to you now. Can you look after him? He needs to see a doctor.'

'Non-authorised personnel are not allowed to hang around the gates.' The guard sergeant roared the words at us.

'We're going,' Micki said. 'Just let Lieutenant Nathanson out.'

The gate opened, I took William's arm. 'Don't let them call the special constables or the police or even Atkins,' I whispered to Micki as she pulled him through the gate. 'Make sure he goes somewhere safe.'

'It was to get you two back together,' he said. He looked from me to Patrick. 'Everything I did: keeping Anna safe, writing to tell you to come, that was why.'

I felt the crimson blush spread across my face, even the damaged part.

I turned my back on them as the gate closed again, returning to the studio, my workplace, where I could just be a person doing a job, fulfilling responsibilities, spared from all the emotional burden expected of a woman. I walked through the door back into my haven, feeling the weight fall off my shoulders.

❧

But of course I couldn't stay in the studio all night. Eventually, when I'd found the actors and explained that I'd have to give them the Clara script the next morning, and when I'd received sign-off from Sefton Delmer's secretary, I had to walk out of the entrance. The Liverpudlian driver had been waiting for me, a paperback and torch in her hands. Guilt washed through me. 'I had a good book,' she said, brushing aside my apology. 'Straight home, sergeant?'

I blinked. 'Please.' I had no idea where Patrick was staying. He'd find it hard locating a bed for the night. I'd be safe from him at Lily Cottage because nobody outside our research unit was allowed inside.

But when I went upstairs to my room to pull down the blackout I saw Micki and Patrick in the garden, sitting on the bench where I'd been the night Beattie came to find me.

I thought of pulling the blind down and pretending I hadn't seen them there, retiring for the night. Exhaustion had filled every cell of my body. But I brushed my hair. Automatically I reached for the pancake. I put it back. A touch of lipstick on my lips, but nothing to hide my face.

I went downstairs and out of the kitchen door into the garden, which smelled of spring flowers. Micki and Patrick lifted their heads as they heard me. I saw a small bottle of what looked like whisky on the grass. Each of them held a tumbler from the kitchen.

There was a narrow space between them. I hesitated. Micki moved along and patted it. 'Here.' She poured whisky into her glass and handed it to me. Beattie's supply had certainly taken a hammering. I could almost feel him protesting from his grave.

Patrick and I were not meeting one another's eyes.

'Micki was telling me about her family,' he said.

'She was?' She hadn't opened up that readily to me.

'Shouldn't think I'll hear much about them now,' she said. 'Last news I had, Jews were being sent east to Poland. That's not a good place for us these days.'

'Perhaps they've found work?' Patrick said.

'They haven't any practical skills. My father was a businessman. My mother was an artist before they married. My older brothers are both artistic types, too.'

'You'll want to know about William, Anna,' she said, after a pause. 'An ambulance took him to London. Patrick persuaded the guards not to send for the police. That man in the smart grey suit turned up.'

I tensed.

'It was all right. He made some telephone calls in the guard house and said William could go to a clinic if they kept him locked up.'

She looked at me. 'What did William do, Anna? Was it Beattie?'

'There was a skirmish near the pond but it was an accident.' I hoped that Micki didn't know about Beattie's fear of water, that she wouldn't ask what had happened to make him go up to the pond edge. I didn't want to talk about my fountain pen and how Beattie had come to have it. 'And I think William was following me for some weeks.' I blushed, not looking at Patrick.

'It was the medication for that back of his,' Patrick said. 'The mixture of pills he was taking. It knocked his sense of reality.'

I remembered what I'd been trying to recall in the pub just after the funeral: Schulte telling me about the combination of drugs some of the guests at his family hotel took. I'd never imagined that someone I worked with might be going through a similar chemical nightmare.

'They'll need to wean him off them all and start again,' Patrick said. 'Poor old Nat, it's going to be bad.'

I felt some pity for William, mourned the loss of the companion he'd been. But I couldn't forget Beattie lying in the pond. I couldn't explain to Patrick why William had been so unhinged by seeing us together that night in my bedroom here. But I didn't want to lie to him, either. I'd also need to talk to Grey-suit Man, tell him what I'd found out today. The scar tissue on my face burned.

The whisky filled me with warmth. Single malt, good stuff. Micki was watching me. 'Don't worry, nobody will know I took it. I think Becker had been at Beattie's supplies, anyway. I'll refill the bottle with weak black tea and put it back where I found it.'

Patrick shuffled on the bench.

'Oh dear, another honest person,' Micki said. 'Just like Anna.'

I shuffled too.

'It took you a long time to come after Anna,' Micki told Patrick. I kicked her but she ignored me.

'I didn't know where you were.' He looked at me properly, for the first time.

'So how did you come to be outside the studio?' I asked.

'Nat – William – telegraphed me yesterday. Told me I had to come here. He'd already sent me some strange letters with a London postmark, asking me things such as the name of the scent I'd given you. I had no idea what was going on. Some of the things he said made no sense.'

'But you still came?'

'He was my friend. I owed him something for the many times he'd brought us safely home.' He looked at me. 'William told me there was a bicycle I could use and where to find it. He said to go to Milton Bryan and wait there, in the lane, for him to come out. When I arrived at the guard post, I met Miss Rosenbaum on her bicycle. We pieced together what William was planning.'

Micki glanced from one of us to the other. She gave a yawn. I'd seen better pretences at sleepiness.

'Long day. I might turn in. Good to meet you, captain.' She waved him down as he stood up.

Patrick and I sat in silence. I ran a hand over the bench seat, picking at the loose bits of wood.

'Burn victim reunited with wounded pilot lover,' I said.

He winced. 'Hollywood would love it.' He leant towards me. 'I didn't have a clue what Nat was up to until Miss Rosenbaum told me he worked at some secret organisation behind the guard post, and you did too. It was only then I knew he was trying to . . . Well, make us see one another again.' He looked down at his whisky.

'Bit of a shock for you,' I said coolly. 'And quite a lot of effort for you to go to.' Patrick might have been seeing someone else, and feeling horribly embarrassed about this.

'When you ran towards me behind that gate . . . Well.' He shook his head. 'And then Nat, so pale and shaking.'

I didn't know what to say.

'If I'd known I'd have prepared a bit better.' He swallowed. 'I think I understand a bit more now about how you felt after the fire, Anna.

Though it's my arm, not my face. And obviously I'm not a woman and so really, what could I know?' He groaned. 'I'm making a complete mess of this.'

'You didn't try to find me before?' I'd made it hard for him, admittedly, fleeing to East Anglia without a word to anyone except my father and then coming here.

'I'd actually been trying to track you down before I lost my arm. The trail went cold when you left Bentley Priory.' He looked around. 'But I probably would have found you myself eventually if you hadn't come here. This place might as well not exist.'

'It's like falling down the rabbit hole,' I said.

'Writing letters and making telephone calls took ages with this.' He twisted his left hand. 'It slowed me down. But I rang the vicarage a few times.'

'Did you?'

'Your father answered. I chickened out. Thought he'd tell me you were married to someone else.'

'Married? Me?' My scar was there for Patrick to see, at its worst because it was the end of a long day and I was tired. Dusk enveloped us, but he would see enough of it.

'And then Nat's letters started coming.' He moved closer, so our shoulders were touching. 'I can't believe you're really sitting here with me.'

'This is who I am,' I said. 'The real me.' I took a deep breath. 'I miss you. Always have done. From immediately after I . . . ended it.'

'I used to be a good batsman,' he said, taking my hand with his left one. I'd forgotten how small my hands were in his, how easily he could cover them. His left hand had been the weaker of the two, now it had to do everything for him. 'And I liked driving that little sports car of mine.'

'I remember your car.' I smiled at the memory of how Patrick had once procured petrol in some illicit way, picked me up from my lodgings and driven me into the West End to see a Laurence Olivier play.

'I was a good pilot.' He said it musingly, without conceit. 'A natural, they said. Switched from Fighters to Bombers, didn't find it hard. I pretend to my family and friends that I don't miss those things, but I do.' I saw a steeliness in Patrick I didn't remember from before. 'I asked myself why someone like you would want a damaged specimen.'

I started to say something, but he cut me off. 'I have dark moods – William isn't alone in that. But I've been lucky as far as the drugs go – my doctor was a bit cruel about taking me off some of them.'

Mine had been too. Thank God. 'Nights can be the worst,' I said. 'When you wake at two in the morning because the wound hurts and your thoughts . . .'

'Aren't good ones,' he finished for me. 'And you know if you drop off again they'll turn into bad dreams.' He swallowed. 'We're not supposed to talk about this kind of thing, are we? We're supposed to be stoic, keep our pain, our fear, to ourselves – move on, do our duty.'

I'd been holding my breath while he talked. I released it now. It sounded like a sigh.

'Is there anything left for us? Be honest, Anna.'

'I haven't been honest for a long time. After the fire I lied,' I said. 'When I told you I didn't love you.'

'I know.' He blushed. 'That sounds as if I'm boasting, but I did know that.'

'I did love you. I do love you. But since then, there have been . . .' I didn't know how to phrase it, how to explain about Beattie, about that intensity of feeling for him and its aftermath. 'So what now?'

'We could try again,' he said. 'It's risky, though.'

We might be setting off on a path leading to shadowy country, where inky-feathered birds pecked over dead things.

I put my other hand on top of his, sandwiching it. Night approached. Patrick had to catch a train down to London. I needed to write notes on the destroyed Clara script so I could rewrite it first thing tomorrow. For a while we were still a team, Micki and I. While we still had our evening airtime, we would carry on.

For now I'd just sit in the gloaming, enjoying the feel of my hand inside Patrick's.

ACKNOWLEDGMENTS AND NOTES

I really could not have written this book without the help of my critique partner, Kristina Riggle, who pushed me through it at a time when life was throwing up some serious challenges: Kris, thank you!

I'd also like to thank my editorial team at Lake Union, especially Sammia Hamer, for bearing with me. My developmental editor, Arzu Tahsin, pushed me into refining the novel into the best version of itself, so my thanks to her. Thank you also to Victoria Pepe, Bekah Graham and Nicole Wagner for their support during the writing of this and earlier novels, and to Laura Gerrard and Melissa Hyder.

Writing a work of fiction about an operation that was both clandestine and riven with internal disagreements and turf wars makes for a complex research process. Sadly the interior of Milton Bryan radio studio was dismantled after the war, but I visited the village and stood at the guard house next to the locked gates, imagining what it must have been like driving here to broadcast.

Much of what I have written about operations inside the studio and in the nearby village of Aspley Guise has been gleaned from accounts written by (the real-life) Sefton Delmer and others, including the novelist Muriel Spark who worked there during the war, as well as from some very useful historical books and other resources listed in the bibliography. Naturally contemporary descriptions tend not to offer step-by-step technical guides to making a 'black' broadcast, so I scoured descriptions of more official 1940s radio stations and studios, examining old photographs to get a sense of what broadcasting then was like, using my imagination to fill in the blanks. Any inaccuracies are my own.

In 2013, before interviewing her for a literary festival, I was lucky enough to read Alicia Foster's beautifully written *Warpaint*, which includes a storyline set in Aspley Guise during the Second World War alongside its main storyline of women war artists. I purposefully did not reread Alicia's novel when I was writing this book in 2018–19, but recommend it for its painterly descriptions of the local countryside and portraits of some of the people, real and fictional, working there.

For the sake of a reasonably cohesive storyline I have simplified and condensed elements of 'black' operations, in particular the use of various radio frequencies, masts and transmitters. It's certainly true, however, that in the small Bedfordshire village of Aspley Guise, houses of German Jews, Czechs, Poles and many other foreign nationals worked on manipulating their German radio audience. If these teams had been able to use Twitter, Instagram and Facebook in 1943, it's not hard to imagine how they would have exploited the opportunity.

BIBLIOGRAPHY

Stephen Bunker, *Spy Capital of Britain*

Edward Stourton, *Auntie's War*

John A. Taylor, *Secret Sisters of Bletchley Park: Psychological Warfare in World War II*

Sefton Delmer, *Black Boomerang: An Autobiography, Volume Two*

David Garnett, *The Secret History of PWE*

Muriel Spark, *Curriculum Vitae*

Tessa Dunlop, *The Bletchley Girls*

Ronald Weber, *The Lisbon Route: Entry and Escape in Nazi Europe*

Neill Lochery, *Lisbon: War in the Shadows of the City of Light, 1939–45*

Fiction

Alicia Foster, *Warpaint*

Websites

Psywar.org

Mkheritage.co.uk

ABOUT THE AUTHOR

Eliza Graham spent science lessons reading Jean Plaidy novels behind the textbooks, sitting at the back of the classroom. In English and history lessons, however, she sat right at the front, hanging on to every word. In the school holidays she visited the public library multiple times a day.

At Oxford University she read English literature on a course that regarded anything post-1930 as too modern to be included. She retains a love of Victorian novels. Eliza lives in an ancient village in the Oxfordshire countryside with her family. Her interests (still) mainly revolve around reading, but she also enjoys walking in the downland country around her home.

Find out more about Eliza on her website: www.elizagrahamauthor.com, Facebook: @ElizaGrahamUK or Twitter: @eliza_graham.